KATZENJAMMERED

Michael Crame

Copyright © 2015 Michael Crame

www.michaelcrame.com

Cover photo by Chris Hammersley

Cover design by Nolan Garrido

All rights reserved.

Raw Head

Chicago, Illinois

ISBN-13: 978-0692418994

ISBN-10: 0692418997

For my parents.

ACKNOWLEDGMENTS

My eternal gratitude belongs to a few people for their talent, honor, trust, loyalty, patience and friendship. Stefan Barkow, a talented young writer and friend, thank you for your critical eye and encouragement. Nolan Garrido, kapatid, thank you for your artistic vision, kick-ass cover design and patience. Chris Hammersley, the voice in the back of my head since college and a true friend, your mix of pitchfork and faith in what I was doing kept me focused through dark days. And finally, to the BDC and the covens before you, thanks for keeping me up late on school nights.

"Every Saint has a past and every Sinner has a future"

-Oscar Wilde

THURSDAY

Chapter One

We are somewhere in the outskirts of the bayou when the Absolut begins
to take effect. Until now I've been wound up, impatient and sleepless. But
with the vodka I'm fortified. The smell reminds me of cotton swabs and
needles and pain followed by immense numbing pleasure.

A familiar comfort washes over me.

The right drug makes it possible to believe anything; like you
haven't been trapped inside a Honda Civic hurtling into the unfamiliar
landscape and a thousand miles of darkness. With vodka I can lie to
myself. Am I really strapped into this little car, just a panicky crash test

1

monkey meant for certain doom? Or am I happily sedated at a dentist's office and wrapped up in a buzzy cocoon from a heady mix of nitrous oxide and a strategically placed syringe?

The dentist fantasy will have to do.

Dr. Feelgood has left the room to let the dope work its magic. Instruments are all laid out on the swing tray; pokers, scrapers, gougers, rippers. There is just enough time to consider it all visually, feel the fluttered rush of the heart panic and be overwhelmed by adrenaline before the Novocain kicks in. Soon a stranger in a mask will violate my mouth with latex fists and metal tools and I will bear passive witness to it all with rubbery lips and empty eyes. This ordeal will be a glorious test of my theory of using depressants to ignore the fear. The high whine of a cold stainless steel drill will crunch bone and tear flesh. The saliva tube will suck oily pools of blood and spit from the corners in my mouth. A little powder on his white gloves will evaporate into the burning air, past his menacing silhouette, and dissolve, along with my dread, into the brightness of the splash shield light fixture above our heads.

Then I will know: I am ready.

Ready for anything.

And totally committed to the lie.

Do your worst, I laugh, *because I can't feel a damn thing.*

Back in the car "I put a spell on you" is on the radio and Nina Simone's desperate voice is filling the air with warning and desire. It unravels the tightly knotted grooves on my brain and I sink into the unforgiving upholstery---comfortably anesthetized and toothless. For a few miles between Roseland and Independence, my thoughts travel forward with anticipation, ahead of the stale darkness inside the car and beyond dim revelations of its dazed headlights. The nagging anxiety of entrusting my personal safety to Seth's driving is gone and I forget I have been sitting for twelve hours staring at a road that will never end.

The signal fades and Nina's sweet cry breaks apart in the dark.

There's a tower high in the black distance blinking its red eyes outside my window. Seth scans the radio until he hears static. Then a scratchy voice: "Don't believe that lie! Who told you that lie? The Lord does not love everyone. He hates Jews! He hates Muslims! He hates faggots! And yes, he even hates Christians. Calling yourself a Christian doesn't make you one. I know plenty of Christians who are going to hell."

I feel Seth eyeballing his peripheral vision. "You may want to listen to this."

"Screw you," I reply.

"But Brother Bob," another voice says. "What would you say to all the people out there who feel that we should love our enemies? That the Bible tells us to love others as we would love ourselves."

"It's a lie."

"A lie?"

"A lie. God is not above punishing wayward peoples. The Bible is full of examples of his wrath upon his own. This call for love is a trick. It's the lie that the devil has sold you and you tell yourself to allow for the moral ambiguity that has destroyed this country. It's the lie of love that sanctions homosexuality, and perversion, and adultery, and fornication, and murder. It's the lie of love that turns this Christian nation into a melting pot of false gods and pagan idolatry. Tell me something…if all God cared about was that we love one another then we wouldn't need God. Isn't that ridiculous? Isn't the logic of that blasphemous? Can you imagine that? How absurd is that? We love eachother so much that we've legislated the consequences out of sin. You really think God is okay with that?"

Seth squirms in his seat.

I ask, "What's your problem?"

"I've got The Bubbles," he groans.

"You shouldn't have eaten that fried crab bucket."

4

He gasps for air and says, "I thought they were crawdads."

I watch him grip the steering wheel with both hands tightly.

"That's what you get for eating shellfish from a gas station," I say and look out the window to ignore his plight.

He pounds his chest. "Fuck...I thing they're crawling back up."

He snorts like a pig and cocks his head up towards the ceiling. The road sways to the left while the car continues to go right. We make slow dangerous slides back and forth across the highway.

This cry for attention goes on for a minute or two before the nasal snorts and chest thumping become a distraction. "Hey. What...what are you doing?"

His head snaps forward. The body convulses in a sudden release of sound and gas: "GUR-HANK!"

He lets the steering wheel go and clutches his throat. "ARR---- Jeheesus Christ!"

The Honda's tiny four liter engine groans in pain and leaps forward.

I grab the steering wheel. "Jesus? Ha! It's too late to change your faith now you awful heretic. Haven't you noticed, Jesus has left the building and I doubt he'll save you now."

He gags for air. His eyes grow wide, wet, and rabid behind his glasses.

The sudden break of silence and mind numbing fatigue of this dark twelve hour drive is an odd thing. It all seems to be happening but not really happening. I cannot contain the laughter and yank at the wheel. "Okay you miserable beast. Listen to me very carefully...I can end this all for you now if you just relax and let the Good Lord take you. As a recreational Catholic I can absolve you of most of your sins. You'll have to pay for the major ones like pagan idolatry and gluttony..."

Seth chokes.

"Come on...pull this damn car right over," I say. "Where's your EpiPen? I know it's here somewhere. Your mama never lets you leave the house without it. I'll stab you right in the heart. We'll triple the dose! Your chest will explode and it'll all be over very quickly."

He continues to fight me as he gasps for air and pulls at the steering wheel with hateful looks.

The car swerves across the white stripes dotting the black landscape.

I stare him down. "You stupid man. Pull this goddamned car over and admit you're having problems. Your foolish pride will kill us both! We all know about your fragile condition."

He clears his throat with a sloppy, wet gurgle. "Y o o u fuh-hucking shit-head! I swear to God I'll stab you with that EpiPen myself!" He puts one hand on the steering wheel and jerks it. "I'm not fucking around with you you drunk. Let go. LET GO!"

There is a brief and uneasy silence followed by mean stares. He declares, "I'm NOT allergic to shell fish!"

"But it is against your people's dietary restrictions to salvation. Perhaps you're being punished?"

"Asshole," he mumbles. I can feel his sullen mood shift with the speedometer's red and orange lights. Pretty soon his internal tachometer will red line and the engine will overheat. Most times he'd ignore me, but the wringing of his white knuckle grip on the car's vinyl wheel makes me believe he'd rather have his wet hands around my neck.

Perhaps I have overreacted.

"LET GO OR I'LL KICK YOUR ASS."

I give up the steering wheel, take a deep breath, and stare out the window at the threatening dark.

Ha! He thinks those crabs are killing him? Wait until he sees those goddamned bees. They're out there. Down South there are millions of them, and they're all invading from Africa via South America, Texas, and Louisiana. You know...the Killer kind. That'll really fuck up his day.

More silence as he wipes his face with his shirt sleeve.

His eyes are damp and his nose is running. "That's not even funny," he says. "Bees would kill me. I could really die."

"Jesus...did I say that out loud?" I suck in my tongue and bite my lips shut. I've heard of ESP happening when confined to a small area with other people for extended periods of time under extreme stress and pressure. No doubt this phenomenon is taking place in Corrine's car as we speed through Louisiana. No doubt those savages at Guantanamo Bay's Camp X-Ray are experiencing the same thing, which probably makes them more dangerous than ever. I mean what's the use of putting bags over the heads of Jihadists if they can read minds.

Seth clears the gravel from his voice. "What the hell are you talking about?"

Oh my God he's doing it again.

"Shut up. Go to sleep. God I can't wait until we get out of this fucking car." His eyes are no longer wet, but intensely fixed on the highway. "Maybe it's not such a good idea to drink nothing but vodka when you haven't slept in a day, jerk-off."

"It's the only thing I can do to ease my nerves," I reply. "I really hate the way you drive." It's a lie. His driving is fine and serviceable. My real fear is of the things that might appear as I sit passively and watch the dark road attack the car's headlights at 85 miles per hour; the suicidal deer, pieces of blown out tires, abandoned cars with no lights, sudden twists and bends in the highway, the driver nodding off.

"You wanna drive?"

"No."

"Of course not. You're conveniently shit-faced so I guess there's no choice."

"Guess not."

"Then shut up. It's too late to bitch about my driving now," he says. "Just sit back and go to sleep."

A flash of blue lights and red lights burst open from the dark road behind us. Head lights chase us down and light up the car's interior. Within moments the sight in the rear view mirror becomes un-mistakenly familiar.

"God-damn-it." Seth sighs and pulls the car to the shoulder.

"Maybe they just want to welcome us to Louisiana?" I laugh. For once this has nothing to do with me. "No sir." I'll smile politely, "I'm just a passenger. I have no control over his reckless driving. He assured me he has a valid license but it doesn't mean he's qualified to navigate this machine at such dangerous speeds."

Seth turns the radio off. "Quick. Help me put my seat belt on or else I'll tell this guy you're an illegal immigrant."

The police officer walks up to the car and shines a flashlight into Seth's face just as he rolls the window down. "Can I see your license and your registration for this car, sir?"

"Yeah sure." Seth fumbles through the glove compartment and his carelessness makes me nervous. It isn't our car. Who knows what the hell has been shoved into the Honda's crevices just waiting to rear its ugly and illegal head. I have been verbally abused and threatened too many times by Southern law enforcement for being jittery when looking for the proper documentation.

It's 4 a.m. and there are no other cars around.

Corrine's old black and silver cell phone leaps from a tight space between the owner's manual and a coiled A/C adapter for the cigarette lighter. It lands on my lap.

My heart stops.

Seth hands him the paperwork. "Here you go."

"Please step out of the car sir," the officer says.

Seth speaks calmly, "Yeah sure."

I close my eyes and take shallow breaths. This is where tragedy begins. This is where bad news gets its origins.

CHICAGOANS SHOT DEAD BY LOUISIANA SHERIFF'S DEPUTIES:

Flying Cell Phone Mistaken for Hand Gun!

The Tribune won't even bother, but the Sun-Times will print it because it's sensationalistic. A front-page headline will blow my cover story and piss off my relatives for saying my gay uncle died as an excuse to ditch work. My boss will know for sure I pitched him a perfect lie; a most outrageous, emotionally difficult, and politically sensitive one the dumb bastard wasn't sure was right to question. But I suppose it won't matter if I am shot dead on this dark highway because I'll have much weightier issues to deal with than unemployment and estranged family members.

A second officer walks up to the car's passenger side with a flashlight and speaks through the window. "Roll the window down." His other hand is hooked against his belt next to his gun.

I give him a blank stare.

He makes a circular motion with the flashlight. "Roll down the window."

I do as he asks and keep the cell phone steady on my leg.

"Uh...Yes?"

"Where you coming from?"

A one-word answer is best, straight, to the point. No frivolous or false sentiment cops need to ask more questions; nothing less than simple syllable words and short phrases to get us moving and on our way.

"Chicago."

"Where you headed?"

I think for a second. Should I tell him the truth or make something up? The truth is we are on our way to Mardi Gras to get irresponsibly drunk and make strange girls do unspeakable things for plastic beads.

The officer shines his flashlight into the back seat. "Who's that?"

I crane my head slowly towards the rear of the car. "Oh. That's just Corrine."

"What's wrong with her?"

I consider the question word by word. Nothing is *wrong* with her; she's a normal girl.

"Hey, what's wrong with her?"

Corrine is wrapped tight in her blanket and dead asleep to the world. I remember how cops are distrustful by nature and this entire episode might look like a kidnapping. "Um--nothing. This is her car. She's asleep."

He shines the light on her face. "Miss, is this your car?"

Corrine sits up. "What's going on?"

"Seth got pulled over," I reply.

The cop points the light at me. "I'm not speaking to you. Miss, is this your car?"

"Yes."

He focuses the light back on her and asks, "Any reason you want to tell me why you're not driving?"

"Because I drove the first half of the trip," she says.

"How long've you been on the road?" he asks.

"MARDI GRAS!" I blurt out.

He trains the light back at me, hands shaking. "Excuse me?"

I whimper, "We...we're going to Mardi Gras."

The officer takes a step away from the window, walks to the back and speaks to the other officer.

"Where are we?" Corrine asks.

"Louisiana."

"How fast was he going?"

"I dunno." I pinch the cell phone between my fingers and ease it onto the dashboard.

Corrine yawns and plops her head back down on the pillow. The officer comes back to the passenger side window. "How long've you been driving?"

Corrine mumbles, "Since 4:30 yesterday afternoon." Trouble has taught her how to talk to cops over the course of her young twenty-two years and she does not fear them at all because of her familiarity with their predictable line of questions. I, on the other hand, have nothing but paranoid contempt for law enforcement. They've used these opportunities to enthusiastically hassle and bully me when they discover I'm a lawyer. The lectures begin with "You should know better," and end with a specious threat: "...And you can get disbarred".

"Any weapons, drugs or alcohol in the vehicle?"

Her face is half buried in the pillow. "No" she says.

"No," I say and smile.

The cop sighs. His shoulders slump and the flashlight droops when he walks away. He is disappointed because he knows we are telling the truth. No chance to hassle these carpetbaggers he probably thinks to himself. Corrine's indifference and my complete attention are enough to break us even in his eyes. Corrine and I are normal people just going to New Orleans for a good time. The wild card is Seth who could easily say the wrong thing and queer this all for us because of the fried crabs erupting in his stomach or the sight of what looks like an errant bee flying in the squad car's head lights. He'll freak out from "the bubbles" or "the buzzing" and cough and gag until his eyes are bloody red and his jaws gnash white foam. The cops will have to subdue him with Tasers and pepper spray while Corrine yawns peacefully and I panic and paw at the window, a crazed dog trapped in a parked car during the summer heat.

Seth walks back to the driver's side, gets in, and starts the engine.

"What happened?" I ask.

"He said I was swerving."

"And?"

"And nothing. He let me off with a warning because we were wearing our seat belts." Seth eases the car off the shoulder and back onto the road.

I am relieved. We are back on our way without the unnecessary trouble. "That's one of the better run-ins I've had with law enforcement down here."

"I'm not surprised," he says. "Why do we always run in to cops whenever we go out of town?"

"I dunno." I reach underneath the seat, grab the Absolut, and take a good swallow. "Ah, sweet Lord." I smack my lips together and sigh. "Let's hope this is the extent of our dealings with the law for the next few days."

"You stupid jackass!" he barks. "Put that away until we get to the city. They're everywhere."

I consider his request and, like a shamed child, tuck the bottle back under the seat. *They are everywhere.* People like that jackass on the radio. Kill Joys. Bad Timers. Brainless swine just waiting for the chance to drag us all down with moral platitudes and dirty looks. Yes...put it away until the city. There will be plenty of time and opportunity to indulge in bad vice at Mardi Gras because in New Orleans we will blend in nicely. They will never find us within the black corners and mysteries that hide cannibals and vampires during the day and draw out the unsuspecting fools and curious virgins into the night to satisfy the thirst. There will be camouflage in Carnival's organic, dirty, nasty, sweltering, salty, sexual, and drunken mess. And *they* will be too afraid to chase us down in the bohemian realm. We will roam free among the city's ugliness and beauty and its sadness and highs while it sweats Southern rain and breathes its old air during another Mardi Gras season.

The getaway is a timely escape and spiritual enema from the nasty, brutal, pre-historic existence of another January and February in Chicago where a lack of sunlight and the unrelenting cold forced us to wonder on the way down through more lush climes why the hell we live there. New Orleans will do well to clear my head of restless and wintry days. We will rendevous with Rio, Roberto and Lenny on Friday. They will come by air, which is brave and stupid considering the headaches involved with random searches, German shepherds, National Guards, machine guns, and the unqualified lookouts at the metal detectors who have unfounded reasons to stop and harass me because of my belt buckle but let nineteen Islamic terrorists pass through with box cutters five months ago. No. I am better off confined to a car for hours with people I know rather than sitting on board a plane with some drunken hillbilly who might wave a Bic lighter against his "shoe bomb" as a sick joke. The drive has gone by for me too slowly despite the initial ease of escaping from Chicago during rush hour traffic. But Seth's gas station shellfish, my need for vodka, and the police have shaken my guts. I am high with anticipation. Closer to New Orleans than further away. Closer to some relief from the last few months and the discordant noise that has made me leery of the universe's intentions. All of it and the uneasiness of cramped spaces are soon forgotten as the vodka sinks deeper into my belly and the sun creeps steadily through Spanish moss and over Lake Pontchartrain's calm waters to shine some well needed warmth on my face.

Chapter Two

The Civic strolls onto Canal Street sometime between 8 and 9 in the morning. Seth is belting out a tuneless version of "Shine on You Crazy Diamond." His mood must have improved because we've finally made it. The singing wakes me more than the crawling thumps of hot tires against broken French Quarter pavement.

"Stop it. You're ruining the song," I say. A few cleaning crews are already at work with long poles and claws. Every morning they will harvest tangled webs of plastic beads from the telephone wires, trees, balconies, and streetcar cables lining Canal. The drunks who've laid waste to the Quarter are responsible for the frenzied mess. It's a thankless task and will repeat itself more and more over the next few days until the bad

19

fruits born out of everyone's rowdy behavior have matured and the trees are left exhausted and barren.

"I had to do something to stay awake. The last thirty miles were long."

I look over my shoulder to see if Corrine is awake. She's still buried in pillows and road dreams. "How's your stomach?"

"Fine."

"While we're here, try to eat things that are cooked."

"Huh?"

"No raw oysters," I say.

"What? The seafood in this town is the freshest. I didn't come all this way just to get drunk."

I shrug my shoulders. "Fine. You've been warned. Just remember, they charge two bucks to use the bathrooms this time of year."

Seth rolls his window down and hangs a free hand outside the door to feel the cool air. "Outrageous. It already smells like vomit. You'd think nobody would care if people were crapping in the streets." He sings and hums and taps his hand against the window frame, *"Where does it go? Where does it go?"*

It is the great mystery of this place. During the night the Bourbon Street establishments toss their refuse onto the streets in neat little garbage piles and boxes. By morning they grow into enormous mountains of plastic, paper and glass. I've seen it all before, the doorways choking on sidewalks of ghastly odors and drunken zombies struggling through the maze. In the Quarter the cops care about people using alleys and corners as toilets and they'll sooner beat you down for squirting a few drops than for grabbing a fifteen-year-old girl's breasts. After the sunrise, an amazingly efficient ritual takes place the zombies rarely see; trucks and armies of sanitation workers, traffic aides, cops, jailhouse detainees, and shop keepers performing a magnificent ballet with hoses, brooms, and garbage picks. It gets washed and hidden away to Lord knows where. It just disappears.

The ballerinas bully and carrel a few stubborn humps of wind blown trash into submission. "I bet the crap gets filtered into the fresh waters where the oysters live."

"Wrong. It goes to a treatment plant or something," he says.

"Uh-huh. Maybe you can't tell they're bad because whenever you eat them you're too drunk to notice a smell."

Seth is looking around for street signs. "Just stop talking. You're bothering me."

"It's green."

"What?"

"The light."

"Shut up. I know where we are." He aims the car to the right and quickly swerves left back to the intersection and straight through the light. A car behind us honks its horn. "Not a word."

We pull into a gas station so Corrine can contact some of her people who are in town for the festivities and Seth can get his bearings. Our plan is to freeload off their hotel room before check out. We can rest, shower up, and find a cheap hotel for the night before getting our posh rooms at The W on Friday.

Corrine and Seth are still in the mini mart when I hear someone peeing near the car. I stretch out and look on with anticipation, "Here we go. Let the weirdness begin." I sit up and catch sight of a fat, old, and swarthy man pumping gas into his Cadillac Deville. He's holding a frozen daiquiri from a local daiquiri shop in one hand and a squeegee in the other. He's missed the gas tank and shoved the gas nozzle between his license plate and bumper. The meter on the pump shows almost three gallons of gasoline already spilled onto the concrete. It is deliciously silly, and I am fully engrossed by his complete ignorance to the deadly possibilities of the moment. "You old drunk." I laugh. "You have no idea how close you are to dying."

Gasoline vapors sneak into the Honda Civic's crevices.

"Good Lord," my heart screams and pumps, *"...this imbecile means to take you with him!"*

I scramble to roll the window down. "Hey you!"

He ignores me and continues to clean his windows.

"Hey man!"

He observes me for a moment pawing at the window and gives me the finger.

"UNGRATEFUL BASTARD!" I struggle to undo the seat belt, "I'M TRYING TO HELP YOU!" I scream. "YOU'LL ROAST US ALL!"

Seth flings open the mini mart doors, charges towards the Civic and yells, "What the hell is your problem now?!"

I squeeze a few fingers through a crack in the window and point at the Cadillac. "LOOK!"

Seth squints for a second. His eyes grow big, "SWEET JESUS!" He makes a careful dash for the Cadillac and delicately pulls the pump away.

The old man steps aside from his car and glares at Seth with glassy, booze filled eyes.

"You're leaking gas!" Seth yells.

The old man sets his drink on the rooftop. He strolls to the back of his car and towards Seth with the squeegee in his hand.

"You're leaking gas," Seth says again.

"Hmm...look at that." The man coolly takes the pump handle from Seth's hands and is unaffected by the dangerous smell lingering in the air.

A red haired cashier steps out from the mini mart's Plexiglas safety to survey the scene and scratches his head. He has an unlit cigarette in his hand he is about to smoke. He looks at me with dull, vapid eyes and sighs.

"Don't look at me," I say. "I-I tried to get his attention but he wouldn't hear it."

Red is unmoved. He will have to wait to smoke his cigarette.

"That pyromaniac almost spoiled *my* day!" I cry.

He puts the cigarette back into his pack and sighs again. "Well...I guess I better clean that up before we all die." He sounds almost disappointed because the entire station didn't erupt into fire and chaos.

My heart and lungs are frantic and about to crack through my chest like the monster in *Alien*. "I-I think he really meant to kill us all. If I were you I'd get on the horn and inform the proper authorities...tell them to check his papers."

Seth shakes his head, steps carefully over rainbow pools of gasoline and walks back into the store. The old man stands untroubled by the moment then treads carelessly through the puddles to examine the car's rear end. "You know what the problem here is...." He pauses and stares at the pump, "...the hose is too short."

I am overripe with fear and grab the Absolut from underneath the seat. Drown *The Alien* in vodka. Keep the beast sedated goddamnit. There is no point in waiting until we get to the hotel for a shower, a clean glass, and ice. No point indeed when this place has already decided to screw with my head before I have a moment to settle down from the drive.

Loni and Sylvia are holed up at a Best Western on the Quarter's north end. They are Corrine's friends and known to me only through Seth's association with the three girls. They came from Chicago via Pensacola where Loni has picked up a young navy boy whom she has no particular interest in other than the fact he is nineteen and dumb. Sylvia is along for the ride and is a New Orleans virgin. It's 9:45 in the morning and check out is at 11:00, but we've decided to stick with the plan to use the hotel's facilities to clean and rest up anyway.

The clerk at the front desk, a young black man, is either dim or high or completely zombified by CNN's "exclusive" gray and white video of an airplane dropping a daisy-cutter bomb in Afghanistan. He smiles at us from behind the check in counter and speaks slowly, "Good morning. Welcome to the Best Western French Quarter on Rampart. Will you be checking in today?"

Corrine replies, "I'm meeting a friend. Can you tell me what room she's in?"

"I'm sorry. I can't give out that information at the front desk. It's for security and safety." He points to a white phone resting at the counter's end. "You'll have to use the house phone and speak to an operator."

Corrine steps to the side and picks up the phone. "Do I have to dial a 9 or something?"

"No...it'll ring the operator automatically."

The clerk trains his slow-eyed gaze at me and smiles. "Good morning. Welcome to the Best Western French Quarter on Rampart. Will you be checking in today?"

"No," I say, "I'm with her."

The phone behind the counter rings. He keeps his eyes fixed on me, picks it up and smiles. "Good morning. This is the Best Western French Quarter on Rampart...how may I direct your call?"

Corrine pulls the phone away from her ear and holds it in her hand.

"Hello?" the man says.

She looks at me. I shrug my shoulders. She places the phone back to her ear and speaks, "Uh...yeah...I'm looking for a friend who's staying at your hotel."

The left eyeball in the clerk's head wanders above and beyond me. His expression changes but his body remains still. For the moment he appears interested in something on the wallpaper behind me the way iguanas do bugs. Corrine's question has triggered a primitive recognition of some sort in his syrupy brain. A slow computation of the situation at hand requiring the proper response in order to facilitate good customer relations; something he's read in an employee manual or seen in a training video. The eyeball finds its answer and darts back to me. He replies, "Do you know the room number, ma'am?"

Seth is on a sofa a few feet away from us and thumbing through a city guide. He takes off his glasses and wipes his eyes. He lets out a small snort and giggles to himself.

Corrine speaks, "No, I was calling to get her room number."

"I'm sorry I can't give out that information."

Seth lets out a frustrated burst of laughter from somewhere deep inside. It renders him crippled and crying. Sitting in a confined space for fifteen hours has finally cracked his mind.

"If I give you a name can you connect me to her room?" Corrine asks.

The man looks down at a stack of papers on the desk and picks up a pen. "Okay go ahead," he replies.

"Loni Cole," she says.

"One moment please." He puts the phone on hold and flips forward several pages. "Yes, hello? Um...is...is that with a 'C'?"

"Yes."

"A moment please." He places her on hold and turns back several pages. "Thank you for holding, I'll connect you."

Loni is in room 324. We are directed to walk across the courtyard and take the elevator to the third floor.

"At least he knows his job," I say in the iguana's defense.

"But does he know where the fire exits are?" Seth replies.

"What the hell does that mean?"

"I don't know. I'm babbling. I'm so tired I can't think. As many times as I've been here nobody ever knows anything more than what's two blocks away. That gets real annoying after awhile."

"That's because everything is only two blocks away."

"No," he says. "There's more than just the Quarter around here but you can never get there because the rubes don't know where anything is."

"Maybe the problem is that most people within a two block radius are all from out of town. Would you live in the Quarter if you were from here?"

"HA!" He snorts. "This is a place you come to to leave. This is no place to plant roots. I'd be dead in a week."

"Of course you'd be dead in a week. You bring too much big city, Mid-Western self-righteousness into a place like this. You're bound to cross paths with death. Nobody cares for that attitude around here. Those types are usually the first to get their skulls bashed in by ornery bouncers and high-strung cops and that's a real tough thing to have happen to you in a lawless place like this."

Seth groans, "Enough. I need rest. Where the hell is this room?"

Corrine walks us towards a staircase across from the pool. "I think it's up here."

Throughout the courtyard, surrounding the pool, and lying among its patio furniture are men and women shackled in beads and the stale air from last night's clothes. It is a familiar scene and I've been there before. Not in a physical way but existentially and many a time after a raucous bout of drinking. At this point the communal hangover is in complete command of this coven of drunks. They are just helpless bodies, passed out or semi-conscious to the morning sun. The undead essence of what they were drinking so heavily just hours before is only now beginning to leave their bodies. They're hiding behind the pool chairs and evaporating shade, and can't muster the strength to make it back to their coffins in time. Judging by the suspicious glaze in their eyes they don't appear to be guests at the hotel. It's reassuring to know you can pass out on a chair next to the pool at this hotel and nobody will bother you for a few hours. I whisper to Seth, "Make note of this sanctuary should you find yourself lost, penniless, and drunk sometime over the next few days."

Loni and Sylvia's room is like the courtyard but without the daylight; the bodies of strangers are laid out on the floor or huddled in dark corners.

"C'mon in," a voice says in the dark, "I'm Marty."

"Is Loni here?" Corrine asks.

Loni emerges from the shadows with a pack of cigarettes. She hurries us out of the room and closes the door behind her. "Anybody have a light?" she asks. "That kid is driving me crazy. I must be nuts."

Seth lights her cigarette. "Who are all those people?"

"Mostly my sister's friends from Bloomington." She takes a drag, "How was the drive?"

"Long," Seth replies. "I need a place to close my eyes for a second."

"Yeah sure," Loni says. "We've got like 10 people in there but you can crash for a while. What time is it?"

"A little after ten," Corrine says.

"Shit." Loni sighs. "We have to check out at eleven."

"I just want to shower," I say.

"Yeah sure...whatever. C'mon in but don't step on anyone."

Once inside I head straight to the bathroom, bag in hand. We have no definite rooming for Thursday night and who knows when or if there will be an opportunity to shower anytime soon.

Once showered, I roll my sweater away and put on a T-shirt, a clean pair of jeans, my jacket and some running shoes. Most everything I've packed is expendable, which makes it easy to flee town if need be with just my money and my wits. I've made the mistake before in bringing things I cared about to New Orleans only to lose them. I have no doubt my favorite pair of sunglasses is still being worn by an Asian stripper named Jada on Bourbon Street who is using them on stage as she whoops it up to "Fire Woman".

The weather is mild but still too cool to wear shorts, and the open-toed, sandal wearers will be in for a great and sobering surprise the next day when they look at their feet and realize they've been walking on garbage during the night. Only the Lord knows what diseased threats lay in the old streets' broken pavement just waiting to gorge on healthy feet. Mardi Gras is rarely a time for cleanliness and no matter what I do to protect myself I am bound to be shit on by the madness. My least personal effects have been brought and intended as my sacrifice to the jawas and strippers.

I repack my bag and head down to the hotel bar for a morning cordial. When I leave the room, Loni's friends are in a mad rush to get showered and packed. There will be no time to rest until we've found and settled into the next hotel. A college kid at the bar is sipping on a fish bowl shaped glass full of rum and Kool-Aid. His bombed-out eyes are watching the television above his head. Nobody else is there except the bartender. She's an older lady, a faded blonde with a bushy and unnaturally yellow plume rising in wisps above her forehead. The plume has accepted the accidental function of filtering her cigarette smoke for years. When I come into view she smiles, "Happy Mardi Gras! What can I get for you?"

"Absolut on the rocks," I reply, "and no limes please."

"Sure thing." She pulls out a tall glass and fills it about half way with ice and proceeds to pour a generous double. "That'll be $3.00," she says.

"God bless this town," I say to her and slip her a five.

I'm halfway through my drink and seven pages into the Best Western "City Guide" when Seth and Corrine sit down next to me at the bar. "So what's the story?" I ask.

Seth puts his head on the bar and closes his eyes. "Everybody's up and getting ready to split. I'm so tired."

"Should've showered. I feel just fine." I smile and chew on an ice cube. "Where are we headed?"

"Some hotel that's not in the Quarter," Seth replies.

"So where is it?" I ask.

"Loni doesn't know. But it's not something we can walk," he says.

"You need something. Something to fire up your Mardi Gras spirit. What are you having?"

"I dunno," Seth mumbles. "What are you having?"

"The usual."

"Yeeacch!" He lifts his head up from the bar. "How many of *those* have you had?"

"For God's sake it's only Eleven O'clock in the morning. What kind of person do you think I am?"

"Is that a rhetorical question?"

"This is my first one." I wave to the bartender and finish the glass.

"First one at the bar."

"Screw you. I'll take my generous spirit elsewhere."

"I can see you're going to be a problem today," he says. "Give me a Bloody Mary," he tells the bartender.

She turns to Corrine. "And you, honey?"

"Mandarin and Seven," Corrine replies.

"I'll have another." I smile.

It's a nice quiet moment in the empty hotel bar, the three of us marinating in vodka and the late morning sunlight. In an hour the place will be packed with alcohol mad tourists waiting to check in, check out, or prime their motors with Hurricanes, beer, whisky, bourbon, rum or anything they can get their hands on before the day's first parade. For the moment it is quiet and the bar, like many bars lately, is an oasis for my peace of mind. I pity the bartender. She'll have her hands full with rowdy and obnoxious foreigners for the next few days and they'll never understand how a bartender in the French Quarter carries a much weightier responsibility than just the simple task of pouring alcohol. To them she'll look like an old stripper from one of the bullet hole bars they've stumbled into on occasion; those small and dark places just off Bourbon Street populated by women worn down by hard living and unwelcome at glossier strip clubs just doors down. She'll shake her old body under black lights and neon, leaving scented glitter sprinkles on their foreheads and get close enough for them to see the bullet holes on her butt from where some mad pimp or deranged lover shot her years ago. To me, however, she is a gatekeeper to the bohemian realm. A conjurer of New Orleans' liquid wonders. The welcoming committee for road weary travelers who have stopped by for a few days of irresponsibility, a clean glass, and some ice.

"Maybe she's not a stripper," Seth says, "Maybe she's just ugly."

"Shut up. Just make sure you tip her well," I reply.

Loni has come down to check out and pay the bill and the bar is gradually filling up with drinkers.

On the television above the bar, two men who resemble the old farts who sit in the balcony and crack jokes on *The Muppet Show* are on a split screen debating the likelihood of success in using a tactical nuclear strike in Afghanistan.

Old fart number one is frothing at the mouth, "I don't see how you could possibly take that option off the table! Who's side are you on? This is a war. We have the technology and capability to attack the enemy with a minimal amount of collateral damage. What the hell have we spent all that money on anyway if we're not going to use it?"

Old fart number two replies and shakes his head, "But Bill, you're talking about dropping a nuclear bomb on an enemy that is mixed in with the indigenous population. By all accounts this is not the type of situation that will lend itself to using sledge hammers to kill flies."

"We're not talking about flies, Randall! We're talking about terrorists and a rogue state that has given them a base of operation and safe haven. For goddsakes they killed American citizens on American soil. Blood has been spilled! That hasn't happened since Pearl Harbor and you know how we ended that damn war!"

"I don't think that situation is analagous as you think to what's going on here, Bill."

"Yes it is."

"No it isn't"

"Yes it is."

"No it isn't"

"Yes it is, and if you think---"

"Bill...can I finish?"

"No Randall! This is exactly the reason why we're in this position! It's a deterrent and the fact you want to take it out of the discussion as a means to an end emboldens these guys! We're not willing to pull the trigger and they know it!"

"Bill, can I finish?"

Old fart number one is red faced and rabid. "No! I've heard enough!"

Old fart number two shakes his head. "Bill, you're a patriot and I understand your feelings but I don't think World opinion would support the U.S. on this. You start dropping bombs on people living in the Middle Ages and I think whatever sympathy and good will and support our efforts in Afghanistan are receiving right now from our allies will surely dry up. It's not how you win hearts and minds."

"SCREW OUR ALLIES! IT'S A GODDAMNED DESERT ANYWAY!" old fart number one blurts out before the local news cuts off the broadcast:

"This morning Daniel A. Hickenbottom pled guilty to one federal count of conspiring to sell drugs."

He had been spectacularly arrested, pinched by the feds with 900 Ecstasy tablets and some Meth in his Jeep Grand Cherokee. He was on his way back to a small town in Florida and a parish congregation of 700 Catholic families. Reverend Daniel A. Hickenbottom was somebody I knew when I lived in Pensacola. Following ordination he began his ministry at my grade school. I was twelve years old. We liked him because he was young and smoked cigarettes. He was nothing like the other priests who wore repression on their faces as if self-denial was something to aspire to. Before the priesthood, his education took him to Notre Dame and Loyola in New Orleans. Maybe that's where the trouble began. He owned a condominium on Bourbon Street's queer end when he was arrested. It must've been a tough thing to explain as a priest and on a $17,000 a year salary. The report continued with a statement issued by the Catholic Archdiocese of Northwest Florida and read by its lawyer:

"It is inappropriate and incompatible with priesthood for a priest to apply and accept membership in a Mardi Gras krewe, which for whatever reason, compromises and undermines his moral integrity and brings embarrassment upon himself, his parish, and the Church."

Corrine asks, "What's a krewe?"

"Social clubs that throw parties and walk in the parades," I reply. "It's an old tradition."

"What's so wrong about that?" she asks.

I reply, "Nothing, but some of the secretive ones are notorious for throwing excessively raunchy get-togethers."

The Archdiocese's statement continues:

"If Father Hickenbottom was in actuality a member of such a questionable krewe for purposes other than offering ministry to men and women struggling with a gay lifestyle, then the shame and embarrassment which the Catholic community experiences upon such revelations speak for themselves."

Poor bastard. Most times when a priest is pinched by secular justice it's because he's a pederast, and the Church makes very little additional commentary about the evil details of his life. In his case it's to be complete and utter banishment and denial of the highest order. They've already started covering their butts by feeding the public and media plates full of innuendo to make him out to be a homosexual speed freak who spends his off days throwing pills and beads from a balcony on Bourbon Street; a self-styled spiritual leader for the pagan and sex fueled ministry of indulgent outcasts who populate these parts. In Florida he has a "good" congregation, and in New Orleans he has his own personal church for gays, lesbians, pygmies, and vampires.

The propaganda is dangerous. It'll set forth precedent. I can see it: *The Hickenbottom Doctrine*. It will be invoked sometime in the near future when a cadre of leaders from varying denominations and faiths are finally cornered by a blood crazed public who demand they address the hypocrisy of their institutionalized beliefs. For every accusation levied against an official for its own religion's thievery, jihadism, Zionism, racism, misogyny, rape, murder, and pederasty they'll boldly cry:

"HICKENBOTTOM! HICKENBOTTOM!! At least we weren't selling speed and faith to the fags and dykes!!"

It will be an acceptable answer to the dispirited masses for their own institutions' failings. Those who don't buy it will be ridiculed and singled out for "re-education" by a unified body of religious Nazis who, while in disagreement about a one true god, can find sufficient vagaries in their texts and teachings to persecute the world's freaks with a 21st Century Inquisition. Salvation will no longer be a question of faith but of blind adherence to disconnected religious figures just as human and frail as this bartender at the Best Western on Rampart. At least what she's doing for me is honest and helpful for my soul, and not religiously sanctioned terrorism. I feel betrayed by the future.

My glass is empty.

"One more?" the lady asks.

"Sure, why not?" I reply.

Chapter Three

By the time we set out for more permanent quartering I am lightly sauced. We attempt to find the Prytania Park Hotel by car, and are dragged tirelessly through the City and into unfamiliar and ghettoriffic territory by Loni, who doesn't know where she's going, and police officers who tell us the hotel is "just two blocks that way." Vehicle and pedestrian traffic is amassing around the Quarter, and eventually major streets like Canal and St. Charles are blocked off and rerouted for the parades. Searching by car becomes impractical and frustrating, especially when my morning buzz begins its death. We park the cars in a garage, convince ourselves we are only two blocks away, and proceed to search for the hotel on foot. Should we never find it or find no vacancies anywhere, we at least have the option of sleeping in Corrine's car in a garage for only $20 bucks a day. An overnight stay in a parked car will make it two straight sleepless nights inside a Honda, which is something I have not done since a week long bender in college. This thought fortifies my determination to find the God forsaken hotel Loni has chosen and the locals are hiding from us.

The Prytania Park Hotel is located, strangely enough, on Prytania Street. Tucked within the Garden District and amongst New Orleans' historic homes, it doesn't look like much and after some intense debate with Seth on the merits of rooming in what, from the outside, appears to be a homeless shelter, Corrine's Honda and the garage closer to the Quarter seem like the better option. Seth and I consider the risk. The hotel is hard to find during the daylight with our clear sight and collective, sober reasoning and nighttime will present greater challenges. Someone will get separated from the group, get lost, or wander off into the darkness under the influence of their virgin awe and too much cheap booze. There are difficulties getting to Prytania Street and cabs are not plentiful. In fact, there do not seem to be many cars passing through the Garden District at all. The hotel does not seem like the right place for us.

"We're taking a bad chance," Seth says.

"With what? Cabs? This isn't Chicago," I reply.

"Well," he lights a cigarette and hands the pack and lighter to Corrine, "Getting lost here is too easy."

"I'm agreeing with you. We can't depend on cabs here." I look to our immediate left. "Let's think about this. The Quarter is in that direction."

"That's about two miles north," he says.

"Wrong, that's about a mile east," I reply.

"No. The atlas says north."

"That fucking thing doesn't even have Prytania Street on it. You can't rely on it to tell you where we are."

Seth grumbles, "Don't diss the atlas. It got us down here didn't it?"

The atlas is yellowed with age and looks like a family relic Seth's grandparents used to drive Route 66 back in the heyday of fine adventure when men still wore hats and it was still safe to pick up hitchikers.

"How old is that thing?" I ask. "It must've been drafted before the continental plate shifted."

"Shut up before I beat you with it." He squints at the sky and unfolds a loose page torn out years before and shoved back into place. He points to our left. "That is north. We're between St. Charles and Camp. Prytania runs parallel."

"Whatever." The plain truth around here is north is west and east is south all at the same time because the City curves like the crescent moon hugging the darkness of the Mississippi River. Try navigating it when you're bombed out of your mind. I put Sylvia's duffel bag on the ground and prop myself up against a staircase running straight into a solid brick wall. "Good Lord. Look at this!" I point at the wall. "What the he--? How the hell am I supposed to find this place if it has no doors?! Is this an entrance? That is definitely going to give me nightmares later!"

"There's another entrance around the corner," Corrine says.

"Eehhhhhh. Maps! Side entrances! What's it matter?" I sigh. "Once the darkness and alcohol hit, it's all irrelevant because this town's geography and soul will change. Then you'll really have more things to worry about than plate tectonics because the whole frigging planet will turn upside down and implode on itself."

He lets out a drag. "No shit. Try getting a cab then."

Loni comes around the corner with the rooming arrangements. According to her there's no way to sneak anybody into the hotel rooms because the staff is tagging its guests with neon green bracelets which have to be presented every time you enter the hotel.

I grumble, "What kind of place is this? Security bracelets?"

"Beats me," Loni says. "We can get an extra room for about $170."

"What's it like in there?" Seth asks.

"Nice," she says. I doubt her sincerity. We've been wandering the City for over two hours and our irritability is noticeable. Seth especially. He was flipping through his map, rolling and wringing it in his white knuckle grip as Loni kept insisting we were headed in the right direction to the hotel. He is sleep deprived and she may say anything to keep Seth from bludgeoning her with the atlas.

"Give us a minute," I say to Loni.

Corrine asks, "Can I take a shower?"

"Sure." Loni picks up Sylvia's bag and hands it to Corrine. "I'll tell them you need to use the bathroom."

The two disappear around the corner.

Seth looks cranky.

"What?" I ask.

"Can we decide what we're doing here before everyone starts taking showers?" he demands.

"What? I showered already. Let her shower. Nobody cares what you smell like. Me? I'm insecure about my appearance and I crave the proper attention from women. I have to look clean."

"Alright already. What do you want to do?" he asks.

"It's only for a night. Tomorrow it's luxury at The W. We'll figure out how to find this poorly mapped corner later."

"What if it's like a YMCA in there?" he asks.

"Does it really matter to you? It's 2:30 and we've been up since yesterday," I say.

"Fine. Whatever." He yawns. "Let's get to the room before they seal the lobby doors up with more cement blocks."

The hotel is better than expected once we make it around the corner. It's small, but from the inside it appears restored from grander days and the amenities described by our desk clerk will do well for the night: Cable T.V., coffee maker, two beds (one pullout), complimentary "prayer breakfast", and no mini-bar which, considering the temptation to booze without care during after hours, is a very good thing. According to the protocol, it is necessary for the desk clerk to tag us with neon bands before she can set us free.

I whisper to Seth, "I bet these things are really tracking devices."

The desk clerk looks at me and laughs. "No, this is just to make sure only Prytania Park Hotel guests are on the hotel grounds. It's for security and safety."

"Uh-huh. I keep hearing that," I mumble. "They'll probably monitor our movements throughout the City."

Seth whispers back, "Shut up. We don't want to get kicked out before we've had a chance to cause some *real* trouble."

I mumble to Seth, "I think she heard you."

We smile at the desk clerk.

She smiles back. "So where are you all from?"

"Kentucky," I reply.

She fastens the plastic jewelry to my right wrist. "First time at Mardi Gras?" she asks.

"First time anywhere." I stare at the band and twist and turn it against the sunlight. "These are much nicer than the ones at the compound."

"The compound?" she asks.

Seth shakes his head and signs the registery. He whispers to her, "Ignore him and forget what you've heard. Between you and me he's never been outside it's walls and he's already said too much."

I wander to the lobby's corner next to a small bank of vending machines and open a glass refrigerator filled with beer and soft drinks. "Say," I am compelled to ask, "is the Prayer Breakfast non-denominational?"

She is confused. "Non-de-no-mi-nation---?"

I grab a six-pack of Miller Lite from the shelf. "You know, not geared towards one specific religion. I'd hate to share a meal with faith crazed Bible bangers. It would really affect my tenuous hold of...things. "

"Uh...it's just what we call the breakfast," she says, "There's no prayer involved. It's kind of a joke. I'm not sure anyone gets it. I think it's kind of like when this restaurant down the street calls their breakfast a 'Gospel Brunch' just because it's on Sunday. You know, with music and such. But there's no prayer involved."

"Thank God." I smile. "I was beginning to think Loni tricked us into joining a cult."

"Yeah," Seth grins. "I was like...'Oops. Not again'."

The desk clerk's well-rehearsed smile withers and she seems frightened.

I place the six-pack on the counter. "Can I pay for this?"

"Umm...you can charge it to your, uh...room."

"Great!" I grab the six-pack and my bag and walk into the courtyard. "I'm loving this place already. Wow! *Laissez le bon temps rouler!*" I cry.

Corrine is still showering in Loni's room when Seth and I settle in. The room doesn't look as big as the clerk described.

"Liars! Where the hell is the other bed?" I groan.

Seth walks past the bathroom and towards the couch. He lifts the cushions. "Well, this is the pull out." Then his eyes roll towards the ceiling. "It's a duplex. The other bed is on the second level."

I walk in and marvel at the high ceiling, "Ingenious. It doesn't look this big from the outside." A corkscrew staircase twists up into a second level. "Hmmm."

"What?" Seth asks.

I point at the staircase. "This is a problem for many reasons."

"What the hell are you talking about?" he asks.

"Well, for one, it's bad Feng Shui," I reply.

"What?"

"It's a corkscrew drilling into the earth. That's very destructive." I say.

"Shut up." He takes his glasses off and dives into the sofa.

I continue, "And secondly, can you imagine trying to negotiate this thing at five in the morning? Someone is gonna die. You might as well stick me in a bunk bed so I can roll off and kill myself."

He spreads himself out over the couch. "I see your point."

"Well as long as you understand the inherent physical and metaphysical dangers in this place I guess I'm okay with it."

"I do. Now please shut up and let me sleep before I'm forced to kill you," he groans.

Seth sleeps for over an hour. I spend the time drinking beer on a communal hotel balcony just above Prytania Street. The neighborhood is camouflaged by drowsing trees and gardens locked behind petite, black, laced iron fences. It feels old and venerable. I suspect within the gardens and painted on every old house is some haunted history. In the distance there are sirens and a marching band playing "St. James Infirmary." There is little traffic or noise coming from Prytania Street. All the action is happening to the hotel's north or west and after a few beers I am ready to rally everyone for a bar crawl through the Quarter.

When I get back to the room Seth is showering. Corrine is watching the same stories on CNN that were on before I escaped to the balcony and wants something to eat before we start drinking. It's a good idea because without food someone is bound to get severely hammered.

"I would like to fight off becoming a zombie as much as possible," I say to Corrine. "I don't remember the last time we ate so we better get a base to absorb all the alcohol."

Corrine grabs a bottle from the six-pack and drinks. "What happened to the vodka?"

"It wasn't much and we had it since yesterday."

She smiles and raises her bottle. "Okay...Cheers."

"To your health."

We leave Loni and the rest at the hotel after they can't decide between having a meal with us or standing on St. Charles Street to catch throws and watch the floats go by. Seth doesn't care about the parades, Corrine wants to eat, and I want to keep my good feeling going. We leave the hotel around 4:30 and plan to meet Loni later.

It's still daylight and we have a general direction to follow. We plan to walk the distance to the Quarter, but catch a cabbie who just dropped someone off from the airport. He takes us as close as he can for five bucks until his car gets boxed in by the crowds of people and the parades.

"This is about as far as I can get you," he says. "Doesn't look like this street is going to open up anytime soon. This parade just started."

Corrine asks, "Is it going to be like this all day?"

He gives her a wide, gold tooth capped grin. "Welcome to Mardi Gras."

We walk through the Central Business District and across Canal to Royal Street and cut through a side street underneath swaths of purple, yellow and green banners and bunting. Drunk men yell and toss beads at Corrine from the balconies embroidered with masks, giant bows and colored garland. She refuses to pick anything up because she thinks she has to give up a flash of the flesh in return. I tell her otherwise but she doesn't believe me. We pass on a small restaurant, a bar, and another bar with an all you can eat oyster platter and a special Hurricane themed drink.

"What's in a Hurricane?" Corrine asks.

"Rum and craziness," Seth replies.

"Depending on where you get one," I say, "it can become something you might have to plan your day around."

The truly raucous attractions are one or two streets over on Bourbon, but I'm not prepared to deal with the madness yet and prefer to walk and find a place on the outskirts and away from the noise where I can sacrifice the last moments of personal clarity for the day. I will give it all up and become a part of the big, lewd and joyous human freak show soon enough. I'm all for the big ticket spectacles on Canal Street, but there are less visible attractions running loose in the Quarter that demand investigation. Like the group of Samoans in diapers wearing Viking horns and drinking beer, or the pack of ladies dressed as pink poodles the Samoan Vikings are chasing after. Why should we stand by on St. Charles and watch floats go by when we can have a few cocktails and be the parade? I surrender to the urges quickly and stop at the closest vendor I see. Seth buys the first round of thirty-two ounce beers at what is not a bar or a street stand, but a doorway to some enterprising local's house with five icy kegs in it. The plastic cups have big blue lettering emblazoned on them: "IMBECILE SIZE BEER".

We stand on the nearest corner next to a mounted police officer and his horse and drink our vulgar beverages. A small krewe walks past us dressed like ducks followed by more hirsute men in diapers and I realize an imbecile sized beer will not be adequate to get a firm grasp of this reality. Seth orders another round and I convince him there must be larger and more obscene quarry out in the streets waiting to be discovered and drank; perhaps a big tank in an alley someplace where the locals quietly drown

54

tourists in beer to facilitate brain death or population control. We move on towards the Quarter's riverbank until I am crippled with pain and a fear my bladder will burst if we don't stop walking. We stop to plot our next move at a corner on Decatur and St. Phillips Street. There is a loose gathering of artists and musicians mixed in with some Hare Krishna just outside the wonderfully fried flavors drifting out of one restaurant's doors.

"Ask them about oysters," Seth says to me.

"They're vegetarians you moron," I reply.

"No...about reincarnation," he says.

I wince in pain. "Shut up. Oh Lord I need to pee. You ask them. I've got to get inside before they grab me and my incontinence is used against me to join the movement."

Seth asks, "You wanna eat here?"

"Why not?!" I cry and force open the doors. "This place seems as good as any and I'll be making an imbecile sized mess in my pants in two seconds if I don't get relief..."

"Alright." He peers inside. "It'll do," he says.

The restaurant has five bottled beers in a bucket for ten dollars a pail. Not as large and cheap an offering as the vendors in the streets, but colder and tastier, along with boiled crawfish by the pound. The restaurant is doing a brisk business. While the Krishna continue to hand out leaflets outside their doors, a small Scientologist card table lurks at the street's end. They have a wired, hungry look about them and seem intent on kidnapping someone to sacrifice to their space god.

"I would like to avoid them at all costs," I say to Seth.

He assures Corrine, "It's all just part of the show. It's not the weirdest thing you'll see in town."

"They frighten me with their alien technology and death rays." I sigh. "I've dealt with them in Chicago and they're quite mad."

"What do you expect, you kicked them out of their church," he replies. "*That's* how shit gets started."

"Don't give me that shit. It wasn't religious persecution, it was business. Everybody has to pay taxes. 'Render unto Cesar what is Cesar's'. Blame the Cook County Assessor's Office. It wasn't like those Buddhists on the Northside who lost a burial ground to a taxbuyer. Those poor bastards couldn't even speak English. That's definitely gonna roll back on someone's head. There's a very special place in hell for taxbuyers; they fall somewhere between liars and pigfuckers."

"I agree," Seth says. "Pigfucking is a dishonorable profession, but you can't blame the pigs."

"Of course not," I reply, "It's not a choice. Pigs are born that way." I watch the spiritless shells of crayfish heads pile up on our plates. "I thought your people aren't supposed to eat this stuff."

Seth barely lifts his head from the feeding frenzy to acknowledge my presence in this one man orgy. He mumbles, "Don't tell anyone."

"Hmm..." I say, "There's something viciously cruel, satisfying, and scary about tearing these bugs apart and sucking the life out of them isn't there? You seem to relish the task. Something in your personality..."

He grabs a crayfish and sucks the well spiced juice out of its head, "Don't worry about me. Worry about the Promise Keepers."

"What?" I scan the restaurant. "They're here?"

"Uh-huh. They were following you but the Krishna chased them off with tambourines and love," he says.

"Screw you. Why would you joke about something like that? Those guys really scare me. Explain to me how you can hang out at a football stadium with a bunch of guys if there's no beer involved? I'm liable to join the Martians just to protect myself from that horde," I reply.

"You're perfect for them," he says, "they love alcoholics."

"Eehhh...what movement doesn't? The goddamned Martians already have me on their 'Watch' list. I get hate mail from NARCONON every month. Pass me another beer."

Corrine takes the last beer from the bucket and hands it to me. "They have oysters here Seth," she says.

"I know." He burps. "I can squeeze a dozen in before we head out."

"Go ahead. I'm too full to argue the hazards of oysters and reincarnation with you." I waive the waitress over. "Can we get another bucket?"

"Sure thing honey," she says. "Miller Lite right?"

"Yes ma'am. Also my friend here would like a dozen slimy oysters," I reply.

"Anything else?" she asks.

"Corrine?" I ask.

"Make it two buckets," she says. "And a helmet with a chinstrap for him."

"Ha! At least you're looking out for me." I laugh. "I know Seth will probably leave me dead in the streets the first chance he gets. Either that or sell me to the Promise Keepers."

"Yeah I will." He sucks the juice out of another head. "And I'll take your helmet with me."

"Judas. I always knew you would betray me." I raise my bottle. "Here's to Red Tide you treacherous bastard, I hope those little buggers come back to haunt you."

"Cheers." He lifts his bottle.

Corrine raises hers and declares, "I feel like a shot. You wanna do a shot?"

I look at my watch. It is 6:15. The Knights of Babylon are about thirty minutes into their parade. In about twenty minutes the Krewe of Chaos will begin their march followed by the Bards of Bohemia. Shooting anything this early will definitely open the doors. Perhaps the food will just absorb it and I'll be fine until after the parades when Loni and Sylvia meet up with us. It will be shot after shot and drink after drink until a plastic helmet becomes a fashionable necessity when things really get going. Seth usually doesn't shoot anything because he's all about the pace. I am like Corrine and drink as long as I feel like it. The food helps. I am buzzed but level headed. What the hell? One shot won't hurt. The other ones will do me in, but that won't be until much later when we'll all be in bad shape and it'll be chinstraps for everybody.

"Better get another helmet," I say to Corrine. "And while you're at it, ask them if we can take a bucket to throw up in."

Seth shakes his head. "Pass."

"You can't pass," Corrine says.

He sucks the juice out of another head. "This isn't a race."

"Forget him," I say. "I'll drink with you. We'll get him later when he's weak with fever and easily suggestible."

Corrine and I leave Seth at the table with the oysters and make our way through the dinning room to a polished and clean bar. It is well stocked with shiny bottles of varying shapes and color, each one filled with mystery and potential chaos.

"Nothing too brown," I say to Corrine.

"Brown?" she asks.

"No. Too many congeners."

She is puzzled.

"Impurities. They're in your whiskeys mostly. It's a little too early for that misery." I wave the bartender over.

"Vodka?" she asks.

I snort. "We could be here all night."

The bartender makes a suggestion, "How about tequila?"

"Uh. Hmm." A siren goes off in my head. For me, tequila is the bad girl whose nauseas mornings spin themselves into gut wrenching afternoons. She's the flirty whore who tests my emotions on occasion. Many a bottle have made me a crazed and jealous ape, temporarily insane, hooting, hollering, and weeping. I have cried many a night with tequila for no reason whatsoever because it felt like the right thing to do at the time. I recall one particularly bad fight with a bottle of Cazadores Reposado. It made me swear to myself never to drink anything from a bottle with an animal's name or picture on it.

"Hmm...I don't really drink tequila." The fear and memories and taste well up my gullet.

The bartender turns to the glass shelf behind him and grabs a bottle that's almost empty. "How about this?"

Corrine looks at me. "Herradura Anejo?"

I lie. "Never heard of it."

He pulls three highball glasses from beneath the bar and sets them on the counter top. He pours shots to fill out half of each glass until the bottle is completely empty. "It's looks almost like gold. See? That's the kind you want to drink."

"What? No limes?" I ask.

61

The bartender shakes his head and tosses the empty bottle into a garbage can. "You going to ruin the taste?"

"I see," I reply.

"This one's on me," he says as he grabs a new bottle from underneath the bar and opens it.

I raise the highball and toast Corrine's.

She shoots the tequila back without a flinch. I taste a bitter burn on the backend. It will haunt me later.

"Not bad." Corrine looks at my soured expression and says, "One more."

I bury my horror and fear with a weak smile and hear a sad voice in my head cry softly,

"Oh...Tequila...(sob)..(sob)...you fucking whore...(sniff)...(sniff)..you bitch... You're a bad girl. And I'm your piñata."

The bartender pours two more shots and one for himself. "Laissez le bon temps rouler," he declares. After we shoot the drinks, the bartender pours two water glasses and hands one to Corrine and one to me. I drink half the glass and drink some vodka to keep me focused and alert.

The bartender looks at me. "You look familiar."

The tequila is warming my face. "I get that a lot," I reply.

"No." He turns around to put the tequila back on the shelf. "I know I've seen you before."

"Impossible," I mutter, "I've never been to Louisiana and have spent the last two years in the Philippine rain forests doing field studies on pygmy marmosets."

Corrine giggles, not because of the marmosets but because she is getting drunk.

"No," he says, "seriously. I'm positive I've seen you before."

"I'm sure you are mistaken," I reply casually. I look away from him to draw attention away from my face. The bartender is deep in thought and continues fixating on my presence with bulging eyes. He has a sinister look about him. Who is this man and why is he so insistent on identifying me? Was offering free shots his method of shanghaiing tourists? Was it all a trick...a false gesture of kindness to make me drop my guard? It was, after all, his suggestion to drink tequila. The blood is racing up my spine and the thin skin on the edge of my ears feels really goddamn hot. Good Lord what *did* he put in that drink? Ruffies? *Was it Ruffies?!*

I grab Corrine's hand and yelp, "I'm with her."

Corrine places her free hand over her face and continues to laugh about nothing in particular.

He looks at me with a stern eye. "Relax buddy, I'm married."

"Happily?" I mumble.

"What?"

"Nothing. I'm sorry," I reply, "it must be the tequila. We only drank vodka on the marmoset reservation and I'm probably having some adverse reaction. It's probably heightening my paranoia. I'm actually a very tolerant person. My best friend is gay."

He turns to Corrine. "Is he always like this?"

She stops laughing and says with a straight face, "Only when he's drinking, and he drinks A LOT."

I snap at Corrine, "TRAITOR! This man isn't interested in my fierce habits." I am compelled to ask him, "You're not from the Promise Keepers are you?"

"The what?" he asks.

"Not that there's anything wrong with that," I say politely. "I'm actually a big fan of the University of Colorado football program. I'm just a staunch Scientologist and don't want any trouble."

He fills my glass with water and eases it over to me. "I'm not sure what you're talking about, but I'm sure you'll need more of this."

"Sorry," Corrine replies.

"That's alright. We get all sorts down here," he says. "But I'm positive I've met him before."

The bartender calls over a waitress, a heavy white woman with an oily forehead. "Charlene, where have I seen this guy before?"

Charlene stares at me for a moment and gives me the once over. "I don't know."

The bartender's eyes light up. "Yeah...I know...you were here before."

Charlene and the bartender's unblinking curiosity make me uneasy. I am probably sweating profusely from the tequila and my aloof composure is not fooling anyone. *Have I been here before?* It's possible I've walked into this restaurant considering the few times I spent in New Orleans; but under what pretext and circumstance? The fact the bartender recognizes me from the thousands who patronize his bar is not a good thing. I probably ventured through these doors sometime ago under the influence of something evil and wrought obscenity, terror, and unpleasantness upon the heads of his staff. They must have been so thoroughly traumatized by my last visit. Only the bartender remembers my face and vowed to avenge his people for my barbaric treatment if I ever dared to darken their doors again. What dumb fate to drink so much Imbecile Sized Beer and end up choosing to use the restroom in a bar where I am wanted dead or alive. Upon her master's command Charlene will hold me down with her oily girth. The bartender will tie me up and order his staff to drag me out into the streets to be horse whipped with plastic beads and stoned to death with used oyster shells. My lifeless body will be left in the gutter next to garbage bags. Seth and Corrine will be too drunk to find me before the morning street cleaning and I will be swept up and treated by the Department of Streets and Sanitation and find myself reborn, covered in horseradish sauce, and lying on a cracker at Mardi Gras 2003.

I say meekly, "Did I forget to pay my bill?"

He laughs. "What? No...not at all. You left a good tip."

"Hmmm. I see. So we are talking about a good visit?"

"You don't remember being here?" Corrine asks.

"No. Well not in this bar but I suppose it's possible." I look at the bartender and try to place his face. "Did I fall down on the floor and hit my head?"

"Uh...no." He walks to the bar's far left end and reaches behind the liquor shelf. He walks back to us and hands a Polaroid picture to me, "That's you, right?"

I take the photo and hold it in my hand. The bartender leaves us to fill the drink orders for some girls at the end of the bar.

Corrine leans against my shoulder to get a look. "Hey, that is you."

The picture is about two years old, the second to the last time I was in New Orleans, but not for Mardi Gras. I was heavily mixed up with a married woman named Lisa who was worse for my soul than anything you might find in the Quarter. It was our last hurrah and we made the most of the cliché by running ourselves into the ground over a four-day stretch with vulgar amounts of booze, cigarettes, sex, love, and self-denial. It was indecent, wrong, and great fun because there was something wonderfully hopeless about our obsession with each other and the four-day ritual in New Orleans gave it a grand and meaningful death.

We spent the day wandering around without a purpose other than the unspoken desire to ignore the end. Lisa heard Etta James singing "At Last" through the restaurant's open windows and wanted to dance. And I wanted what she wanted. We stayed for a few drinks before being sent free shots and drinks as a courtesy from the bar.

Lisa sat across from me at a table next to a tall window opening out to Jackson Square. It was a late weekday afternoon and the light in the City was cooling from orange to blue. The restaurant was not busy and the waitress kept putting five-dollar bills into the jukebox to keep things lively.

"I'm being seduced," I said to Lisa.

"That's because you're easy," she said as she looked out through the window at some street musicians walking by.

"I'm being seduced by this city," I said.

She kept looking out the window and a faint smile broke from the corner of her lips.

I laughed. "Oh...you thought I was talking about you?"

She turned back towards me and smiled with her eyes. "Why is that?"

"Why is what?"

"Why do you think you're being seduced?"

"I don't know," I said as I took a sip from my beer. "I grew up three hours away and being down here reminds me of it all."

"Why not just go to Pensacola instead?"

I considered her question and shrugged. "I don't know. This was the first big city I ever saw and I guess it's still a great mystery to me."

"You should move down here...you seem more relaxed," she said. "Nevermind. Bad joke."

I laughed. "This place would just break my heart."

"Uh-huh."

I looked outside at the sleepy mules waiting across from the Cathedral of Saint Louis to pull their carriages.

She asked, "What's on your mind?"

"Nothing."

She sunk back into her chair and stretched her legs across and underneath the table to rest on my lap. We were at Café Du Monde earlier in the afternoon and the beignets left powdered sugar on her red, nail polished toes.

"What?" she asked again.

I smirked. "I was just thinking. You should never get involved with a beautiful woman in New Orleans."

"And why is that?" she said as she drank her beer.

"Because it gives them the advantage."

I thought we had settled the matter. At least in her heart. But New Orleans plays a trick on you. Your life sounds, smells, looks, and tastes better and you can't imagine the alternative once it ensnares your senses and you start day dreaming again.

That morning I was mesmerized by the brown landscape of her body laid out against the hotel's white bed sheets. I drove my hand along the slope of her hips and down across her belly following a slivered trail of daylight peeking through the blinds.

"I hate this," Lisa said.

I whispered into her ear, "Hate what?"

She took my hand and locked it into hers. "This. I want to leave New Orleans and you're making me fall in love with it again. Like it was when I first moved here. Like it was when we first met. Before I got married."

"Oh." I kissed her neck. "I'm sorry."

"No you're not."

"No." I replied. "I'm not."

"That's the problem," she said. "This place makes us not care about anything else. There are no consequences until you leave. I can't stand Bourbon Street. I don't even come here unless you're here. But I don't care when I'm with you. It scares me."

"Why?"

"Because I just can't forget about my life. I just can't forget who I am. But this place tricks me into forgetting and not caring about anything else."

"So what should we do about this?"

Lisa pulled me close and tucked my hand against her face. Her eyes were wet. She said nothing and breathed deep against my body.

My eyelashes brushed the light hairs along the nape of her neck and I breathed in her skin.

"It's over," she said.

"I know," I whispered.

She kissed my hand. "But not today."

I kissed her neck. The light through the window had already moved on. "No…not today."

Back at the restaurant, the waitress, a pretty, light skinned, Creole girl named Katey, walked up to the table. She had a sweet easy way about her and moved playfully, occassionally dancing by herself around the restaurant floor. She spoke with a slow, subtle, twang, "I told the bartender what a nice couple you are and would like to buy you a round of drinks."

Lisa looked at me and smiled. "That's sweet. Thank you." She stood up. "Order whatever you want honey, I need to make a phone call."

I ordered more beer and the bartender threw in a few easy shots. Lisa was still outside on her phone when Katey brought the drinks. "Where's your girlfriend?" she asked as she placed the beer on the table.

I took the shots off the tray and sighed. "She's not my girlfriend."

"Really?" she said. "Huh...You look real good together."

Lisa was standing on the Square's cobblestones with the strangeness of fortunetellers, street performers, artists, mimes and magicians swirling around her. I would miss it all, and knew real addiction came from being tangled up with a woman I could never truly have. In the end she left me alone in the Quarter, unconscious and hungover on the hotel room floor with a $1000 hotel bill and a pack of Marlboro Lights.

Corrine holds the picture between her fingers, dangles it above the growing wreath of alcohol above my head and asks, "Who's the girl?"

"I don't know," I say. "Just some chick I had some shots with that night. You know me...I always end up drinking with women or because of them. We must've whooped it up for these guys to take a picture."

The bartender comes back to us and asks, "Jog your memory?"

"Vaguely." I snag the picture away from Corrine and look at it one more time before handing it back to the bartender. "Did you ever see this girl again?"

"Naw," he pours me some Absolut with fresh ice and pours Corrine another shot of Herradura. "Here. I learned this in Spain," he says proudly, "Bebemos a olvidar, pero no olvidamos a beber." He hands me the glass and eases Corrine's shot over to her. "To good times."

"Good times."

Corrine puts the shot down and draws the attention of a guy sitting two empty stools down from us. He's says he's impressed with her drinking the way most men are when they have nothing interesting to say but need an icebreaker to make a move and buy the "next" drink. I suppose I should be offended he's hitting on a girl he's assuming isn't my girlfriend, or maybe to him it doesn't matter, but Corrine is a free agent and my interest in her is limited to her willingness to let us borrow her car to drive down to New Orleans as long as she could come with. She's been hanging out casually for almost a year now after one of my associates made the same move on her at a bar in Wrigleyville. Until the long drive our friendship only seemed to exist in the context of bars and the hazy recollections of the next day. Her would be suitor gets the low down on her vitals while I continue to ward off the flirtatious banter with more vodka. I could spare us all the wasted oxygen and blurt out in my slowly creeping tequila delirium that she's five-six, 22 years old, half Spanish,

73

half Polish, fair skinned more than olive. No, "this guy" is not her boyfriend just her friend. No, she's never been to New Orleans before and she doesn't care how you have a "thing" for brunettes. Bastard. You may be able to see things but you observe nothing. Can't you tell this woman has been around bars and knows what the score is? For God's sake you've seen her drink tequila. Do you really think she would buy into such amateurish attempts to win her favor?

"Hmm...." I slur, "...you're very pretty."

"Don't get weird on me," Corrine says.

"No...I'm just saying...as an observation."

"You're drunk."

"Ehhh you're probably right."

"Thanks."

"Like I said, 'with them or because of them'."

"Huh?"

"Uh...women and drinking."

"Right."

After a few more drinks, Corrine and I walk back to the dining room to find out if Seth expired from eating bad oysters. He is sitting, stretched and reclined back, with a fat, happy smile on his face and about two-dozen empty shells scattered over the plate and table.

Corrine asks, "How were they?"

He pats his stomach. "Great."

I pull up a chair and sit down. "They taste horrible coming back up," I say. "Sometimes they come up through your nose and you don't know the difference between your snot and the oyster."

"You guys took long enough," he says.

"We were chatting with the bartender." Corrine gives me the evil eye and nudges her shoulder against mine. "He's been here before."

Seth asks, "Are we in trouble?"

"No, idiot," I say. "We got free shots."

"Oh. Good. Shots of what?" he asks.

"Tequila," Corrine replies.

"Yeaachhh!" Seth sits up and grabs a beer from the bucket. He turns to Corrine. "Your phone kept buzzing."

"Who was it?" she asks.

"I don't know. I answered it but couldn't hear anything. It's too loud in here," he replies.

She looks at the number. "It's probably Loni," she says. "I'll call her when we get outside. Are we done?"

"Yeah," Seth replies.

"We've still got a few beers left," Corrine says.

"When the check comes ask the waitress for some plastic cups and we'll take it with us."

Corrine asks, "They'll let us do that?"

Seth lights a cigarette and nods his head.

I smile. "God Bless this town."

Chapter Four

The meal's final tally for breads and circus are a modest $98.07 with tip----

drinks at the bar not included. From that total the food was only $27.00 and

the beverages came out to about 8 beers a person. We take four with us in

plastic cups and venture into the creeping darkness. The tequila-vodka-beer

experiment is kicking in and I am pleasantly numb, slightly obnoxious, and

light on my feet. I feel like dancing with the Krishna and picking on the

Scientologists. Seth can sense bad ideas emerging from my brain's blacker

corners and takes the initiative to steer us away from the religious and back

down Decatur Street towards the drunks. On Decatur I will easily blend in

as just another boogey man.

Loni and Sylvia are done with the parades and drinking somewhere on Bourbon Street at a bar they believe has no name. On our way there, Corrine becomes the temporary infatuation of an old man with sex crazed eyes. He spied her a few yards ahead and comes crashing towards her without care for the people walking around him. His neck is fully beaded and the trinkets shining underneath his overgrown beard barely cinch the boiling lust in his Viagra fueled brain. Corrine is stunned. He is the troll she has always heard about in the Grimm Brothers' fairytales; the trickster who lures naïve girls deeper into the forest and steals away their innocent, bare-chested souls. I can see them all, barely legal nymphs from Mardi Gras of the last twenty years, forever imprisoned in his VHS and now digitized trove of masturbation material hidden underneath a bridge somewhere.

He aims his camcorder at her and walks backwards to shoot us.

"Sssshow me yore tittssss."

"Christ you freak! Get away from us!" I growl. I push Corrine along and we keep walking.

The man stalks us for half a block pleading even louder now, "WHU-HITE shirt! WHU-HITE shirt! SSSHOW ME YORE TITTSS!"

Beads fly from above and behind us and whack me on the head.

78

It begins, I think to myself. Impending darkness. Bars with no names. Religious wars. Crazed boogey men. Trolls with camcorders. Dizziness. Hurricanes. Nakedness. Claustrophobia. And beads. Beads being whipped at me by unprincipled opportunists, raging alcoholics and sexual deviants. We lose the troll or he loses interest and he quickly becomes an afterthought in the thickening crowd and darkness.

"I hate the way they've commercialized it all," I grumble.

Seth asks, "Commercialized what?"

"The tease around here."

"What are you talking about?"

"The tease...the subtle suggestion. The burlesque...With the camcorders and the crap."

"You have those tapes," he replies.

"They were a gift. Their value to me is strictly informational. It's a fine example of the privacy problems we face...legally speaking."

"Uh-huh." Seth keeps walking and ignores more cameras behind us chasing a tall blonde girl with a cowboy hat and red vinyl pants.

Someone yells above our heads from one of the balconies, "RED PANTS TAKES IT UP THE ASS!" A shower of beads rains down on us.

I am distracted for a moment at the ruckus and realize all the walking and all the drinking is making me short of breath, "No really...you should watch out for the free roaming camcorder. It's a miserable consequence of unchecked technology and the state of the world. If the government isn't watching you then some unscrupulous tourist with an onanistic sex life is."

"Uh-huh," Seth says.

"I'm serious. I could get disbarred for anything with the appearance of impropriety. Gossip and rumor is hearsay. Video would be objective proof. The Attorney Registration and Disciplinary Committee would love to get their filthy hands on me."

"You're paranoid."

"There are too many lawyers in this world. The market dictates that they gotta get rid of us somehow. All they need is a lurid videotape of me asking some cross-dresser to show me his tits and it's all over for me. Video would definitely give them cause to bring me in for interrogation."

"I'll keep that in mind."

"Judas." I eye him suspiciously. "You *would* do that to me wouldn't you?"

He stops walking and hands me his beer. "Idiot...the tequila is fucking with your mind. If you start bawling I'm out of here. Drink this instead, it'll set you straight."

"God maybe you're right." My chest feels tight and I take a deep breath and drink the beer slowly until the cup is empty. "I'm feeling cranky as hell."

"Stop doing shots," he orders. "I'm not going to drag your drunk-ass around the Quarter. I'll leave you to rot in the streets with the lunatics if you become too much to handle."

"You really shouldn't frighten me like that," I reply, "but I understand."

"You sure?"

I nod my head and give him the most composed smile I can muster. He stares at me for a second with uncertainty and shakes his head and continues cutting through the parade route's thinner edges.

More people fill the Quarter.

Corrine pulls out a business card with the hotel's name and address on it and hands it to me. "Here. Put this in your pocket. If you get lost just find a cab and tell them to take you back."

"Bless you," I reply, "but you might have to staple it to my forehead so I don't lose it."

"Just show them the wristband," she says.

"My God you're right." I look at the wristband and read the hotel address in black lettering. "I forgot about this thing. If I get lost I'm sure they'll track me down and haul me back to the compound."

Loni and Sylvia are instructed to meet us at Bourbon and Iberville. When we find them we are told Marty has been arrested. Loni is glad to be rid of him. He was becoming a drunken pain in the ass and refused to pay two dollars to a Chinese lady renting her door space for port-a-potties. The local deputies took him away when he tested the natives' threshold for unsanitary behavior by urinating in a very non-discreet corner off Bourbon Street. The right thing to do would be to bail him out but it seems pointless to chase after him. As soon as the cops discover he is Navy, he will be handed over to the MP's. They in turn will tag and release him back into the Quarter because they will have their hands full with more pressing matters like unsolicited ass grabbing by horny sailors and the resulting fist fights. It will be a fine test of Marty's military training to locate us, and Loni reasons if he does find us he will have earned his right to drink with the cool kids.

Loni did the right thing in letting him go without a fight. If there's anything to be learned from Southern gatherings, it's that police down South have hard-ons for carpetbaggers and know-it-alls. My knowledge of this old law enforcement tradition has come from attending the grandest redneck rituals from Mardi Gras to The Kentucky Derby where one year Seth and I witnessed an associate of ours receive a royal Southern ass-whuppin' at the behest of a pissed off female cop. After our friend refused to let the police take his brother-in-law away for public drunkenness, he was attacked by a pack of nightstick wielding hyenas who jumped on him like he was a confused water buffalo in a nature video. It was my first instinct to save him, but my culturally sensitive side realized at one point during the exchange that once you cross the Mason Dixon line you become fair game to any chawbacon with a badge who is still hell bent on winning the Civil War. Best to let it go, take your beating like a man, and let a good Southern lawyer play Jedi mind tricks on your tormentors in a court of law.

The sky looks like it might rain and Bourbon Street is becoming dark. There is neon and street lamps and light coming from the balconies and from the entrances of restaurants, bars, gifts shops, and strip clubs, but I am still disoriented by the looming dark. There are too many people

moving around the street and the signs and landmarks lose their
significance and purpose.

I have experienced this feeling before. After a time everything on
the street will look the same and a dangerous mood will creep into the
Quarter. It is the uneasiness brought on by the apparent chaos surrounding
you and the irresistible notion you should do something just because you
can probably get away with it. By then it might be too late to save you
from the impulses drawing you into New Orleans' godless corners to get
cannibalized by the insanity. It's not unusual to see women weeping in the
streets from the sheer, drunken panic of being lost in such a scary place.
Aside from the heightened testosterone levels brought on by fistfights,
cheap booze, and nudity, it must be pretty horrifying to be lost in the dark
with strangers screaming at you to show them your tits.

It is eight o'clock and I hear a voice in my head say, *"I'm thirsty"*.
Shortly thereafter, my sensibilities go down. I fall hard into the alcohol and
the Quarter becomes a demented landscape. The outside world is a
nauseous blur. I am in the midst of satyrs and many more unknown
creatures with human bodies but the heads of birds and beasts and I'm
looking for any bar to take my money and protect me from these monsters.
Eventually I find myself rooted to a stool on Bourbon Street's northern end

surrounded by plastic palm trees, Christmas lights, a badly airbrushed

sunset, very large parrots, and a dead shark suspended in the air gnashing

its teeth. There is a green octopus spreading its arms around the room

above my head. It has mad red light bulbs for eyes. The parrots squawk

loudly and randomly, and look close to freaking out from the thick

cigarette smoke invading their air. I am sucking on something green from a

plastic half yard glass called a "Grenade". It is sticky and potent business. I

am halfway into it when the only thing I am certain of about this place is

the rum, melon liquer, grain alcohol and some swarthy foreigners in the

corner directly across from me with a camcorder and bad looks about them.

I've been told recently to be suspicious of this exact scenario by the

mannequins on cable news. They could be conducting reconaissance for

"Non-State Actors" looking for soft targets to film and eventually attack

with bombs. In this case the foreigners are hounding a blonde cheerleader

in a blue and white skirt with their accents and insisting on trading beads

for the opportunity to immortalize her pale, Western flesh on their cameras.

It makes me uptight and cranky until the rum sinks deeper into the blood

and turns my spine into warm goo and fuzzy feelings. In their homeland

these poor bastards would probably be sentenced to death for their amateur porn so why not leave them be and let the ladies bare all as a gesture of good will to our democratically deprived guests.

As the xenophobia fades, my head fills with sleep and dizziness. It is not a place I want to be. I refocus my attention and efforts on ordering something to get my blood pumping and more oxygen to my dull headed brain.

I command the bartender, "Absolut on the rocks!"

"Do you want a lime or anything?" she asks.

"No," I reply and hand her five bucks. I pass the Grenade back to her. "And please take this godawful thing away from me."

She is surprised more than offended. "You didn't like it?"

"No, actually I loved it but it could be a real problem if you know what I mean."

She looks confused and I have no idea what I am saying but continue blabbering away, "I should keep my feet firmly planted on the ground and drink only those things I am comfortable with...at least for the moment."

She slides a plastic cup with my usual in it and shrugs her shoulders.

I hear a voice in my right ear say, "Maybe you shouldn't drink so much."

A middle-aged white man is sitting next to me. My forehead is heavy and I can feel the weight of it resting on my eyelids. I look for Seth and the others but don't see them. I turn my attention back to the man and observe him for what seems like a very long time. He is staring straight ahead and smiling at nothing and this makes him seem disingenuously kind. In weaker moments his white smile might garner my curious sympathy with all its gloriously capped teeth. But I suspect it is a lure. Like those vampire fish who dangle bright lights in dark waters to naïve and wayward creatures. His head is long like a tear drop, narrow at the top with a high forehead, but full, round, and thick at the bottom. His face looks red from too much sun and his long jaw is strangely cartoonish. The wrinkles above his eyebrows are thick and tight and look shaped by a man used to purposely twisting his polite expressions into sudden, explosive rage. His eyes creep and dart like black lizards underneath the eyebrow canopy. All the facial signs are subtle warnings. The odd contradiction to all this is his hair. His hair is a nicely manicured gray and seems dusty underneath the Christmas lights. It swoops up and back and remains undisturbed by the kinetic expressions quietly boiling below.

He turns to me.

"Holy shit!" I yell and clutch my chest. "I thought you were a statue."

"I said maybe you shouldn't drink so much."

"Oh, thank God." I take a few sips from the plastic cup. "I thought the voices...you know?...uh...never mind."

He raises an eyebrow. "Are you a true believer?"

"I'm a firm believer," I reply.

He nods his head up and down and takes a sip from the plastic cup in his hand. "Great!" He turns to address me and smiles all teeth, "It's always nice to meet a true believer."

"Wait---" The heaviness on my eyelids spreads to the rest of my face and I try my best to keep the dead weight of my head from slumping onto the bar top. "What are we talking about?"

"God," he says.

I ask, "What about God?"

"You're a believer," he smiles.

"Oh. No, no, no," I reply. "I thought you meant a believer in only drinking things I'm comfortable with."

His face stiffens. The teeth disappear. "I see." He pauses and takes a deep breath and extends his hand. "Bob Whittaker. My friends call me Brother Bob."

"Okay Bob." I shake his hand. "Seth," I reply.

"Say, Seth," he asks, "do you drink a lot?"

"Oh God yes," I say. "I'm all about the buzz."

"I see." He nods his head. "Did you ever think to consider you might drink too much? You do real evil to yourself by giving into these temptations."

"All the time," I reply. "But I can't really help myself right now. It's really my lawyer's fault. He dragged me to this godforsaken town and is slowly killing me with cheap booze and bad oysters and I think he's sleeping with my wife."

Bob's black lizards search the bar. "Where is he?"

"I don't know," I say. "But if you see a Filipino mad man running around here with a fourteen year old girl and a bottle of Absolut crammed in his face you have my permission to turn him in to the proper authorities."

The lizards freeze. Bob contemplates my revelations with horror and disbelief.

"The fourteen year old is my wife's daughter from a previous marriage," I reply.

"Oh I see," Bob says. "How old are you?"

"Twenty-nine," I reply and take a deep sip of vodka. "Yes, we're here to find my wife and serve her with divorce papers. Damn whore. Truth be told I think he's humping them both."

"Who?" he asks.

"Jesus, Bob...my lawyer," I reply. "To tell you the truth, this moment in time is a historic opportunity to purge our land of all sorts of deviants. I hope I nail the bastard!"

He shakes his head. There is a grumble of disgust. "They should keep people like that out of our country. That is just...perverse."

"Absolutely sickening," I reply. "But apparently in his country it's customary to have sex with minors as part of the retainer. So you understand my dilemma and why I need a drink."

Bob is searching his inventory of moral truisms to pull Seth back from his unseemly disclosure. He pauses for a moment to reorient his thoughts: "Well, I can see why you drink. But why do you have to drink?"

"Weren't you listening to a word I just said? CHRIST." I shake the glass in my tight fist and thrust it at him. "THIS JUST GETS ME BACK TO NORMAL, MAN!"

Bob spills his cup and aims a slow smoldering glare at me but regains his composure. I can sense where this is going. As far as Bob is concerned we are locked in a struggle to save me from having a good time.

The bartender rushes over. "Settle down," she says.

"I'm sorry Bob," I reply. "...What are you drinking?"

"A COKE," he says sternly and wipes his hands with a cocktail napkin.

"ARE YOU SHITTING ME?!" I roar with a laugh. "IT'S MARDI GRAS!"

A fat, black gentleman, presumably the bouncer, comes in from outside the bar doors, blocks the doorway with his stomach, and looks at the bartender. She turns to me and says, "I won't tell you again."

"I'm sorry, ma'am," I reply, "...may I please have a Coke and another Absolut rocks."

She turns away to get my drink order. The bouncer moves from the doorframe and leans his enormous weight against the wall directly opposite the bar. I can hear him sucking huge gulps of air from the room with his breathing. He crosses his arms and eyes us suspiciously.

Bob is rigid and severe. "Now. I've been polite with you my friend haven't I?"

"Absolutely Bob...a complete gentleman if you'd allow me to say so."

"Well then you'll forgive me for saying I'm truly offended by your use of the Lord's name like that. It's a sin...it's blasphemy," he says.

I put a hand on his shoulder. "I'm just having a hard day. Nothing personal against you and your God," I reply.

"He's your God too, Seth. Tell me, have you accepted Jesus Christ into your life as your Lord and sav----?"

"HOLY SHIT!" I scream. "The cheerleader isn't wearing any panties!"

Bob unflinching, doesn't bother to even look in the cheerleader's direction as she puts on a beaver show for the whole bar.

I give Bob my best solemn look. "You were saying?"

"I was saying he's your God too, Seth." Bob places both hands on my shoulders and gently squeezes the way I suspect childmolesters do before the molesting really begins. "Tell me Seth, have you accepted Jesus Christ into your life as your Lord and savior?" he asks.

I place my own hands on Bob's shoulders. We are now locked in an almost embrace and I give him a gentle shake. "Bob?"

"Seth?"

"I'm Jewish."

It seems an odd revelation to him. The word 'Jewish' tweaks his ear and tightens a screw in his brain with its syllables. He drops the almost embrace.

"Don't let my ethnicity fool you," I reply and pat him on the shoulder. "I converted at a very young age."

"I see," he says. "Well...we can't all be perfect." He laughs. "Right?" He laughs again this time with a little creeping hostility.

I let out a tiny laugh and nod my head.

"I mean," he says and smiles again with the teeth, "you got to know that your time is running out."

The bartender slides the Coke and ice to Bob. She pushes the vodka and ice at me. "Six dollars."

"SIX?!" I reply. "How much is a Coke?"

"Two," she says.

I dig into my pocket, pull out a bill and hand it to her. I carefully lean my head to the side to sneak a glimpse at the bouncer. He is still pressing his back against the wall, his fat arms crossed and resting on his stomach. I turn to Bob and raise my glass. "You were saying?"

The bartender interrupts, "This is a five."

My eyelids are heavier than they have ever been and I strain to focus on the money in her hand. "Hmmm. My bad. It's the new bills...they all look like tens to me." I sift through the wad of crumpled dollars in my fist and give her two singles.

Bob interrupts, "I've got a ten here Miss but I'm not paying for him."

I smack his hand politely. "Don't you dare, Brother Bob! Your money's no good here!"

The bartender takes the money. "Thanks," she says and moves her attention to the bar's opposite end.

Despite "Seth's" obvious religious disability Bob is determined to keep his company. He begins a slow grumbling complaint about non-Christians. It starts with him intellectualizing the geopolitical reasons for the world's problems and how they could be corrected with evangelism. It is his reason for throwing himself into the unholy land this time of year. I think he should lighten up and when he isn't looking pour vodka into his drink. I sheepishly nod as he babbles on. He takes a sip, spits back into his drink and slams his cup into the bar. There is a silence and the waves of wrinkles above his eyes begin to tighten. Bob lashes out, "You people have no respect for anything!" He wipes his tongue with a cocktail napkin. "Things like piety, abstinence and sobriety. You come here with your godlessness and spit all over the people who belong here! Well I won't let you ruin my country!" He balls up the napkin and flings it at me.

My forehead is hot and as Bob spouts his firebrand declarations into the air and pokes a crooked finger at me, the wall behind him bends to the right, over and over and over again. Corrine's tequila shots are bashing my head. Seth and the others are nowhere, and without the proper supervision I wig out from the squawking parrots and squawking Bob. "Respect?" I say, "No. Because you evil bastards won't be satisfied until everybodys a Christian. Am I right?! Perhaps instead of picking on Jews, half-breeds, effeminate heterosexuals, masculine homosexuals, whoremongers, alcoholics, drug abusers, aborigines, and pornographers you should focus your self-righteous rage and inexhaustible crusading towards cannibals, rednecks, the deaf, and pygmies!" I shove him on the shoulder. "What do you think Brother Bob? Perhaps your annoying proselytizing has a divine end we heathens don't yet know about or are too ignorant to comprehend. Maybe your loathing will rally all those people you've offended and the World will finally unite in one effort, one love, and one mutual hate towards you; whom history will later re-examine, reconsider and ultimately praise as a unifying force of the highest order. Yeah Bob...you'll be a fantastic scapegoat...delivered into pagan hands to ridicule and murder because nobody likes you!"

I squeeze the plastic cup eagerly in my hand. Fully intent to baptize Bob with vodka. It will put an end to our religious debate and indoctrinate him into my glorious faith in alcohol. "OR MAYBE YOU'RE JUST WRONG YOU STUPID BIBLE-BANGER!"

The big green and yellow bird closest to me lets out a deafening noise and the bouncer springs into action. He is exceptionally light and quick on his feet for a sweaty, fat man and takes little effort to lock me into a rough chokehold. He drags me across the floor towards the doorway. Hopelessly outmatched to resist this bum's rush, I yelp like a stray dog on its way to be gassed, "WAIT! WAIT GODDAMNIT! YOU DIDN'T SEE THE WAY HE WAS PROVOKING ME! ASK THE PARROTS! THEY WERE THERE!" I struggle to get loose and make a wild grab at Bob's gnashing teeth as the bartender holds him back and he spits out all sorts of Un-Christian like words.

"YOU GODDAMNED FASCIST!" I yell. "YOU'LL GET YOURS!"

The Bouncer has no trouble at all in carrying me out and speaking to me at the same time under his heavy breath, "You were warned...now get the fuck out before I call the police!"

"I'M NOT FIGHTING YOU!" I declare.

"And I appreciate that," he replies as we pass through the doorway and into the cool night air. Curious onlookers outside the bar seem to annoy the bouncer more than me because they are in his way. As he drags me along, we bump into a giant smiling green pineapple.

"HOLY CRAP!" I laugh. "WHAT THE HELL ARE YOU?!"

It is actually someone dressed up as a grenade to promote the bar's signature cocktail. The grenade snaps and pushes me back. "HEY! Don't grab the costume!"

"WARMONGER!" I scream. "AT LEAST LET ME GET MY DRINK!"

The bouncer lets me go on my feet and shoves me in the back and off into the street. He calmly pushes his way through the crowd with thick, dark, arms and heads back towards the bar entrance.

"ANTI-SEMITES!" I scream. "WATCH OUT FOR THOSE PARROTS 'CAUSE THEY'RE REALLY PISSED OFF!!"

There are a few boisterous laughs and smart-ass remarks from the crowd, but after The Grenade steals away into the bar for safety, nobody outside seems to care much for the spectacle. Being thrown out of the bar makes the spins in my head worse. The Creep has finally settled into the Quarter and my clarity is gone. There are too many people out tonight. Too much laughter, and darkness, and bad alcohol and weed. I get dragged along at the crowds' whim. The others have disappeared but I know if they are in the bar, there is no way for me to get back in to find them. Not with The Grenade and those freaking parrots watching the door. I am certain if my colleagues saw me getting the boot at least somebody would've followed me out.

I stumble and slice a path through the crowd, stopping to hold onto the side of a building when the dizziness crushes my brain. My survival instincts kick in, and I tuck myself into a vacant space between two, overfilled, garbage cans and lean against the building's old brick wall to keep from completely falling down. The closest street sign in view keeps bending to the right over and over and over again. My eyes are marbles in a liquor bottle, rolling around my head. I cannot read the sign clearly to save my life. I convince myself it says "Rue Dauphine." I don't know where Bourbon Street is. I have no idea which direction on Dauphine I am facing or remember if it runs north, south, east or west. The time on my watch reads "10:20 p.m." and I have lost two and a half hours of memory, my associates, and my balance. The crowds get louder and rowdier. The planet is falling off its axis and I will soon be violently hurled out into the coldness of space to be lost among the beasts and monsters.

Chapter Five

In the universe of Egyptian mythology "Seth" is the god of chaos and can,

at times, embody hostility and evil. He is typically depicted as human with

a head of unknown origin although it does look something like an aardvark

with its curved snout, boxed ears, and a forked tail. In one story Seth

murders his brother Osiris and subsequently has his testicles torn off by

Osiris' avenging son, Horus. In another story Seth accompanies Ra the sun

god on his nightly voyage through the underworld's darkness. As Ra's

guide, his duty is to battle the Apophis snake----the eternal threat to Ra and

the cosmic order.

At the present moment, in this universe, Seth is pretty much the

same manifestation, and while he may not look like an aardvark I am convinced he has been exhibiting the same qualities as his murderous namesake; an ever-present social companion and quiet threat to my safety as I embark into the night's darkness searching for booze. I don't remember him being drunk even though he was drinking a lot, and somehow, as the world was really spinning beyond my control he was remarkably non-existent and most likely quietly observing it all from a safe corner at the bar. Perhaps he witnessed the rant and disavowed any human relationship with me at all.

I could picture the bars' partons surrounding Seth:

"You there!" Brother Bob said. "You are known to travel with him."

"I'm sure I don't know what you're talking about," Seth replied.

"LIAR!" the green parrot squawked.

"This man is with the Drunk," a swarthy foreigner said, "We have him on video speaking with him."

"I swear to CHRIST! I don't know him!" Seth insisted.

"INFIDEL!" the green parrot squawked.

Bob yelled, "You dare invoke the Lord's name?! SAVAGE! Your speech betrays you! He is definitely with him." He turned to the hushed crowd and commanded, "FEED HIM...FEED HIM TO THE BEES!!"

"WAIT! THIS IS A TERRIBLE MISTAKE!!" Seth screamed.

Before he could run, the big, black bouncer locked him into a chokehold and whispered in his ear, "It's too late to change your faith now, heretic."

Gasping for breath Seth pleaded, "I swear to you! He just followed us in here! Can't you see he's completely cracked from the vodka! He drinks it like vampires drink blood! You must believe me!"

This seemingly innocuous detail about my drinking habits will be enough to convince them Seth knows me well, and therefore should be crucified. Treacherous bastard. Death by bees is too good for him. His allergies will force him into anaphylactic shock and he'll black out from the pain. He won't suffer slowly like me, wandering the Quarter in the throes of a ruthless tequila buzz, abandoned by my colleagues, and driven mad by the spinning and paranoia. My life will be left to a poor fate and very little chance. I am convinced that I, like Blanche Dubois, will have to rely on the kindness of strangers to make it through.

I secretly loathe him. He is the type of drinker to be leery of because he will never tell me he is snookered and I will nonchalantly follow him down a bad path of mad drinking just to keep pace. He has a quiet animosity and contempt towards me because I can be "disruptive." I throw up in my small shelter between two garbage cans, and recall, within my dizzy brain, his overt threat to abandon me. I feel purposely misplaced.

After the puke I feel better but irresistibly drawn to lay my head down in a soft nest of garbage next to my feet. It's a nice springy mound of crushed plastic cups and boxes. On the ground inches away from the nest is a message branded into this street when the cement was still wet, probably ages ago. The directive seems eternal and reads: "STAY THIRSTY." I could die a peaceful death here and be an omen to anyone who might come across this edict from the street. *Why not just go to sleep?* I think to myself. It is a reasonable solution to the controlled riot surrounding me in every direction. Hide. Wait out the storm. Just shut the body down and wake up refreshed and in a better place. Anything hidden in the garbage though will be scooped up without regard to its importance and will not be found and properly buried. For the sake of my soul I cannot give up the ghost and leave my body in this dark place off Dauphine. I throw away some beads dangling from my neck. It will only take one errant slip to hang myself off the sharp lattice work of a wrought iron fence or worse yet, get hooked to the crowd and dragged mercilessly through the Quarter by my throat. I head back onto Dauphine where the crowds happily crush and pull me to wherever they are headed.

103

Right seems a good direction and I consider simply asking where Bourbon Street or Canal Street are but am suffering a severe speech impediment brought on by twelve hours of drinking and sleep deprivation. It will be too much personal horror to hear myself slur while still climbing out from the depths of this bad drunk. That sober moment might seem obscure to the rest of the world but will be psychologically traumatizing for me. Hearing yourself slur when drunk is a threshold event; a nexus in time and space when sober Dr. Jekell and drunken Mr. Hyde share the same space within your liver and brain. You see what everyone else sees: you are a blabbering and drunken idiot and not some smooth operator in liquor ads charming the ladies and joking with the guys. Pay attention you fool, because this is the *you* friends and the cops will tell you about the next day when you can't remember why there is puke in your shoes and dried blood on your face. I stay tight lipped but career off one person and onto a large woman in the middle of the street. I could easily bury myself into the comfortable folds of her fatty goodness, hide in the warmth, and sleep off the drunk until daylight comes, but she shoves me aside and snarls, "Watch those hands, asshole!"

I give the beast an empty eyed look and raise my hands to shield my face from her flailing hooves. The alcohol has robbed me of speech.

With palms together in a weak gesture of apology I move on; staying the course of passive and mute penitence. Open my drooling mouth to the wrong people and I might wake up from a narcotic coma years later in a straight jacket at the Louisiana State Psychiatric Hospital.

I remember Dauphine runs north and south and take a right turn knowing the walk will eventually intersect with the wide landmark of Canal Street. I can regain my orientation there, catch a cab on the corner and have the driver speed me away to the hotel and safety. It's only eleven o'clock but I quit and let reason claim victory over thirst. I want sleep, and quiet, and can wait to suck the marrow out of Mardi Gras tomorrow. If I make it to Canal everything will be fine.

I follow a fraternity and let them block and push through the crowd with camcorders, imbecile sized beers and Greek letters. They are looking for Bourbon Street and I linger in their background like a remora would a school of juvenile sharks. It is a fruitless endeavor. They are too preoccupied to care where they are---stopping and going every second in awe at the sex languishing from the balconies. The street is grid-locked and I abandon Dauphine and cross through side streets to access the most lightly traveled paths I can find.

I pass across light and dark doorways until I reach Bourbon Street's queer end. I thought I've been traveling north the entire time but have ended up further south from where I started. Since the Parrot bar I've traveled in a meandering loop and gone just one block east of Dauphine. This is where the Church believes Daniel A. Hickenbottom met his spiritual demise, a street dominated at night by muffled dance music, whispers, giggles, stares, and things most straight people would never grasp or get their thrills from.

Further down on Bourbon Street looks darker and I walk a few steps back towards the brightness and noise, keeping my head down and feeling doomed, directionless, fearful and silent. I quicken the pace. Sluggish footfalls follow my own but I am too drunk to force a way through the crowds on Bourbon and turn left onto the closest street with less traffic, less paranoia, and more hope. From the corner behind me there are, shadows, garbage, and the old troll who chased Corrine earlier in the night. He stands on the edge of Bourbon Street breathing heavily and yelling at me, "WHITE SHIRT! WHITE SHIRT! SHOW ME YOUR TITS!!"

Turrets. This man is obviously crazed with Turrets or some rare type of repetitive behavioral disorder. Never mind that *I* am wearing a white-shirt like Corrine. I can't find my colleagues but somehow this perverted troglodyte----manic, wild-eyed, and obviously insane----has remembered me and managed to track me down because he is trapped forever in an endless loop of lust and memory.

"Filthy monster!" I scream. "You'll keep your distance if you know what's good for you!"

He stands breathless underneath a gas light, his plastic beads reflecting different shades of orange. Perhaps Bourbon Street is his boundary because he seems trapped, and abandons the chase. After making a bold sign of the cross in my direction he waves me off. Frustrated.

Damn devils, I think. Will they ever stop trying to save me?

I continue walking without much care for direction and operate on faith. The good Lord will somehow steer me towards something familiar. This might explain why the troll has chased me out of Bourbon Street. I feel closer to a place where I might easily catch a taxi thanks to the troll.

The dark and narrow street opens into a wide and poorly-lit boulevard. It is too quiet to be Canal Street but it looks familiar. There is little traffic and the prospect of a cab passing through this intersection seems remote. I keep walking until I realize there are no street signs. No storefront signs or buildings with a street name on them. The next intersection is barren and without life until a cab buzzes through the intersection giving little pause to break or stop for my frantic hand waving. Maybe they just don't see me, I think, so I keep walking, all the while waving at more vacant taxis speeding by. Finally a lone taxi cruising down the street in the opposite direction passes by, breaks hard, and makes a u-turn. It speeds up as I wave and passes me before stopping half a block away. A heavy set black man exits the driver's side, straightens his shirt and grabs a jacket from the front seat before closing the car door.

I am breathless. "Thanks for stopping."

He stands silent for a moment and zips his jacket.

"The Prytania Park Hotel," I say.

"I'm off duty," he replies.

"Are you kidding me?"

"Nope." He turns and walks across the street towards an all night liquor store.

"WAIT!" I plead. "I've got money!"

He keeps walking with his back turned to me. "I'm done for the night."

"But I'm trying to catch a cab!"

He stops and turns around and stands in the middle of the street shaking his head and laughs. "You ain't gonna catch a cab here boy."

"What street is this?"

"Rampart," he replies and continues to walk towards the liquor store.

"Wait!" I plead, "Where's the...where's the Best Western?"

He waves his hand to his right and without turning around replies, "Two blocks that way,"

Impossible. I have just come from at least eight blocks "that way". Obviously this man has been sent by the devil to punish me and prolong my agony. In Chicago the liveries would be crawling all over themselves to take my money unless I was black and looking for a ride to the Southside. "Wait! Where's Canal Street?!"

He keeps walking but turns around long enough to point in the direction behind me.

"LET ME GUESS," I yell, "...TWO BLOCKS THAT WAY!"

The man keeps walking and dissolves into the liquor store's red and blue neon lights. I have no idea how far down Rampart I've gone or how far away the Best Western is. The drunk is fading. A hard ferocious headache is taking shape and pouring itself into the emptying space where the alcohol was once braising my brain. Now my skull is just hot and pulsating. I turn around and head back into the French Quarter to suffer the crowds again. By midnight I find the Le Meridian Hotel. It is two blocks from Canal Street. The parades have long since gone but Bourbon Street is just beginning to lure more people. Canal has been split in half with metal barricades used for the parades and by some sick twist of geography everyone is forced to go in one direction only: back into the Quarter. I can see taxis on the opposite side driving away from the Quarter and decide to squeeze through the barricades while the police are not looking. Cabs ignore and continue to pass me by until a brown taxi pulls up a few feet away from me. I pull on the door handle and find it locked.

The driver rolls his window down. "Where are you going?"

"The Prytania Park Hotel," I say and pull on the handle. "The door is locked."

"Sorry." He takes his foot off the break and almost speeds away with my fingers.

Just as quickly as the brown taxi leaves, a minivan screeches to a stop at my feet. "Where are you going?" the driver asks.

I stay on the curb and away from the door handle. "The Prytania Park Hotel," I say.

He shakes his head and drives one block down from me to pick up some girls staying at Le Meridian. I can do them a favor by telling them their hotel is five minutes from the curb but the headache and my frustration consume my sympathy. On a corner further down I try my luck at a Popeye's Fried Chicken where some bad drunks are hassling normal people waiting to cross the street. It doesn't seem like a corner any cabs will stop at for a fare so I continue the walk until I am underneath the I-10 overpass. Prytania is past the interstate and I will brave it and try to find the hotel without assistance. The experience of searching for the hotel in the daylight when I was sober and in a much better mental state was damn difficult. A real fear and confusion grips my heart. It's past midnight. I have very little desire to keep walking and I finally begin to understand why you see people, without care or consequence, just passed out on the streets in New Orleans. Perhaps I will have to do the same, pack it in, or maybe find a bar to sit in and wait six hours for daylight to clear a path.

At the moment when I feel ready to surrender my efforts, a yellow minivan rounds a sharp corner and pulls up alongside the curb. "Where are you going?" he asks with a thick Nigerian accent.

I raise my head, expressionless. The passenger side window is rolled down but the doors are still locked.

"Where are you going?" he asks again.

I am comfortably rested against a newspaper box and don't bother stepping away from it. "The Prytania Park Hotel," I reply.

"Which one?" he asks.

I am dumbfounded and about to abandon my tenuous hold on reason. "There's more than one?"

"Which one are you going to?" he asks.

"The one on Prytania Street?" I say.

He is puzzled.

I pull out the business card Corrine has gave me and pass it through the open window. "I don't know," I say, "but it's this one."

He takes the card, studies it and looks over his right shoulder through the rear window to see if there are any other fares he would rather drive. He looks back at me. "How much money do you have?" he asks.

"Enough," I reply.

"Okay fifteen dollars," he says.

"Fine." I step off the curb and put my hand on the sliding door. It is locked.

"No, okay fifteen dollars?" he says again.

"What? No. I mean 'Yes'!"

The door unlocks and I jump into the rear bench seat before he can change his mind. Once I'm strapped in, he speeds off and speaks to the dispatcher. I close my eyes and sit quietly in the back seat. Irritated but relieved. Soon I'll be asleep in a bed. The cab stops.

"Okay fifteen dollars," he says.

I look to my right and see the hotel entrance and doorman. The minivan has traveled no more than two blocks straight and two blocks over.

I dig into my pocket, pull out a nest of crumpled dollar bills and sort through my singles. "Are you Nigerian?" I ask.

"Yes Nigerian, yes," he replies.

I continue to count the money.

"You know," I say, "I took a cab earlier today from the hotel to the Quarter and it only cost five dollars. But now you're charging me fifteen dollars for a ride that took thirty seconds."

He eyes the doorman, who stands at watchful attention over the minivan paused at the parking lot entrance. The driver turns his attention back towards me and smiles.

I stop counting. "Nigerian..." I say, "...lots of Muslims in Nigeria. How long have you been in the States?"

He speaks but is slow to answer. I hold seventeen singles neatly folded and loosely stacked in my hand.

He stares at me and says, "One year."

"You know," I say, "in Chicago your country men are a lot smarter than you."

His stare is blank.

"I'm from Chicago," I reply.

He smiles nervously.

"I'm a lawyer for the Immigration and Naturalization Service."

The smile disappears for a moment and reappears a bit crooked and fake.

"Goddamn have we been busy lately. We've been kicking a lot of people out of our country whose paperwork just doesn't look right. You know...all that JEE-HAAD business..." I say.

He looks out the window again at the doorman and then says with a slight laugh, "Okay...okay...ten my friend."

"In fact, the reason I'm here is because we're detaining and deporting any foreigners who've over-stayed their visas. Know anyone like that?"

The smile vanishes and his eyes go wide with fear. The smile appears again.

There is little said between our fake smiles and our measured breathing.

I lean forward and hand him the money. "Personally, I don't think we need your kind 'round here. This place has enough troublemakers and price gougers don't you think?"

He sits silently with his body twisted against the seat belt and scratches his forehead.

I lean over to look past his shoulder and squint at the identification card on the dashboard. "Here you go----Olfemi." I smile. "Even though I don't appreciate being bled I left you a tip."

He holds the money in his hand reluctantly, counts out five, and hands back twelve dollars to me. "My friend...this is...a misunderstanding," he says, trying desperately to squeeze out another fake smile.

The doorman squints into the window and creeps towards the cab. He puts a hand on the locked door.

"No misunderstanding here," I reply. "I know exactly what's going on. You hate us all don't you?"

He pleads, "N-n-n-no, no, no sir-----a misunderstanding." He waves the bills at me and tries handing me all the money.

I undo the seat belt and open the door.

The doorman steps back.

"Keep it...and save every American dollar because you're gonna need a good lawyer. If they'll even let you have one." I step out onto the street, put my hand on the door handle and growl, "Have a nice trip to Cuba asshole."

Olfemi tears off his seat belt and runs from the driver side door. "MY FRIEND! MY FRIEND!" he pleads. "My mistake! I have accidentally overcharged you." He stuffs all the money into my hand and lets it go. A few bills float to the ground and he quickly picks them up and tries again to shove them into my hand. He runs around the front of the minivan and scrambles into the front seat. "Please forgive my mistake," he says and speeds off onto the street without closing the sliding side door.

The doorman is now standing next to me and together we watch the van travel down half a block before breaking abruptly. In the headlights I see Olfemi run around the front of the van, close the sliding side door, run back to the driver's seat and flee into the night.

I look at the doorman. "Uh...he was provoking me," I say. "Usually I'm not really like that."

The doorman sighs, shakes his head and walks to the hotel entrance.

I follow him and plead innocence. "No really," I say, "I'm all about the Melting Pot. My uncle is an immigrant."

He stands silent and opens the door.

I shuffle past him waving the neon green bracelet and sweep through the lobby without incident.

The hotel room is still. Outside I hear muffled voices and car horns. I take off my shoes and leave them far away from the couch. There is a warm beer hidden with the empties on the corner table next to the sofa. I twist it open and throw the cap up into the loft above my head. There is no sound from the loft and I sit in a semi-drunken peace, relieved to have a quiet room all to myself. I drink from the bottle until there is no more and sink into the soft sofa. A replay of Ashleigh Banfield's nightly television reports from Afghanistan is lulling me to sleep. Lately I've found myself easily drawn in by the seeming explosion of cable news sirens who present the war to me on a daily basis. Where did all these vixens suddenly come from? It's a contradiction for sure, so I usually mute the volume and just watch their lustful eyes and glossy lips move and pretend like they're talking about something pleasant. But Ashleigh has a really nice voice if you turn the volume down a few notches...even-toned...intelligent and feminine. I wonder how her day went.

FRIDAY

<u>Chapter One</u>

A katzenjammer. I recall Rio spitting that old-timey word at me as we fought over the last beer in a case of Bud Light before I passed out on a boat in Lake Geneva. She declared she should have it because mixing different beers with different types of liquor all in the course of one evening plus a boat ride would leave me crippled with a most unforgiving hangover. She was partially right. It wasn't the boat ride. The boat did not move at all save her jumping around on it like a mad woman as it sat restlessly in its slip. The boat bounced slowly in darkness and still night waters until the unsettling sway in my brain and her incessant chatter brought on sickness. The following day was one of the worst

katzenjammers I'd experienced----ever. Hangovers. Katzenjammers. It's

all the same, just me and the pains. I've assigned numerical values to such

misery. The numbers help me gauge the body's distress level, what can be

done about it, and whether the drinking went too far the night before. Lake

Geneva was a nine out of ten.

I am experiencing a seven on the hotel room floor, half covered in

a bed sheet, fully dressed except my shoes, and hard pressed to remove my

face from the seat cushion I passed out on. The pull out bed is set out but I

am on the floor, drunk but awake and restless and because of this know I

am scheduled for a day-long hangover. It will be miserable. The

unprocessed alcohol from last night will continue to chew away thin layers

of my brain tissue throughout the morning and I will function throughout

the day with temporary amnesia, phantom head trauma and misfiring

synapses. I will have the impulse to move body parts for simple things like

walking but do so poorly because the nerves are no longer connected to the

brain. It won't amount to the shakes, which is a very public warning sign to

others of one's ferocious habits.

Lenny has the shakes. The first time he noticed was during his

brother-in-law's bachelor party in New Orleans. It was eight in the morning and he woke up at a bullet-hole bar with a squirting dildo in his left pocket, a disposable camera in his right, and some poor girl's breasts bouncing listlessly above his head. He tells himself and me it was the bayou heat in August making him twitchy; the "goddamned heat" and poor hydration kept his muscles so tight they shook. But there's no bayou heat in Chicago and the lie he tells himself about it seems less humorous now.

It's 9:00 a.m. I have time to recover before Lenny casts a dark and shaky shadow on the Quarter. He will arrive at seven tonight, along with Rio and Roberto. The prospect of having us all together in New Orleans for Mardi Gras is ripe with co-dependent doom. They will ride into town on winged chariots like the Apocalypse and I will end up checking myself into a clinic. My friends are not the type who should be around too many vices and the chicanery running through this town like poison through veins. Sooner or later somebody will have to be sacrificed to New Orleans in order to appease the local appetite for exploiting bad behavior. Not counting Corrine, Seth is the most sane amongst us. He will no doubt just sip his Hurricane and quietly watch us run crazy through the Quarter which I am certain he did last night as I suffered the indignities of a bad drunk.

Seth is asleep on the pull out bed and looks peaceful enough to fool anyone he is free of guilt. I weigh the evening's events in my head, his threat to let me rot with the monsters and consider grabbing a pillow to smother him with.

I could do it right now. Take the big fluffy one next to his feet meant for my aching head...take it and place it over his face. He would struggle at first but if I sat on his chest he would have no choice but to relent and give up the ghost. As long as I left no bruises on his body there probably wouldn't be a coroner's inquest.

"Dead you say? But he was so full of life yesterday," I would weep.

"Well he appears to have suffocated in his sleep," the coroner would reply.

"Oh Lord," I would cry, "He always wanted to go that way, peacefully, and in his sleep."

The coroner would scribble something in his notebook as they carried his lifeless corpse out of the Prytania Park Hotel. "Tell me," the coroner would ask, "was he allergic to anything?"

I would sob uncontrollably and cry, "Yes. Oh God, yes! If it wasn't bees then it was definitely the crustaceans or bad oysters. He ate a ton of them yesterday at this very nice restaurant where the bartender knows me as a kind hearted and well-liked individual. He bought us shots while Seth gorged himself on half shells."

"Really?" the coroner would ask.

I would reach into my pocket and produce a receipt. "See, right here, $27.00 on crayfish and oysters. Oh you poor stupid bastard. God is punishing you for not keeping Kosher. Why couldn't you just leave the oysters and crayfish alone?! WHY?! Was it worth your life you stupid, stupid bastard? Oh Lord, he should've been born a Catholic! WHY oh Lord, WHY!?"

"What are you doing?" Corrine asks.

I crane my head up towards the loft. Corrine is staring at me from above.

"I-I'm sorry?" I reply.

She laughs. "What are you doing?"

"Oh nothing." I put the pillow down and look around the floor.

"What are you looking for?" she asks.

"Why was I on the floor?"

"You said Seth had the 'Jimmie Legs' and if he kicked you while you were sleeping one of you would end up dead in the morning."

"Okay, but why was *I* on the floor?" I ask.

"Rock, paper, scissors," Seth mumbles. "Rock always beats scissors."

"What happened last night?"

"We already told you what happened," he insists.

"I don't believe you," I reply. "Corrine, what happened?"

"We went into the 7-Eleven to get aspirin and cigarettes. You said you would just wait for us outside and we didn't see you the rest of the night," she says.

I stare at Seth.

"It's true. You can ask Sylvia and Loni," he mumbles with his face buried in the pillow.

"LIAR!" I declare. "We didn't even meet up with Sylvia and Loni!"

"Yes we did," he says.

I crane my head towards the loft where Corrine is nods vigorously. "Look in the closet," she says.

Seth takes the pillow I was hoping to kill him with and tucks it underneath his legs. I stumble to the closet, my legs still wrapped and twisted in the bed sheet on the floor. The closet is cracked open with light passing through a small gap between the door frame and the sliding door. I pull it open.

Corrine is laughs.

"Seth?" I ask.

"Yes?" he mumbles.

"What's this dead white boy in his underwear doing in our closet?"

"You don't know?"

I consider the question. Corrine's laughter echoes from above. "Um...no," I say. "Did I kill him?"

"No." Seth replies.

I mumble, "Did you kill him?"

"No."

"Who is he?"

Corrine is in tears and breathless. "It's Marty."

"What's he doing here?" I ask.

"Loni kicked him out. He had nowhere to go," Seth mumbles.

"Why is he in our closet? And why is he in his underwear?"

"I don't know," Seth says. "He was going to use the bathroom and we didn't see him after that."

"I see." I turn the light off and pull the closet shut.

"What time is it?" Seth groans.

I sit down on the floor and search for my shoes. "Nine."

"It's too early for your crap. Go back to sleep."

"I'm going out to get a drink," I reply.

He screams, "ARE YOU NUTS?!"

"Something *to* drink. Jesus, you have a really low opinion of me, don't you?"

"Yes."

"I need water, jackass. If I don't hydrate soon I'll cramp up and suffer horribly."

Seth mumbles, "Let's hope so."

"I can already feel my cells shrinking...my lips are dry."

He stares at me for a moment and grabs an aspirin bottle from the floor. "You're an idiot."

My shoes are next to the aspirin and underneath the fold out. They are blackened with sticky crud and a dark red paste. "What do you think? Hurricane or sorority girl vomit?"

"Get those fucking things away from me," Seth growls. "Go outside and bother the people at the prayer breakfast."

"I'm sure it's already over," I reply. "Those bible-bangers are early to rise. They're probably running around the Quarter right now plotting their conversions for the day."

I wash my shoes off in the sink before leaving the room. The weather outside is cool and the prayer breakfast is over. I cautiously work my uncooperative legs down the staircase, through the courtyard, and into the lobby where I can purchase relief in the form of the largest Gatorade bottle sold along with a Snickers bar and a Doritos bag. A six-pack is tempting and sometimes the only solution for a hangover, or a really mild joint. Although I am all about the buzz and less often about the high, I decide against either indulgence.

Check out is at 11:30 and our check in at The W won't be for almost four hours later. I will have to find uncomplicated diversions to ease into the day and let the hangover run its ugly course. After 3:00 I can easily lay in state at The W for a few hours until the others arrive from Chicago.

The desk clerk is tagging new arrivals to the Prytania Park when I slip into the lobby. She is explaining the neon bracelet procedures to some girls who have a problem with being "labeled" as one pudgy blonde has put it. They are from Chicago and the blonde interrupts the desk clerk to chat incessantly about nothing important to the world:

"Well..." she begins, "Loren showed up sporting a pair of cute jeans, a button down and a black jacket. I give him about a 'B' for the outfit. As for looks he was cute but on the shorter side and his hair was a little too long but let's not dwell on that. So for looks, I'll give him another 'B.' Car? BMW. A *great* car, he gets an 'A' for that. As for the place we went to, another 'A.' An excellent date place. I was never a wine connoisseur but I'm thinking I can become one. This summer we *must* hang out on Randolph. The date ended with me getting intoxicated but not like crazy. I'm assuming he was fairly intoxicated but since he was driving I didn't want to know. As for myself I get an overall 'A+' for how damn cute I looked. I was a BABE. My worries of not being cute were so swept under the rug with the outfit I pulled off. I stayed the night only because I semi-passed out on his couch. I just said he could take me home in the morning. Nothing happened. Only a kiss derived from this date and it didn't even happen at his place. I think it may have happened at the restaurant. I might have mastered French kissing. I can execute a pretty intense kiss. So where do I stand on Mr. Loren Callahan? The car, the money, the job, the cute apartment, the boat....which only seats six people

128

so I *really* don't consider that amazing. He probably locked in another date but unless he cuts his hair and sends me gifts it won't lead to much. I need to keep my options open right?"

Hmm...I know your type, I think to myself. You get an "F" for being a "fucktard". Do you plan to be an idiot your whole life? You live in Lincoln Park and drive a red Jetta no doubt. Good you're here. This town is a great equalizer and will gladly chew on your spoiled carcass like hyenas do brainless wildebeests. Drink a Hurricane and you'll have more than a green "label" to worry about especially when Mommy and Daddy see you on the internet sucking your girlfriends' tits for plastic beads.

An awful silence fills the room.

The desk clerk is stunned.

"Jesus did I say that out loud?" I turn my attention back to the open refrigerator. My throat tightens and I become momentarily deaf from a mysterious flat ringing tone bouncing around my head. A prickly sensation of tiny bugs crawling underneath my skin overwhelms my arms and I scratch them slowly. I wipe the sweat off the Gatorade bottle and run the wetness through my hair and over my forehead. Still more silence and even more disapproving looks from the ladies. Perhaps I should just leave the bottle in the refrigerator and crawl back into the miserable hole I have come from. *Just ignore the reactions to your mumbling observations and say nothing more, idiot.* It could easily be played off as incomprehensible nonsense from a disoriented wretch and not even worthy of a response. *Just maintain.* I place the Gatorade back into the refrigerator and skulk towards the exit and my hotel room's safety. Halfway to the lobby door I feel the gravity of female contempt eyed upon me. The body goes numb and erupts into a million tiny itches. "Ah!" I scream and tear at my arms. "Fucking aphids! Why won't you just leave me alone!"

The desk clerk breaks the silence while I rub the bugs off. "Excuse me, sir?" she asks.

I raise my right hand over my head sheepishly to display the green bracelet without making eye contact. A pungent mix of metabolized vodka, fried food and night sweats fume off my gray skin. I do my best to avoid giving off the bad airs by sticking close to the walls farthest away from her perch.

"Excuse me, sir," she says again.

"What? No thanks," I mumble as I try holding in my boozey breath. "Got enough towels."

"Are you okay?" she asks.

I am almost through the door but turn around. She waves me over gently and I oblige. I am in no condition to flee and she will be able to call security before I make it to the courtyard.

"Are you okay?" she asks. "You don't look so good."

I approach the counter and lean against it for support. The wildebeests take a collective step back, say nothing, and remain sharply vigilant.

"Are you alright?" she says again.

"Hmm," I mumble to her, "Well I suppose physically...I'll manage..."

I dip my head to the side to glimpse the girls, "But mentally...." I shrug my shoulders.

"Is there anything we can get you?" she asks.

"God bless you," I say. "You're much too kind and I've already embarrassed myself with that slip of the tongue. I'll just go back to my room and wait for the medication to kick in. I don't like to make a big deal about it but I suffer from a repetitive behavioral disorder much like Turrets and from time to time I find myself saying things I shouldn't say. I don't want sympathy. I'll just go back to my room."

I turn around and step cautiously towards the courtyard door.

"The Gatorade." She asks, "Would you like to get one?"

"Well..." I turn and look at the blabbering blonde who might be attractive if she lost fifteen pounds. I feel no sympathy for her life's dilemma. She is making her journey through the universe thinking she is relevant because she drinks wine and shops. No doubt poor Mr. Loren Callahan will fall for her bullshit and together they will single-handedly keep The Pottery Barn and Starbucks in business for years to come.

"Sir?" the desk clerk asks.

I turn my attention back to the front desk. "Umm...yes...the Gatorade...right...well perhaps the electrolytes and sugars will help speed the delivery and absorption of medicine into my central nervous system," I reply.

"We can charge it to your room," she says.

"That would be fine." I smile politely and slide back to the refrigerator to grab the purple bottle, a six-pack of Miller Lite and a fat Snickers bar. "Room 220. The beer is for my nurse. She's had a long night caring for my eccentricities and deserves a little relief."

"Oh," the desk clerk replies as she totals the goods in her head, "certainly. Anything else?"

"No more prayer breakfast huh?"

She shakes her head.

"Hmm...I see. I guess that'll be all then." I clutch the hotel's spoils close to my chest and scurry off.

"Wait--,"she says, "What room was this under again?"

"324," I reply. "It's under Loni Cole."

The desk clerk clicks through the computer registry. "Who is Loni?" she asks.

"My nurse."

"And who are you?"

"I'm her patient," I say.

She insists, "Wait--I need your name."

"Marty." I reply and slip out into the courtyard with goods in hand.

My eyes are closed and New Orleans smells like mischief this morning. It is a sweet smell like funnel cake, kettle corn and hot dogs. There is a tickle of anticipation growing in the pit of my stomach for the day's local wonders and inebriant mysteries to unfold.

Halfway up the stairs to the hotel room my legs and feet break down into slow, heavy, and sloppy steps. The veins in my head are tight and a hot sweat glaze is breaching the delicate gray pores on my forehead. The tickle in my stomach turns vicious. I am no longer in control of my own body and in the throes of the big spit. Within a few agonizing seconds the hangover's vulgar and prolonged effects are a lifeless vomit on the Prytania Park Hotel's stone tiled courtyard. It is a violent and unpleasant solution better undertaken willfully with an index finger and toilet, but I have been forcibly exorcised and reborn by fate so why dwell. I can feel the blood and color return to my face but now I'm paranoid about the mess. I consider the importance of reason and accountability in light of the kindness shown to me by the desk clerk but convince myself no one saw me. I steal away to the room without detection and pick up the complimentary morning paper left at our doorstep. My associates have gone back to sleep. I set the six-pack and newspaper next to the coffee maker on the bathroom counter, drink the Gatorade and grab a fresh shirt and jeans from my bag.

The hotel phone rings.

They've found me. Somehow, they know it was my doing in the courtyard.

The phone continues to ring.

Ignore it and it will go away----the ringing. Or maybe it's not even the phone but a din lost somewhere in the vagaries of your brain.

Seth lifts his head from the pillows and squints at me. "Are you going to answer that damn thing?" he asks.

"I don't know."

The phone keeps ringing, now even louder.

"Answer the phone," he insists.

"No."

"You're closer," he replies.

I shake my head.

Seth stares at me, baffled.

The ringing stops.

"Must have been a wrong number," I say.

He mumbles something, rolls over, and covers himself with the blanket.

Corrine's voice echoes above my head, "It's for you."

"How do you know?" I reply.

"Because he asked for you."

"Who is it?"

"I don't know."

Seth groans, "Just pick up the damn thing."

I place my hand on the gray phone and bring it to my ear. "Hello?"

The voice on the other end is reedy and familiar, "So you *are* alive?"

"Hmm...yes, physically I'm fine. How did you find us?" I ask.

"You left a message on my voice mail last night screaming about foreigners and parrots," he says.

"I see...anything else?"

"Yes, you said the goddamn parrots weren't strictly ornamental and you couldn't find the hotel and were convinced someone was following you."

"And then?"

"And then you said you were going to forget about the hotel and head straight for the airport and board the first plane to Bhutan."

"I see," I groan. "You know I hear it's quite a place; the last true Buddhist Kingdom on the planet."

"Sounds great," he says. "Any girls?"

"I don't know. It's not really a place you go to meet women."

"What's the fucking point?"

Seth is grumbling from underneath the blanket, "What the hell are you blabbering about now?"

"Nothing."

"Who is it?" Seth asks.

"Aaron."

"What does he want?"

"What *do* you want? What are you doing calling me so early in the morning?"

He replies, "I'll be there in a few hours."

"WHAT?" I look out the window first and run to the front door to stick an eye through the peephole. "Where *exactly* are you?"

"The plane."

"You know, it's against FAA regulations to use cell phones in flight. You'll bring the whole bird down, you stupid bastard."

"I'm in the bathroom," he replies coolly. "They can't hear me."

"I see." Good Lord, I think to myself. This will lend unnecessary fuel to the engine currently dragging me up and down Bourbon Street to quench the thirst. Aaron is unapologetically free from guilt and prone to a love of strippers and gambling. He is wealthy but not ostentatious; a true man of leisure. His chosen distractions tend to be things he can purchase and consume in large volumes and varieties. He will usually only go as far as Vegas with his immediate compulsions. On one rare occasion he ventured into the Midwest for a twisted bachelor party in East St. Louis; a place which makes up for St. Louis' lackluster tourist draws with it's own overabundance of vulgar sex, cheap booze, and provincial riverboat gambling. Sometimes he can put the fear in me like he was doing at this very moment because he will do whatever he wants to just because he can.

I insist, "Umm..er...I don't think you need to check on me. I'm fine really. Stay in California."

"Well...I've never been to New Orleans and it sounds like you're all having a good time. Plus I've got nothing going on," he says.

"I see...well...I guess that that's that huh?"

"Uh-huh."

"Fine. But I must warn you they don't take kindly to bad behavior around here. Especially during this time of year."

"You're a lawyer...as long as I have a lawyer with me I'll be fine right?" he says.

"HA! Who told you that miserable lie?"

"You did."

"Oh no..no..no! We're a cursed profession. Besides, it's all Napoleonic Code here. In fact they still behead aristocrats in public so I advise you stay away before the locals find out how much you're worth."

"Good one. Should I call your cell phone or the hotel?"

"Neither."

"What hotel are we staying at?"

"Uh..."

"Come on asshole..."

"The W..."

"Nice. I'll call you when I get in." The line goes dead.

"Err…wait…damnit. Hello?"

I put the phone down.

Seth is now up and visibly annoyed with the noise I'm making. He puts his glasses on and looks around the room for his cigarettes. "What'd he want?"

"He's coming," I say.

Seth is horrified. "HERE?!"

I nod mildly and turn my back on any lingering questions now filling Seth's groggy mind. I walk into the bathroom with the six-pack and close the door.

The bathroom feels safe. I have my doubts he is on the plane because of my own fears he is already here, lurking in the lobby or the courtyard waiting to attack me. I can barricade myself in here with wet towels, toilet paper and tiny soap bars and Aaron will not be able to sniff me out. He will easily by-pass the bathroom once he sees Seth and grab him first, dragging him along on whatever impulse is being concocted within his restless mind. Seth will grab and claw at the carpet and walls while Corrine continues to sleep, as always, unbothered. I will be forced to stuff wet toilet paper into my ears to spare myself from hearing Seth's terrified screams for help. Good. Excellent. Let him suffer like I suffered the night before, left to wander aimlessly and mad with booze as he went grocery shopping at the 7-Eleven. Maybe we can sacrifice Marty to Aaron instead of Seth? Marty will present a difficulty though. The military will have to get involved.

I take a beer and calmly turn the bathtub faucet on until there is enough steam to draw out a good sweat and sit on the floor with the newspaper to distract myself with whatever godawful things are happening in the world today.

Chapter Two

It is noon and the front desk has called several times to pester me with their 11:30 check out. House keeping has come around and given us up to the authorities since we declined their services throughout the morning. My approach in dealing with them is more cordial and diplomatic while Seth simply yells at them through the peephole to go away. We are on our way out, bags in hand, when I do a clean sweep of the room and make sure nothing valuable is left for the help to scavenge.

I hand Seth an ATM receipt lying on the nightstand.

"Just throw it away," he says.

"I don't trust this town," I reply. "Everything gets recycled around here. You'd best keep your documentation to yourself."

"You're paranoid."

"Never leave anything behind they can use against you."

Seth slides open the closet door. "What about that?"

"Hmm...good question...is he still breathing?" I ask.

"Well his foot just moved," Seth replies.

"I'd hate to leave a sailor behind. My Dad served in the Navy as a doctor and his buddies were the first to introduce me to the decadent world of late nights, drinking and swear words. Perhaps this is where I repay the debt."

"Yeah but your old man was an officer...this guy is an enlisted man."

"Good point. But we're all in this together, right?"

Seth asks, "When did you get patriotic?"

"Patriotic? I'm talking about Mardi Gras. Remember: 'patriotism is the last refuge of the scoundrel.'"

"Whatever." Seth takes the receipt and tosses it into the garbage can. "I'll go and stall the front desk until you can return this jackass to Loni."

Corrine stays and helps get Marty's bearings back after he throws up in the bathroom sink.

"I never understand why people throw up in a sink," I mumble to Corrine as Marty struggles to find his clothes. "A toilet always presents a bigger and much easier target to throw up in so why bother climbing to the sink when you're already crawling on the bathroom floor?" Marty's puke refuses to slide down the drain. "No matter...that'll teach house keeping to screw with the complex inner workings of a hangover. They should've let him sleep it off and work around him."

Loni is still passed out when we return Marty to her room. Sylvia allows him to sleep it off on the floor. They have reservations at the Prytania for the weekend and will reach out to us once they can agree on venturing into the Quarter. It doesn't matter to me if we see them the rest of the time or not. I prefer not to be around Loni once she sees the room charge for a five-dollar bottle of Gatorade, eleven dollar six pack, and four-dollar Snickers under Marty's name.

We wave goodbye to the Prytania Park Hotel and the Garden District as parade enthusiasts claim temporary real estate along St. Charles Street. Aaron will soon blow into the city but I know there will be enough bizarre distractions to keep him preoccupied while I escape to a nondescript bar in the Quarter. The last time I saw him was in Chicago. The end result of that vodka and rum inspired evening involved stealing a life sized papier-mâché fishing boat Captain from a seafood restaurant, the

Chicago Police Department, and a pack of crazed Mexican Valets who

gave chase yelling "EL CAPITAN! EL CAPITAN!" while we fled down

Wells Street with the good captain in tow. I can only assume the Captain

found his way back to his waterfront home, but rumor has it he ended up

standing at the intersection of LaSalle and Superior until someone realized

he wasn't a public arts work project but the victim of a half-assed

kidnapping. I left Aaron at a bar known for late nights and bad violence on

Clark Street where eventually he sobered up and caught a plane back to the

West Coast in the morning.

We walk the distance to the Quarter's outer Southern edges and

store our bags in Corrine's car at the La Quinta garage. It's one o'clock and

we have a few hours before check in at The W on Chartres. Seth is

wrestling with a headache and is more indifferent than usual to the noise

and sights surrounding him. Corrine is collecting beads and super balls

thrown to the public by Krewes on their floats.

Physically I am fine and mentally my head feels screwed on

straight for the first time since leaving Chicago two days ago. I am

nostalgic having been to New Orleans during Mardi Gras with my parents

on several occasions. Back then I was sternly warned about the lure of the

French Quarter but most times couldn't hear or see anything beyond sounds of Dixieland jazz and the purple, gold, and green tinsel floating by me. I was only allowed to pass through Bourbon Street during early daylight hours and spent most of the time at the French Market with my mother haggling for rarities and eating beignets while she sipped her coffee at Café Du Monde. After a time I was old enough to wander around with my sister. I remember her purchasing a red and black voodoo doll for $4.99 at a quiet shop lost somewhere in the memory of a naive mind. She used the doll to torture me with threats of a cursed life whenever I refused to do her bidding. That is the moment I began to sense the Quarter's potential for personal doom.

Seth, Corrine and I cross Canal Street by the River Walk, steer clear of Bourbon, and walk to St. Peter Street and onto Pat O'Brien's third floor terrace at the Jax Brewery Millhouse overlooking the river.

"Absolut on the rocks please," I say to the waitress.

Seth is at first expressionless, lost in the throes of his hangover until The Natchez river boat wails.

He puts his hands to his face and rubs his forehead. "WH---WHAT THE HELL-----WHAT THE HELL IS THAT?!"

"The New Orleans Steamboat Company," the waitress says. The Natchez is sitting in the water fifty yards away from the terrace and blowing "Darktown Strutter's Ball" through its pipe organ. It's cheery and festive and most definitely twisting the inner fabric of Seth's delicate mind with its bubbly tones.

Corrine asks the waitress, "How long does it play for?"

A sour and painful expression is slowly overtaking Seth's face.

I smile. "Long enough."

It's a quiet lunch save The Natchez's sweet treacle and random car sirens and marching bands romping throughout the streets. The noise and racket are extremely detrimental if you're suffering from a hangover, but I am too preoccupied with drink and food to fully appreciate how much the chaos is tearing Seth's brain apart. I eat two butterflied-fried shrimp plates and drink three Absoluts before losing myself in the Mississippi's sleepy, dark brown crawl. Corrine is the last to finish her meal and Seth hardly eats the fried crawdads lying sacrificed, curled up, and crunchy in their plastic basket. He pokes at a few but says he will eat later. It has been more than two hours since I spoke with Aaron and I can only hope the authorities stop him at the airport and detain him for a lengthy interrogation and strip search. It will give me time to prepare for the inevitable run at bars and strip clubs.

We walk to the water after settling the bill with the folks at Pat O'Brien's. The Natchez's jubilant songs are now traveling and floating down the river much to Seth's whiny relief. A warm breeze passes along the river banks and although the Mississippi is not much to look at it feels good to be close to the wide expansive space. It's thick and muddy. But maybe that's the way it should be. It starts as a clear trickle somewhere in Minnesota, a leaking wound bubbling out from the Country's underbelly. As far west as Montana and as far east as New York, arteries of water drain into it and swell and run a course from the Midwest down into the South's whispering trees. It's a geographic and metaphysical scar on the land and conscience. There are still black ghosts in the Mississippi Delta swinging by ropes in trees waiting to be set free and bad memories of war and violence lurking in the Southern air. All that flows through New Orleans--- the last grand stop before the river confesses the collective secrets of the nation to the Gulf of Mexico and the world.

Seth's color and demeanor have returned. "What the hell is that?" He asks and blocks the sun's glare with his hands. "...Old Man River?"

At the river's edge and hiding behind leafy bushes and pine trees is a white statue of a man rising almost two stories above the ground. He was inconspicuous from the Jax Brewery Millhouse. The squared chin and shoulders are turned away from the Quarter and his arms are raised up to lift the sky.

We walk to the base of the statue. A plaque bolted to the ground reads:

OLD MAN RIVER

I turn to Seth. "Huh."

My cell phone rings.

I try to make out the caller ID against the sun's glare.

"Answer it," Seth growls.

"Hold on."

The phone continues to ring.

"Answer it."

"Relax, I will...."

"Answer---"

"Would you---shutup. It's Lenny. Hello?"

"What are you doing?" Lenny asks.

"Nothing."

"You hungover?"

"No. Not at all...physically I'm fine. Where are you at?"

"I just got off work. I'm at O'Hare," he replies.

"When does your flight arrive?"

"Seven fifty-five."

"What about the others?"

"Rio and Roberto are on the same flight and are supposed to get there at 10---I think," he says. "Did you hear from anybody else?"

"Uh...no."

"Where are we staying?" he asks.

"The W."

"Which one?"

"What?"

"There are two," he replies.

"What?"

"Two W's. There are two. One in the French Quarter and one on Poydras next to Harrah's."

"The casino?"

"Yeah...the casino."

It occurs to me. Aaron is already here.

"The rooms are under your name, right?" Lenny asks.

"No...Seth's..." I reply. "We're at The W on Chartres."

"Chartres...right...," he says, "...okay."

It is 3:15 and we can go to The W once we retrieve our things from Corrine's car.

I call the hotel to see if anyone has checked in.

The voice on the other end is soft, southern, female and mechanical, "Good afternoon you've reached The W Hotel French Quarter. Please hold..."

A lisping man picks up the line. "The W French Quarter, this is Charles."

Charles leads on that he is too busy to answer my simple questions but is able to let me know a "Seth" on a reserved room list was allowed to check into room 308 at around 2:30.

"I see..." I reply. "Is he still there?"

"I have no idea," Charles says.

"Well...can you call his room to see if he's in?"

He sighs. "I guess."

Charles lets the phone ring several times. "There doesn't appear to be anyone in the room. Would you like to leave a message or is there anything else?"

"Wait---are there any messages for me?"

Charles sighs again. "Hold please...there's one message from a mister 'Lance Manley'...It says: 'Gone Drinkin'. There's a line underneath 'Drinkin' "

"I see..."

"Anything else?"

"No, thank---" the line goes dead.

"What's up?" Seth asks

"Nothing. The phone got cut off. Lenny's at the airport. He'll be in around nine."

Aaron was in town already. "Lance Manley" was one of his annoyingly but less often employed aliases. He had used 'Lance Manley' or a variation of this to score free lap dances from some strippers at a gentlemen's club in Louisville. He played up the role of a ridiculously wealthy Silicon Valley wunderkind and I his hired security detail sworn to keep the job duties professional and separate from the distractions associated with the client's personal habits:

"*Lance seems to be a really cool boss,*" Cassandra said as she stood on a metal stand next to my chair, bent over and squeezing her thigh.

I was distracted by the glitter shining unevenly on her toes and was very impressed by her ability to move so effortlessly on a metal box while wearing high heels. "*Yes, well Mr. Manley is one of the firm's more easy-going assignments. Every time he's in this part of the country he requests my service,*" I replied.

"*Where's he from?*" she asked.

"*I'm not at liberty to say. Let's just say its West,*" I said.

She widened her stance and winked at me from between her legs. "*The other girls says he's a computer big shot,*" she said.

"*He does dabbles in many things,*" I replied. "*Let's just leave it at that--*"

"*Oh right, I know...your 'client's privacy'...right,*" she said.

"*Well I hope you understand. I'm really not supposed to accept lap dances from you let alone discuss a client's business but it does help me blend into the environment...*" I replied.

She turned around, faced forward and stood between my legs. "*Well I think you're doing a fantastic job,*" she said as she buried my face into her chest and left me bedizened with gold sprinkles. *"Are you supposed to be drinking?"* she asked.

"Oh, yes...the vodka. Again...part of the cover. I've been trained to drink straight vodka, often quarts at a time without feeling a thing." I smiled.

"And you're the only one here...I mean watching him?" she asked.

"No. There are two more gentlemen in a car outside and three more in here I am not even aware of---their identities that is. It's better I don't know who they are unless they show me the sign."

"The sign?" she asked as she sat on my lap.

"Again...company business...sorry," I replied.

"That's okay, you do your job and I'll do mine," she replied.

"Fair enough," I said and slipped a twenty-dollar bill into her g-string.

Cassandra pulled out the twenty and gave it back to me. *"Uh-uh."* She smiled. *"Mr. Manley says it's all on him."*

I gave Aaron a look. He was sitting in a chair not too far away from me with two girls vying for his attention and money. *"God bless that man. It's that sort of generosity that keeps the economic engine of this fine country running,"* I said as Aaron raised his glass to me and grinned.

Cassandra asked, *"You're not carrying any weapons are you?"*

"Oh Lord no my dear...you can't bring a gun in here without getting into some serious trouble," I replied.

"Then how do you---" she asked.

"Let's just say I've been trained," I said.

"Hmm...me too," she said.

In understanding my friend's proclivities towards certain vices I had a fairly decent guess as to where Aaron was. He was most likely flying solo at the casino upon mistakenly attempting to check-in at The W on Poydras or entertaining himself at one of the many gentleman's clubs in the city. It wouldn't be unusual for him to work out his intial urges alone much the same way a serial killer might satiate himself within strange and virgin territory. The "me" time would help him burn off some of the mad enthusiastic fuel pent up as he sat anxiously on the plane for a few hours.

I dial Aaron's number and get his voicemail.

Seth is bored. "What are we doing?" he asks. "Are we going to stand around here all day or check in? Let's get back to the car and into the hotel before all the weirdness begins."

"Yeah, good idea," I say as I watch Seth and Corrine leave Old Man River and head back towards the Quarter. "Ha! Weirdness," I mumble to myself. "Too late."

Chapter Three

The W on Chartres is quiet. The lure of this place occurs to me while slipping into the sweet vodka haze of an early Friday evening; watching the night's long shadows chase away daylight. The shade is becoming blue, longer, and wider by the sips. It's an old building; a secretive and perpetual wood and brick shell disguising a refurbished interior of velvet, polish, and deep red and gray colors. It is hardly noticeable on the street and at night can be easily missed unless the dim spotlight hanging above Chartres happens to catch the reddish and orange 'W' in the right way. There is a fountain bubbling in the cobblestone courtyard's center. It hypnotizes the mind and drips over itself like a slow rain. The water echoes, multiplies, reverberates, and eventually breaks apart against old brick walls. At night the courtyard functions best, as a place of meditation, worship, and pagan drinking rituals. From the street the subtle call is irresistible and inviting.

My cell phone is off but next to me on a patio table. A few people are out savoring the light breeze. I purchase a bottle of Absolut for fourteen dollars at a souvenir store at Canal and Exchange Place and am enjoying the pleasant burn by the pool with an ice bucket and a clean glass until The W staff informs me they can't allow breakable containers near the swimming area. I politely state I have no intention of breaking anything but take myself and my afternoon cordial to a table and some chairs a few feet beyond the black iron lace guarding the fenced in pool. Seth has taken an afternoon siesta rather than watch me drink. He bought a case and a half of Miller Light from the same store for almost thirty bucks. The cost is absolute piracy, but who are we to argue when it is obvious the thirst has us under its thumb. We reserved three rooms on separate floors and were able to upgrade one room to quarters with a small patio overlooking Chartres Street. Having slept in a duplex loft the previous night, the upgrade was the natural space Seth and I agreed we needed in order to maintain our psychic boundaries. The rooms are equipped with all the necessary amenities: cable; honor bar (fully stocked); Playstation; iron and board; plush terry cloth bathrobes; coffee maker; coffee and Earl Grey Tea;

24 hour adult movies with five minute pre-views; and a compact disc player with an R&B CD Seth has sworn to steal. The beds are highly stacked and thick with pillow top comfort. It is perfectly suited for my needs. My only concern is the toilet. It hisses and moans at random and the difference between the humidity and cold water in the tank makes it sweat; not just a light condensation on its porcelain skin, but a nervous, fearful, panic sweat. There is a hotel bar next to the in-house Italian restaurant but I prefer the courtyard's cheap drink and relative freedom. Aaron has not called yet, and after a few glasses of vodka and some gentle weeping from the fountain I am relaxed and turn the phone back on, curious to join him in whatever distractions he's found for himself. Corrine is wandering the Quarter with Loni and Sylvia. Marty is gone, back to Pensacola, no doubt. Or jail.

I am undergoing a solitary and peaceful metamorphosis to 'drunk' when a Texas drawl spills into the courtyard to break the fountain's hold over me. "Hey! Yer at that strip club last night, man."

I open my eyes to squint over my sunglasses. They have slipped during my trance and sit at the edge of my nose.

He says again, "Yer at the club last night, man." His name is Dave, and I have no idea what he is talking about.

"Man, yer fucked up---I can't believe they didn't kick you out sooner. If you hadn't fallen off the bar stool you'd been all right---" Dave is a crew cut with an untreatable leg twitch from just outside of Fort Worth. He is stocky and is wearing denim shorts and a white t-shirt that reads: "Panama City Beach Rocks Spring Break '98!" He has been in the sun too long and is the radiant pink pigs can get when they are excited and aren't covered in mud.

"Boy," I say sternly, "you got ants in your pants? Sit down before your leg falls off."

"Yessir," he replies.

"Please. No formalities. It's too nice a day to ruin things with false sentiment." I push the chair across from me out to him with my foot.

He sits down and eyes the Absolut bottle resting next to the ice bucket. He is enthusiastic and exclaims, "You drank all that? Man, I knew yer nuts!"

"Actually no. I mean yes, but not all today."

"You don't put no cranberry juice or nothin'?" he remarks.

"No."

He exclaims again, "Man, yer nuts!"

"Yes...well... I suppose the days of drinking anything on the rocks as a gentleman's pursuit are over, huh?" He has no idea what I am talking about but nevertheless, smiles and nods in agreement.

The vodka never hurts you. It is the things people throw into it to make it taste better that screw with the mind: the lemons, limes, olives, fruit juice and whatever extracurricular distractions are the fad. To really enjoy New Orleans' hard edges on a typical Friday night it is vital to allow the vodka to temper itself on the rocks, alone and unspoiled.

I am unmoved by his presence. "You were saying?"

"Oh nothing." He grins. "Naw man, yer really fucked up last night."

"Apparently." I finish the glass, grab some ice from the bucket and pour myself a double.

"This is a nice place," he says as he gives the courtyard a 360-degree once over.

"Yes...it'll do." Dave watches me drink for what seems like an eternity before I speak, "You know you'll have to refresh my memory. That fall I took last night may have affected me."

He leans into the table, eyes wide and whispers, "X---man."

I stare at him and shrug my shoulders.

He whispers again, "You know anybody who wants to score?"

"Oh...drugs. Sorry, I can't help you there." I take off my sunglasses and place them on the table.

"Damn!" He whispers, "I got so much X....I don't know what to do with it. I come over for the weekend with my brother 'n sister-in-law and 'bout 500 tablets and ain't nobody in this town doin drugs 'cept weed. You sure you can't help me out?"

"Afraid not..." I raise my glass to him and shake the ice cubes at him. "...I'm all about the buzz."

"Yeah I figured. You got that drinkin look 'bout you. Say, yer from Chicago right?"

"Yes."

"Ain't nobody there you can hook me up with? I got lots more where this come from...good ole' Mexico."

"No, not really. But my attorney might. He's been known to associate with low lifes, liars, and thieves."

His eyes grow wide. "He criminal de-fense?"

"No, he works for an insurance company."

Dave looks confused.

"Never mind," I say, "Nowadays you'd best find some alternative source of income because it's getting harder to bring anything into the country, let alone drugs."

He looks even more confused.

"You know," I say, "because of the jeehadees..."

Dave scratches his head.

"The war."

"Oh yeah." His knee bounces up and down. "That sucks. There ain't no drugs in Chicago?"

"Oh no, there's plenty, but I don't make enough money to start a serious coke habit and am really not the type of person who should be around drugs. I've got a doctor's note."

Seth appears from his nap with a plastic garbage can overflowing with ice and packed full with Miller Lite bottles. He looks groggy and lost. He stares in our direction from a distance until he recognizes me.

"Dave," I motion at Seth. "I'd like you to meet my physician Dr. Lance Mannion." I whisper to Dave under my breath, "----nerve specialist."

Dave stands up, turns around and shakes Seth's hand. "Doc," he says politely.

Seth looks at me, shakes his head, drops the garbage can next to the table and sits down. He pulls out a beer and offers one to Dave who turns him down by saying, "Naw I'm cool."

"You travel with yer doctor?" He exclaims, "Man, I knew yer crazy!"

"Exactly...now you understand why I can't do drugs." I grab a beer from the garbage can and shake the water off my hand. "It's bad for my synaptic fibers and overall mental health."

Seth says nothing and slouches back in his chair after putting down half a beer. It is quiet and Dave's knee bounces faster than before. Seth continues to stare at him without saying anything. I drink the beer and stare at Seth staring at Dave.

Eventually Dave takes the hint and stands up. He extends his hand to Seth. "Nice meetin' you, Doc."

Seth shakes his hand and nods.

Dave turns to me. "Good talking with you Mr. Seth."

Seth glares at me with a stern eye.

"Yes...well..." I smile and firmly shake Dave's hand. "...sorry I can't help you out."

"Well," Dave replies, "if you change yer mind just look me up at the Sonesta room 406."

"The Royal or Chateau?" I ask.

He looks confused. "Yeah..."

"Well which one is it?" Seth asks.

Dave's leg twitches. "Oh the, uh, Royal---but hell, I'm sure I'll see you around."

"I'm sure you will," I say.

Dave walks away and waves his hand as he disappears into the dim lights on Chartres Street.

"What the fuck was that about?" Seth grumbles.

"Narc," I reply and sip on my beer.

"That guy?" Seth lights a cigarette and blows out a drag. "He's too dumb to be a cop."

"Well, not him per se but they're using him. Dirty fascists. They should all be flogged for taking advantage of that imbecile. That dangerous retard is bound to take down some unfortunate drunk with his plea bargain."

"Corrine didn't come back yet?" he asks.

"No," I reply. "What time is it?"

"A little after seven."

"How long have I been out here?" I ask.

He picks up the Absolut bottle and examines the contents. "Since about four-thirty." He puts the vodka down and grabs my phone. "You haven't heard from anyone?"

"No." I stand up and the earth moves sideways and to the left before I am able to stretch my arms out for balance. "Good Lord did you feel that?!"

"What are you talking about?"

"The earthquake. I need food---quickly---before the next one hits me."

Seth shakes his head. "You drank too much. You should slow down."

I lean against the table for balance and collect my thoughts. "Don't lecture me. Goddamn plate tectonics. I just need something to keep me grounded before the continent drifts."

"Well let's get something and bring it back."

A pleasant woman named Jennifer whose voice is the sweet southern message recorded on the hotel's automated operator directs us to a Taco Bell/KFC for a quick bite.

"You can't miss it," she says as she leans over the front desk and points to her left. "It's right next to a sex shop."

It's already dark and we walk down Chartres for a distance to find nothing. As we backtrack to the hotel Seth suggests we head to Canal Street where he is sure there is a McDonald's. I am convinced this is a bad idea because of the crowds gathered for the late parade, but my head goes dizzy and I realize food will be the only salvation from another night with screaming parrots. We leave Chartres and walk onto a dark side street made smaller by parked cars blocking the curbs.

"I don't get it," Seth grumbles. "How could we miss the place? She said it was right around the corner."

"It's The Creep I tell you. We probably keep passing it but just don't see it," I reply.

He is puzzled. "I mean shouldn't there be a sign or something?"

"Yeah, it's next to a sex shop," I say.

A syrupy and slow lisp breaks from a few cars behind us on the street, "You boys lookin' fo' the sex shop?"

Seth and I turn around.

The voice is young, black, thin, and smoking a cigarette. "I said you boys lookin' fo' the sex shop..." he lisps.

"Actually," Seth says, "....we're looking for something to eat."

He is leaning against a parked car and waves his cigarette in the air with his left hand to point behind him. "There's a Krystal ova' there..."

Seth shakes his head. "No. We are not going to Krystal. I'd rather starve to death."

I plead, "Yeah but I'm so hungry I *could* eat Krystal."

He speaks again, "Well *we* got food...." He points at a Taco Bell/KFC storefront sign. It is made of wood, dimly lit by a small spotlight and nonchalantly situated next to the Adult Emporium Triple X window. "...But all we gots strips and tacos," he says.

"Wait, where's The W?" I ask.

He casually waves his hand to his left, leaving smoke whirls twisting in the air against the light. "Two blocks that way." He takes a long drag, puts his cigarette out with his foot and walks into the restaurant.

Inside, the cashier, a young black woman, is standing but asleep and leaning against the counter. The young man who was smoking outside casually strolls around the counter top and heads for the kitchen. "Brandy git up...," he yells, "we got company..."

At this instruction, Brandy comes to life, slow, drowsy and stiff, like a coin operated, Ouija divining carnival machine. "Welcome to KFC/Taco Bell may I take your order."

The young man bellows from the back, "Brandy we got nothing but strips and tacos!"

Brandy speaks, "All we gots strips and tacos."

The alcohol is ready to turn against me so I order fifteen tacos and a diet Pepsi that has very little life left in it. Seth orders chicken strips and a large handful of honey mustard to hide the dry and stale taste.

We sit in the hotel room and eat quietly until the floor and side table are littered with taco wrappers, hot sauce packets, napkins and empty beer bottles. I do the change up, abandoning the vodka for the moment and switch to Miller Lite. With beer I feel grounded, comfortably stable and safe as I sit on the floor with a bag of tacos. The television is on and we watch opening ceremony highlights from the Winter Olympic Games in Salt Lake City. Controversy is brewing. Apollo Ohno has just been accused of tanking a short track speed skating race days before so his buddy would qualify for the U.S. Olympic team.

The games will end seventeen days from now and will probably be remembered mostly for the paranoia and disillusionment generated by terrorism, blood doping, bribery, sporting fixes, formal protests, steroids, and curling. As commentary and analysis is being made as to whether a fix is in I can only imagine the Mormons breathing a collective sigh of relief once they are able to kick the liars, cheaters, and politicians out of their town.

"It's all just falling apart isn't it?" Seth says.

"What?"

"Amateur sports," he replies.

"Don't kid yourself," I say. "It all went to hell with the Dream Team in Barcelona but The Fix was in a long time ago." I collect the wrappers on the floor, ball them up and stuff them into the brown Taco Bell bag. "The moment they let Hitler use the '38 games for propaganda it was pretty much over. They should've ended the Olympics right there. At least with professional sports you know everyone's driven by greed and not competing fascistic ideologies."

"What in the hell are you babbling about?" he growls. "Stop talking."

Lenny materializes from the unlit entrance to the room. "Yeah, just what the hell is he talking about now?"

Seth grabs his chest and leaps from his chair. "CHRIST!" he screams. He takes a breath and laughs. "Where the hell did you come from?"

"I've been standing here listening to you idiots for the past five minutes," he says.

"Doesn't anybody knock anymore?" Seth asks.

He sets his bag down next to the closet door and passes into the light. "What the hell do I have to knock for? I've got a key."

I slowly crane my head up and to the left. He appears upside down to me at first, bald headed, brown, and slightly menacing. I offer the last wrapper to him. "Taco?"

He has a disgusted look on his face. "No."

I raise my other hand. "Beer?"

"Yeah," he says and sits down on the bed. "What the hell is wrong with the toilet?"

"It has a life force of its own," Seth replies.

"What's it like out there?" I ask.

"It's getting crazy."

The highjinks in the Quarter were spreading and Lenny abandoned the cab he was in to walk to the hotel after the driver found himself gridlocked by the crush of pedestrians. As Lenny passes on to us a few details about his route through the Quarter, Seth sits at a table next to the open door near the patio. He stares at the ceiling. "Wh--What was that?"

Lenny and I watch Seth from across the room. His body is still but his head and eyes canvas the space above his head furiously.

Lenny looks at me.

I shrug my shoulders.

"There!" Seth insists, "Did you hear that?!" He carefully closes the door and flips the wooden plantation blinds next to him and looks out and beyond the window framed doors.

Lenny asks, "What are you---"

"Shut up!" Seth cries. "Turn down the volume on the T.V."

I grab the remote control and press the mute button. The room is quiet except the sound of air passing through the vent overhead. There is a muffled humming.

"THERE!" Seth says. "THAT! WHAT IS THAT?! THAT BUZZING SOUND?!"

My cell phone is sitting on the nightstand, buried and vibrating underneath a plastic grocery bag from the souvenir shop.

Lenny stands up, walks to the nightstand and makes flapping motions towards Seth with his hands. "OOOOOooooo...BEES...BEES."

Seth springs out of the chair and runs into the bathroom.

Lenny picks up the phone and answers, "Hello?"

I can hear the nasal whine on the other end of the call.

"Where have you been?" Aaron says.

Lenny is puzzled. "Who is this?"

"Aaron."

"Why are you calling?" Lenny asks.

Aaron replies, "I'm at Jacque's Cabaret."

"What---" Lenny holds the phone to his chest and looks around the room. Seth is still locked in the bathroom. I remain silent and focus on muted images from the television. The Olympic torch is raging away in the cool darkness of the Utah night.

"What are you doing here?" Lenny asks.

"Who is this?" Aaron asks.

"Lenny."

Aaron's laughter is loud and grating. "Get over here. It's on Bourbon Street. Ask the concierge."

"Yeah, I know where it is." Lenny sits down on the bed before handing the phone back to me.

The line is dead.

"So..." Lenny says.

"Hmm…" I stare at the display on the phone. It is nine-ten.

"So..." he says again.

"Yeah, I know. I called him last night," I reply.

"He's at Jacque's Cabaret," he says.

I sip my beer. "Uh-huh."

Lenny thinks for a moment and snorts. "That's unexpected."

"I'm sorry," I reply. "I couldn't stop him. He tricked me, the goddamned bastard. He told me he was feeling unhappy and restless and unloved in his mansion and his wealth had alienated him from common men. I felt pity for his choice to live an aristocratic lifestyle and invited him to debase himself here in order to assure himself of his humanity. Little did I know it was just an excuse to ogle strippers he's never met."

We drink a few more beers each before Seth's apiphobia passes and he comes out of the bathroom. Lenny is ready to get outside the hotel and deal with Bourbon Street. I am sedate, a bit drowsy, and definitely weighed down by vodka, beer, and tacos. I am feeling very slow and stupid and reason that a quick shower will bring me back from the feebleness that only comes from sitting and drinking without care for hours on end in front of a television.

We are waiting for the elevator on our way out when Lenny stops me and shakes his head. "What are you doing, jackass?"

"What?"

He stares and points at the plastic Taco Bell cup in my hand. "What is that?" he asks.

"Diet Pepsi."

"Lemme see it," he insists.

"Fuck off."

He looks at his watch. "It's 10:15. Do you really think you're gonna last?"

I consider the question:

It was all very well to say 'Drink Me', but the wise little Alice was not going to do that in a hurry. For she had read several nice little histories about children who had got burnt, and eaten up by wild beasts and other unpleasant things all because they would not remember the simple rules their friends had taught them. She had never forgotten that if you drink much from a bottle marked 'poison,' it is almost certain to disagree with you sooner or later.

"Duly noted," I reply. "However..."

...this bottle was NOT marked 'poison' so Alice ventured to taste it and finding it very nice she very soon finished it off.

"What a curious feeling!" said Alice; "I must be shutting up like a telescope."

"You idiot," Seth says. "You'll rot with the crazies. Remember what happened last night?"

...This curious child was very fond of pretending to be two people. 'But it's no use now,' thought poor Alice, 'to pretend to be two people! Why, there's hardly enough of me left to make one respectable person!'

"Hmm...I see your point," I reply and walk back to the room.

Although it isn't marked poison, I can see the sheer volume of alcohol disagreeing with me sooner than later so I listen to what Lenny says and what Lewis Carroll has taught me and pour the vodka I am prepared to carry to Jacque's back into the bottle. Corrine, Roberto, and Rio have not shown up yet so I leave the Absolut, an ice bucket, and eight Miller Lite bottles on the desk with a "DRINK ME" note. It will give them something to do before heading out to join the tea party in the Quarter.

Outside the air is warm. In the distance people are laughing and shouting and playing music. "Down, down, down, the rabbit hole we go," I say as we turn a corner and walk towards Bourbon Street.

Chapter Four

Jacque's Cabaret has high ceilings. It's an odd thing to notice in a strip club but it's the first thing I realize when I pay the twenty-dollar cover. Maybe I *am* shrinking and the ceiling's height is actually normal, but it is unusually high and looks much smaller from the outside. It's airy, cool, and lit with blue light. Sexual fantasy is wafting through the vents and around silhouetted, naked, lavendered and baby oiled bodies. Occasionally bright lasers cut through the blue shadows to reveal tan female bodies swimming in the dark depths beyond reach. The tease is enough to get the men off their chairs and take their curiosity to corners where strippers stand: strange, soft, luscious, inviting, fleshy, and overpowering, all swaying to Guns and Roses' "Patience" and re-igniting prepubescent fires in their heads of what women were to them not too long ago before marriage, children, or doomed relationships.

We find Aaron distracted by the pricey entertainment in the VIP room with two champagne magnums, cigars, and a host of beauties whispering in discreet tones the phrase: "Thousand dollar lover" to one another.

He rises from his sofa, grabs me by the shoulders and calmly tells me:

"I NEED THREE HUNDRED AND FIFTY DOLLARS."

"What?!"

"GIVE ME THREE HUNDRED AND FIFTY DOLLARS."

Eight hours in New Orleans has eaten away the natural fear visitors wear as armor to guard themselves from the anxiety of the new geography. Aaron has abandoned the fear and embraced the decadence.

"Give me your money," he insists.

"You're depraved."

"Don't make me take it from you," he says. "You'll just drink it away. I'd rather have you donate it to my cause." He looks at me as if I should be able to read his mind and answer the question myself. "It's for THE SPECIAL man...THE SPECIAL..." he says.

"What the hell is 'The Special'?"

He pauses to think about it for a moment and shakes his head. "I don't know, but it costs three hundred and fifty dollars and is special."

"You lecherous fool...you're drunk."

"No. In fact I don't think I've ever seen things so clearly." He points to a curvy blonde wearing black French cut bikini bottoms and a matching laced top. She is at the bar, and as most flesh under dim and champagne fueled lighting appears, is dangerously inviting. Her name is Karen, and last year as an entertainer she made over a hundred and twenty thousand dollars---mostly in cash and mostly undeclared.

He says, "She's giving me investment advice."

"But you're the rich guy, " I reply.

"Yeah but...she's really savvy?"

"Did you just say 'savvy'?" I ask, "How much have you had to drink?"

"No, let me finish," he continues, "so she says she took in about a hundred and twenty thousand dollars last year, mostly cash and undeclared."

"Uh-huh, you told me that already."

"Oh right." His eyes are glazed over, strained from alcohol and ogling the pretty girls for hours. "Karen got me thinking that strippers have a lot of liquidity and probably do little investing but not Karen because she's savvy. But most probably don't invest."

"Uh-huh."

"So when I get back to California I'm going to start investment seminars for strippers." He smiles proudly.

"And you need three hundred and fifty dollars for what? Fliers?"

"Oh, well, no. She'll only take cash and I don't have that much on me right now and I don't want to use the ATM here and well...The Special...I mean just look at her..."

A "Three Hundred and Fifty Dollar Special" typically ends up costing about twice as much in a place like this so I buy him a lap dance instead and a seven dollar beer at the bar. Drinking at a place like Jacque's is dangerous and expensive. There will never be enough money to satisfy your needs if you are addicted to booze or sex. The club is too manicured and the talent too well versed in the art of the tease. Sooner or later everyone will get fleeced. This is apparent to me when I negotiate a lap dance for Aaron. Karen informs me Aaron is running a tab on drinks and dances.

"What's the bill?" I ask.

"Well," she says, "what time is it?"

"Eleven."

"It was about two thousand dollars half an hour ago."

My head goes heavy and my face cold. "Good Lord." I gasp. "But it's just him."

Karen smiles. "Yeah, but he's a really fun guy."

"I need a drink."

"Sure," she says, "what are you having?"

"Vodka on the rocks. Absolut."

"A twist?" she asks.

"No. Nothing."

"So I'll just put this on the tab?"

"Sure why not? You know what?" I shrug. "Make that a double."

The bartender fixes my drink. He is pouring the vodka with an electronic shot dispenser. It is an unfriendly practice I consider sterile and lacking human kindness.

"Where is Aaron?" I ask.

Karen replies, "Huh...he was here just a minute ago. Maybe he's in the bathroom."

Bastard, I think to myself. What a cruel joke. It would be unconscionable for Aaron to initiate this spectacle and duck out to let us sweat out the bill while he lays low at the black jack table down the street at Harrah's. He's had plenty of time to disintegrate into a drunk amnesiac by now and forget the bill. Seth and Lenny will be too wrapped up with the nudity while I observe, carefully calculating the dances in my head along with the drinks. Sooner or later we'll have to pool our resources to settle the tab. Things will get horrible, turn ugly and we will all realize we are in over our heads by even indulging the thought of Three Hundred Fifty Dollar Specials.

I stay at the bar, finish the Absolut quickly, have another for courage, and feel my nerves settle. I order my third when a large man places a heavy hand on my shoulder. Here we go I think to myself, the people running this place know we've hit the limit. Somebody's ordered a lap dance or a drink and when they ran the charge through, those bastards at Visa decide enough is enough and put a stop to Aaron's scheme to earn airline miles off strippers and booze.

"Just not the face," I mumble as I clench the drink in my hand and turn to face him.

"What?" the man replies.

I take one last gulp from the glass. "It's vodka."

"On the rocks, huh?"

"Yes."

"How many is that for you?" he asks.

"Three."

"You know," he says, "those are nine dollars a drink. There's champagne over there."

"Too many sulfites," I reply. "Lord knows what that'll do when mixed with all the grains...." There is a moment of awkward silence as his sweaty paw weighs down on my shoulder and my spine's ever decreasing ability to remain upright. "So what's this all about? What's the score here?" I ask.

"It's at twenty-six hundred."

"Dollars?"

"Uh-huh. Are you having a good time yet?" he asks. "We can set you gentlemen up with some good company for the night."

"That depends," I say politely as he waves the bartender over, "who's paying for all this?"

"Lance Manley is." The bouncer gives me a drink on the house and says I should thank Mr. Manley.

"Have you seen him? Where is he?"

"Right over there. He'd like to speak with you."

"God bless that man." I raise the glass in relief. "He's a true philanthropist."

Aaron had left to get something quick to eat outside the bar. A girl comes over with a running bill that he looks over and nods at. "So I'm paying for things I can see outside for free." Aaron laughs. "Compared to the street this place is like church!"

"You're probably right. We should settle up and leave," I say.

"Yeah, yeah, whatever," he says. "But you have to get a lap dance before we go."

"Save the thirty bucks and buy me a drink."

"Live a little."

The vodka begins to kick and the movement around the VIP room slows to a blur. I sit in a dim corner lit with a tea light. It is quiet and cool. I am content to remain silent and let the alcohol mellow out a bit while curved silhouettes tease and negotiate fees all around me. When the candle goes out, I take it as a sign I can disappear into the shadows and take a nap. A girl named Cindy drops into my lap.

She is from Hawaii, Asian, athletic, and on a one-month stint in New Orleans from Super Bowl XXXVI to Mardi Gras 2002. My guess is she is twenty but under the vodka spells, warm flesh, and temptation in dark rooms like this it's always hard to tell. In the end there is very little to remember about a lap dance or a stripper unless the circumstance, the song, or the stories they tell strike a chord.

She relights the candle. "He said you were shy. Like your privacy, huh?"

"Just some quiet time. I can feel the beginnings of a bad hangover."

"I drink a can of Pedialyte to avoid hangovers," she says as she moves the chair next to me aside and pulls up a black metal box to perform her dance.

"Pedialyte?"

"It's what babies drink when they're dehydrated. It works better than Gatorade or water."

"How's it taste?" I ask.

"I like the cherry flavor."

"Hmm, does it come in grape?"

"Uh-huh."

"That's brilliant. I'm all about the buzz, but lately the hangovers are murderous. I might have to give it a try. When did you figure all that out?"

"My daughter drinks it."

"I see. How old is she?"

"Eighteen months," she says as she removes her silver, silk slip and tucks it deep into my t-shirt in workmanlike fashion. She keeps her g-string and white heels on.

"You mind if we wait until the next song?" she asks.

"No, not at all."

Cindy is physical and smells like French Vanilla ice cream. Trisha Yearwood is singing "How Do I Live?" when I begin a smooth descent into the spell of her professional charms.

"What are you wearing?" she asks, breathing into my neck.

"Uh...cologne...."

She giggles. "I mean what kind?"

I begin to speak but forget the words; too much vodka or too much Cindy. I am distracted, hypnotized by shadows and the fickle candlelight. It hides, reveals, melts, and bends her tanned curves. There is no point in talking. It is one of those instances where even polite talk is forced and insincere unless I am completely drunk.

She runs her fingers through my hair. "You smell nice...whatever it is..."

"I showered." I mumble more unintelligibles and close my eyes while she lowers her body onto mine.

She pulls back quickly and puts a finger over my lips.

I open my eyes.

She leans forward and moves close enough to whisper in my ear, "No biting." She continues her vertical slide against my chest.

Good Lord, did I just bite her? I place my hands underneath my legs and away from her body. I taste nothing salty or soapy on my lips. No glitter or French vanilla Cindy. Biting has happened once before in Chicago but under the influence of some very bad drinking and not so tempting a woman. I wasn't aware I had done anything unusual until the next day and was convinced Lenny fabricated the vicious lie just to shame me into submission. But who is to say now he was lying? My mind is not so bent on vodka so as to lose all the reason and civility I normally conduct myself with when a naked woman sits on my lap for money. This has to be latent vampirism or, God forbid, cannibalism. If it comes down to it I suppose vampirism I can live with; I enjoy late nights and hardly ever go to Church. But cannibalism will be a different lifestyle and commitment altogether. It requires isolation, power tools, and a working knowledge of anatomy. A cannibals' life seems very lonely.

"Maybe you're just horny," Cindy whispers.

"What?"

She is reading my thoughts.

She laughs, pulls my hands out from underneath my legs and places them on her hips. "I don't think you're shy...that's just your game. You like to bite? So do I."

"N-no, really," I reply, "...that's very nice of you to say, but you shouldn't encourage me."

"But honey," she says confidently, "that's my job."

It is probably the only true statement uttered in that bar. The rest...who knows? Her daughter is in San Diego with her mom and is passed from relative to relative while she tours the country. She may be lying about her kid and herself, but I'm not dumb enough to search for truth in strip clubs.

The music ends.

"One more song?" She asks as she reaches into my shirt and slowly pulls out her slip.

I take a deep sip and order another drink. "Sure...why not?"

Although I am supremely inspired by Cindy's attention, the nine dollar Absoluts begin to weigh more heavily on my brain. I lose count sometime after Trisha Yearwood and before ACDC's "Givin The Dog A Bone." It is time to leave here before we become unsatisfied with just the tease and are rendered penniless and vampiric by their feminine wiles. The total amount is twenty-nine hundred dollars for seven Absolut on the rocks, two magnums of Champagne, 42 Miller Lites, miscellaneous Mandarin and Sevens, Captain and Cokes, shots, a VIP charge, and an infinite string of lap dances. Back at The W the concierge has called Lenny to let him know Rio and Roberto have arrived. The coven of drinkers is now complete. It is time to find cheaper thrills and cheaper drinks.

Chapter Five

Seth is afraid of Rio. He fears her the way dogs fear cats. It's not a physical fear so much as a psychological one. While a dog may be master of its domain in its own right it's acutely aware and knows at any given moment a cat, if compelled or even on a whim, will not think twice about turning around and scratching the shit out of you for kicks. Perhaps in a past life they knew each other and have been locked in a primordial struggle between predator and prey that spans the ages. Seth fears her and she knows it, which makes me a happy and sadistic observer when they are in the same room together.

To me, Rio has always been Nordic. She is blonde, fair skinned, blue eyed and appears taller than she actually is although she swears she is only 5'9." I've seen her fight with women and men and can only reason her aberrant behavior is reinforced by a deeply embedded Viking gene laying dormant in her brain until first triggered by a chemical reaction between the hormone which the gene controlled and the alcohol which polluted her virgin lips. She claims no such ancestry, but I've seen the horrified expressions of her victims' faces in illustrations of Norse invasions and comic book renditions of Valkyries. This fear can only be a byproduct of an encounter with someone who harbors within her blood the berserker rage and believes in the cult of Odin. Like her Scandinavian forbearers, she lives big, takes freely from the planet's smaller, peripheral inhabitants, and has a thorough lust for high adventure and good times.

She was drinking on the plane and had not been on Louisiana's terra firma for less than twenty minutes before terrorizing some young boys who demanded to see her tits:

"What did you say to me you little shit?" she asked from the taxi *cab window.*

The boys were petrified.

"Wait---What did you say to me?" she screamed. "You...What did *you say? Do you even know what real tits look like?!"*

"Oh God," Roberto muttered to himself as he sunk lower into the taxi's backseat. He eyed the boys and pitied them. They stood silently on the airport curbside, shocked, embarrassed, and fearful. The cab was stuck in a traffic line leaving the arrival terminal and was moving too slow for Roberto's comfort and the driver's patience.

Roberto grabbed her shoulder to talk her down. "Uh...Rio..."

She smacked his hand away. It was too late. Half her body was outside the window and she was pointing her finger and threatening them with a vulgar eloquence that only comes from experienced shit talkers and brawlers. "What've you got there, little man?!" she yelled. "Do you even have hair on your balls yet!?"

"Uh...Rio..." Roberto pleaded.

The cab driver, a swarthy foreigner, stopped the car and turned around in his seat. "Young lady...would you..."

She turned on the driver. "Did you hear what they said to me?!"

"Miss...please...into the car...please," he said.

"You heard what they said to me!"

"Miss...please get in or get out of my taxi I do not have time for this," he replied.

She pulled her head back into the cab and glared at the man. She rolled her eyes at Roberto and opened the door. "Fuck all this! I don't like your attitude and this car stinks...we're leaving!" She yanked Roberto out from the backseat and slammed the door, staring at the driver for what seemed like an eternity until she barked, "Open the trunk."

The cabbie refused.

"Open the trunk now or I'll drag you outta that car and kick your smelly ass back to whatever Third World shit hole you escaped from!" she growled.

Roberto struggled to pull her away from the driver's side window as she prepared her fist for a wind up. "ARE YOU CRAZY?!" he screamed.

"No, look at him." She laughed. "Doesn't he look like his ass smells? You probably eat a lot of chick peas you hairy camel fucker! That'll definitely make your pucker stink!"

The driver swore something in his native tongue and opened the trunk.

"Thanks," Roberto said as he pulled her towards the trunk to get their bags. "Thank you."

Rio redirected her rage on the boys. They scrambled when she leapt from the car and retreated towards the luggage carousel and airport security.

"You better run!" she yelled. "Didn't your mommies and daddies tell you to stay away from girls who use drugs?! Fucking hillbillies."

Stunned bystanders looked on with disbelief. The boys scattered into the terminal.

"I'M A DRUG USER!" she declared. "I PEE BROWN!"

"...and I swear," Roberto continues as he sits on the bed drinking a Miller Lite and staring intently at the television, "...the look on that poor guy's face when she told him his ass stunk was the funniest thing."

"Yeah," Aaron says, "but he shouldn't take it so badly, I mean...what ass doesn't smell?"

"Great," Seth groans. "Keep that crazy bitch away from me."

I pour some Absolut into a fresh glass with ice and ask, "Where is she?"

Roberto says nothing. The silence is deliberate. Our current animosity towards one another has turned from explicit to subtle. He laid into me weeks before by telling me in front of this coven of drinkers I was an alcoholic and should get help. At first I considered it a clumsy joke and an excuse for rude banter. We were at a bar during this conversation and he was drunk and almost under the table. It degenerated into a yelling match about who was worse and who should be preaching sermons about the evils of drinking. I freely admitted I was all about the buzz but would eventually stop before it became an entanglement. In the end I was thrown out of the bar for accidentally knocking over the table but not before I threw a balled up ten dollar bill at him to "buy a clue." We had not really spoken since.

Lenny asks, "Anybody know where she is?"

"Uh...upstairs with Corrine," Roberto says. He pretends to be preoccupied with previews for the adult channel while he drinks his beer but I suspect he'd like to choke me if he got the chance. "Y'know, this is bullshit. They cut off the movies just when everything gets good."

"You have to pay for the rest," Lenny says.

"Oh..." he laughs. "Well fuck this. Let's get out to a bar or something."

"What are you eating?" Lenny asks.

"A Kit-Kat," he replies. "There's some in this little 'fridge."

"You moron...That's the honor bar."

"The what?"

"How much is that Kit Kat?"

Roberto shrugs. "I-uh...I don't know."

"They're seven dollars. They cost a dollar at the convenient store next door."

"Man if you can spend three grand on strippers then I can eat a seven dollar Kit Kat," he replies.

"Durry notareded...retarded...," I say and stir the vodka and ice in my glass.

I think I hear Roberto speak but am not sure. But I do hear a familiar voice say in a repetitious and louder tone, "What did you call me?"

I am about to say something more when I look at the bottle and realize its contents and my ability to speak have slowly diminished. Seth shakes his head from across the room. Lenny and Aaron talk Roberto down from delivering a throttling, which based on Seth's glare, he thinks I probably need. I don't see why the apparent misunderstanding should matter because I myself am ignoring my babbling.

"Ahhh...what's the point?" I hear myself slur. "We've got to go. There's no need to be offended by my words and good cheer. We should go out and drink. Instead of sitting and watching him argue pay per view rates with the television."

"Come on, jerk...let's go," Aaron says and hustles me out into the hallway and off to the street.

There are too many bars to consider on Bourbon Street and the relentless stop and go winds my brain so tight I cling to light posts, walls, or strangers as we push through the crowded pavement. I am praying someone will show mercy and pick a venue where we can stop. Corrine is dragging me by my wrist while Aaron holds me upright with an occasional shove from behind. After a time I don't seem to be walking at all. I am legless and floating down a fleshy stream of bodies, beads and arms until the Quarter disintegrates into blurry silence.

I feel myself propped up against a black, iron table. A flash from a camera brings my mind into focus and I am in a courtyard on Bourbon Street, surrounded by bars, beer tubs, and dance cages. A fountain at the entrance is bubbling water and shooting out blue and orange flames. I observe this beast for a few seconds before it acknowledges my presence with a boiling hiss of hot spit.

Lenny yells at me, "What did you say?"

"The dragon. It's going to be trouble...later," I mumble. He has two plastic cups in his hands.

"What?" he asks.

I raise my arm and make a faint motion towards the fountain.

"That thing there. Over there. I said it's going to be trouble. It looks pissed."

He walks up and hands a cup to me. "Just stay away from it. You'll only make it angry if you keep glaring at it."

I look down into the cup and see ice and vodka, "I should go home."

"You've been saying that for the past hour. You can't go home idiot, you're not in Chicago."

"Where am I?"

He points at the cup in my hand. "It's water. Drink it."

I sniff the cup and sip slowly. "God bless you."

"Wait here...I gotta piss." He hands his drink to me.

"What is this?"

"Mandarin and Seven."

"Back on that again are you?" I reply. "Will you never learn?"

"I'm not stupid enough to drink it straight."

"Yes you are, you hypocrite. But that's your own goddamned problem," I mutter. The ground moves and I feel rubbery. My knees are soft and the Earth's gentle orbit affects my balance.

Lenny shakes his head. "Lean against the table. And for God's sakes try to stand still, jackass." He points at his drink. "And don't drink that."

I nod and set the cups on the table. Rio, Corrine and Roberto are on the dance floor. Seth and Aaron are talking to a bachelorette party. One girl is carrying a giant blow up penis almost as tall as she is. After a few songs the sway in my head slows down and I am supremely confident I am improving. Rio hands me two small test tubes filled with dark, cherry red liquids. She grabbed them from one of the many shot girls pushing the poison around the bar.

"Drink it," Rio demands.

"No."

"It's a girly shot. Drink it."

I grip the table with both hands. "Those are the worst kind."

She shoves the vial in my face. "Do it. Everyone else has."

Lenny comes back just in time to save me. "Christ, Rio, what are you doing? You're gonna kill him." He takes the vial away from her hand and drinks it.

I let go of the table and ask, "What is it?"

A pained expression twists his face. "I don't know," he says.

I laugh, "Whoa! You're fucked now, bitch! Drinking anything in a test tube is just wrong. Something like that should be a warning to keep it out of your body."

Rio drinks the other shot. "That was good." She pulls over a heavily tattooed shot girl passing near us and points at her tray of test tubes. Her eyes light up with thirst. "What's all this?"

The shot girl points at the tray. "These are Jagermeister and Stoli raspberry."

"What about those?"

"Watermelon and vodka."

Rio shakes her head. "No...We need something to wake him up."

The shot girl looks at me for a second and realizes the girly shots won't revive this drunkard. The Celtic tattoo banding her arm moves across and towards the back of her tray. "This is 151 and pineapple. The bartenders make it just for us to drink and keep things lively. But you can have them."

Rio bursts out, "We'll need three of those!"

Lenny smacks a hand to his forehead and rolls his eyes. "Oh God you're gonna kill us all."

I am about to creep away into the background when the shot girl snares me with a painted arm and sits me down in a chair next to the table. "You're going to have to sit for this one." She licks the test tube's sides and shoves it between the Captain Picard tattoo and Mr. Spock tattoo facing one another on opposite sides of her breasts' cleavage. She straddles my lap and presses Picard and Spock against my face. Human and Vulcan are now one. And before I am able to ask the obvious question of why Spock instead of Kirk, Rio hits me in the head with an open hand and cries, "DRINK IT!" Most of the shot goes down badly. The rest spills over my chin and onto the girl's tank top and breasts. I rest my tight forehead against her wet body like a boxer in a clinch. She is hot, salty and soft. Somewhere in the world Patrick Stewart and Leonard Nimoy are dizzy and becoming drunk for no comprehensible reason.

Rio yells, "Holy shit that's awesome! Do me next!"

Having just gone where many men had gone before, I am still sitting in a dazed stupor when Rio gets on her knees to do a shot from the girl's unzipped crotch. There are people howling all around us. A guy standing behind me wearing a hat with a dead alligator's head on it grabs my shoulders like he knows me, shakes me and yells, "I luh-hove the lesbians!"

The shot girl pulls me out of the chair and sits Lenny down for the last shot. She puts the test tube in her mouth, straddles him and pours it into his. His eyes grow wide and fearful. He leaps out of the chair on fire, screaming and choking, "JESUS CHRIST!", and runs to the bathroom clutching his throat.

Rio is dancing up and down and trying to speed the rush of alcohol into her system. "That's good, huh?" She laughs.

The after taste from the rum is swishing around my mouth. I gag, my eyes water and my face goes cold. "No."

She grabs my wrist. "Come on! They're playing my song! I must dance!"

The planet spins upside down and the courtyard rises unmercifully to meet the back of my head.

There is silence. I recognize Aaron standing over me for a moment while I stare at the night sky. It is dark and purple. The giant blow up penis is standing next to him fully erect. Aaron grabs the penis and rams my face with it. I try rolling away but am dazed.

"You homo," he says. "I knew you liked the cock."

A girl from the bachelorette party gasps. "Omigod...Is your friend okay?"

"Who? Him?" Aaron laughs. "He's not my friend. He's just the driver."

I feel alright despite the gravity, but "feeling alright" isn't enough to assure the bouncers I'm not a liability so we leave as soon as Lenny stops choking on the 151. We find a nice bar without the chaos of a dance floor and shot girls. It's called The Alibi. It has tables and chairs and a juke box playing good music. It is peaceful enough to set my head straight for the hour or so we're there until I get to the bathroom. I pay no attention to the heavy breathing coming from behind me as I go about my business in the cramped space. There is just a urinal, a sink, and a toilet with no stall. I turn to the sink to wash my hands and a man is standing in front of the door and next to the toilet. He is young, white, balding, and tall. He is standing against the door with his arms crossed, glaring at me.

"How's it going?" I say.

He lingers in front of the door.

"Sorry. I'll get out of your way. I have this whole ritual about touching bathroom faucets after I wash my hands." I look around the bathroom for paper towels and find none.

He growls, "So you've got nothing to say to me?"

I consider the question. "Uh...no." I wipe my hands on my shirt. "Should I?"

"You've got nothing to say to me!"

I reconsider the question. *Did I have something to say to this man?* I suppose it is possible I may have offended him in some way but have no idea what I've done.

"Uh...who are you?"

His face grows tight, and a twisted vein on the side of his head grows and pulses. "You've lost all rights to say anything about me in front of my wife, you hear me!?" he screams.

"Wife?" I say as I lean confused against the sink. "I...*really* have no idea what you're talking about. Really."

I walk towards the exit.

He turns and locks the door.

My heart beats badly. A punch to the face will hurt despite the anesthetic effects from the alcohol and I don't want to lay unconscious and bleeding on this piss and muddied floor. A flurry of thoughts scatter throughout my head. This man is totally insane. Tragically mistaken. Maybe this is a bad karmic boomerang catching up with me? Payback for my fling with Lisa. An anonymous husband seeking revenge from someone he thinks is his wife's lover for making him a cuckold. It was bound to come, the beating, even if I am the wrong man. The universe is going to teach you your indiscretions do not exist in vacuums but contribute to the culture of infidelity which has ruined this man's life.

I calmly say, "I don't know who you are."

"DON'T LIE!" he screams and punches the wall behind him.

"I'm sure you're mistaken. I get that a lot."

He eyes me suspiciously, gives me the once over, and for a moment his face softens and I believe reason and sanity have triumphed over the tragedy of a mistaken identity.

I creep towards the door. "No harm done, man. Everybody makes mistakes." When I move around him to unlock the door, he raises his arm and shoves me back.

"You're not going anywhere until I get an apology from you!" he huffs and crosses his arms.

I squeak, "What in God's name are you talking about?!"

"Y-you know, all that shit that happened a couple of months ago between us," he says.

I scratch my head and shrug my shoulders.

He sighs. "I thought it was special." An eerie and deliberate calm settles over his face.

Special? I think to myself.

He smiles. "You're not leaving this bathroom until I get what I want."

He moves towards me.

I put my hands up. "HOLY CRAP! WAIT WAIT." The mind races. I blurt out, "Look, I'm not going to apologize while you're threatening me so forget about it. You want an apology, fine, I'll give you one. But it's not going to be sincere and that's no good for anyone, is it?"

He thinks about it for a moment and says, "Okay. Then you and I are going to get together tomorrow, sit down at a bar, have some drinks and talk about this."

"Talk about what?!" Suddenly the conversation's fabric is clear to me and I am consumed with the fear and realization. "Uh...Hey...I hate guys...I love women," I say. "My...girlfriend is outside and she's a tall, blonde, jealous, Nazi type who will beat the devil out of you if you touch me. Maybe you saw her? She was harassing the Jewish kid with glasses."

He is confused.

I back up against the sink. If he comes charging at me I can deliver one swift kick to the groin. It will be enough to stamp out this maniac's burning need for love, appreciation, and extramarital anal sex.

Someone bangs on the door. "WHAT THE HELL IS GOING ON IN THERE?! SOME OF US NEED TO PISS, YOU HOMOS!"

The man is startled, distracted, and seems to shrink. I run around him and unlock the door.

A white-haired, thickly set, old man busts in, shoves his way through us and charges straight to the urinal. "CHRIST I GOTTA PISS!" he screams. He lets out a huge gasp of relief and grumbles, "AHHHH...FUCKING SODOMITES! Sometimes I can't stand this fucking town!"

I slide out of the bathroom and back to the table's safety.

"What the hell was that about?" Seth asks.

"Madness," I reply. "If it wasn't for that white-haired homophobe I'd probably be the victim of a deplorable personal violation." My heart is still pumping wildly. "Where's my drink?"

Seth looks over his shoulder, confused, and slides the vodka across the table to me.

I take the glass. "It's warm. Are you trying to kill me?! You know I need ice!"

He groans, "It's the same drink you've been nursing for half an hour jackass."

I stare at the glass suspiciously. "Well this won't do at all considering what I've just been through."

"What are you talking about?"

"Nevermind. But if you or I have to use the facilities anytime soon I suggest we work with the buddy system. You don't have to go in with me, just guard the door and leave me about my business. I don't trust the people in this place." I flag the waitress down and order a Miller Lite with the bottle cap still on.

The waitress looks at me. "You want the bottle cap on?"

"Yes," I insist. "It's my OCD. It's impossible for me to drink anything in a bottle unless I open it myself."

208

She is puzzled.

"You know," I continue, "germs and Ruphies, Ruphies and germs."

Suddenly she seems to understand and leaves us for the bar.

Seth lights a cigarette. "You're freaking out."

"You'd think so but I know exactly what I'm doing."

A young, blonde girl approaches our table and sits down without saying a word. She is spaced out and most definitely seeing the planet from different angles than the drinkers at the bar. I stare at Seth. Seth stares at me, blows out a drag and shrugs his shoulders. She stares at the ceiling for a very long time before refocusing her attention on the wall across from her.

"Hi," I say.

Seth shakes his head.

She aims her attention at me and speaks with a strong British accent and a drug induced speech impediment, "I'm Janice."

I motion across the table from me. "This is Seth."

Seth is uninterested and rolls his eyes.

"Having a good time?" I ask.

"Oh...yesssss," she replies.

"Before we begin I need to know if you're here with your husband," I say.

She makes a snorting sound and says, "I'm not married, silly." She continues to look upwards, distracted by imaginary somethings floating above her head.

I look up and see nothing. "Here with friends?" I ask.

"No."

"Lost?"

"No." She refocuses her gaze at the table.

"Not from here, are you?"

"No," she says. "I'm from England."

"I've never been," I say.

"Suckssss," she replies. Her eyes slide across the table slowly. "It's so much more fun here."

"That's why I'm here," I say. "Is this your first time in New Orleans?"

She nods weakly.

"First time in the States?"

She nods again and reverses herself. "Um...no...actually, no...I was a foreign exchange student here. Not here, here, but in Oklahoma. Tulsa."

Seth says, "You know Tulsa spelled backwards is 'A-S-L-U-T'?"

I give him a stern look.

"I'm by myssssself." She sighs sadly.

"That's very brave of you," I reply. "Can I get you something to drink?"

She nods and slurs, "WWUUHHTTIIR."

I shrug my shoulders.

"WWUUHHTTIIR."

I hear Seth's voice in my head, *"Are you insane? Can't you see this chick is totally whacked out of her mind? If you keep talking to her she's never going to leave. You buy her drinks and she'll end up following us the rest of the night."*

I glare at him. *"Heartless bastard. Obviously this poor girl is lost and completely deranged from the experience. You have no compassion. At first I thought she might be a hooker but you can clearly see she's a virgin and needs the kindness of strangers."*

He fires back. *"Of course she is. She's too ugly to be a hooker."*

"Get out of my head," I say aloud.

Seth takes a drag from the cigarette. "What?"

The girl taps my arm. "WWHUUHHTTIIRR. W-A-T-E-R. WWHUUHHTTIIR."

"Yeah...Sure thing," I reply.

The waitress comes back with a Miller Lite, bottle cap on. I request the largest water glass they have, order another beer to pacify Seth, and tip her well for her services. The English girl continues to babble on about nothing important. I see this as an opportunity to practice my small talk but Seth sees this as a bothersome and needless diversion. I suspect Seth was late in his development as a child, and perpetually inscribed on every report card from K4 and beyond under "Teacher's Comment (s)" was the phrase *"plays poorly with others."* He continues to display boredom and a quiet animosity towards her, so I drag out the conversation as much as possible in hopes this will irritate him.

Janice continues the slur through her water, "Is this your first time here?"

"No," I say.

"What are you doing here?"

"I'm doing a field study on alcohol induced vomiting and gravity related head trauma. There's a lot material to work with."

"You're an idiot," Seth grumbles.

Janice is dazed and unimpressed. Her eyes light up with an odd

recognition and settle down again. "Fasssscinating," she says. "You some

kind of doctor?"

"No, I design helmets."

Seth stares at her and says nothing.

I whisper, "Don't mind him...he has a thing against foreigners."

She looks confused and possibly offended.

"Oh believe me," I assure her, "it's nothing personal. He's just

suspicious of everyone lately. You know, because of the war."

She slurs, "Awful thing."

"You didn't have any trouble getting into our country did you?" I

ask.

"Of course not silly...I'm white," she says.

"How true," I reply. "Fortunately I was born here, but even *I've*

been randomly searched four times."

"At the airport?"

"God no, on the streets of Chicago," I say. "Don't dare go there.

The bad weather just aggravates the natural suspicion and hostility that

exist in an urban environment. Besides, there's no way you'd get me up in

a plane nowadays. Not unless they allowed everyone to carry guns. I'm not a big NRA fan but if everyone were armed and you knew it, would you commit a crime?"

Her eyes become big and concerned.

"Of course you wouldn't!" I declare. "You'd be too worried about someone shooting you. I'm talking about detante, 'you don't fuck with me and I won't fuck with you.' Makes sense right? It seemed to work during the Cold War didn't it? Now we *wish* the Commies were still our boogey men, right? Sure they were a godless people, but you can't even begin to understand what you've got on your hands with a God obsessed martyr. I mean what with the jeehadis and all. Remember, 'The devil you know is always better than the one you don't.'"

Seth shakes his head and walks to the bar with his beer.

"Don't mind him," I say. "The dull hatred in his expression is strictly ornamental. His sullen animosity is a defensive posture, a sad consequence of cowardice and a religious handicap. He's not a God Fearing Christian like you and me."

She is now stiff with concern.

"Don't let my ethnicity fool you. I'm a firm believer in a Christian God as long as he let's me defend myself against the filthy heathens of this world. The Romans had it right. We've got to go out there and crush the barbarians. Hell, we're an empire too, right?" I motion at Seth. "Oh, he'll get his, you'll see...humorless bastard..." I drink the beer and wink. "Don't get me wrong. I'm all for keeping God's justice within his own divine hands, but sometimes you have no choice...and you're forced to teach these pagans something about his earthly reach!" I slam my fist onto the table top. "'Keep your friends close, but your enemies closer.' I think Sun Tzu said that...or Vito Corleone."

"I'm sorry," Janice says, "What's your name again?"

"Bob Whittaker, but my friends call me Brother Bob."

"I...uh...Nice to meet....have...to go... Bob," she says and picks up her big water glass before scurrying away.

That ought to sober her up. Nothing like small talk with a Neo-Christian fascist to make you think twice about sitting down with strangers at a bar in the French Quarter at two in the morning. Now she can wander the Quarter with the proper anxiety. It will keep her safe and weary of the unknown.

"Are you done making an ass out of yourself?" Seth asks as he comes back to the table.

"I've done my good deed for the night," I reply. "You should consider being more charitable. It'll balance out your bad karma."

"I don't believe in karma."

"I'm not surprised."

"Let's go." He finishes his beer. "Aaron went to that bullet hole bar around the corner."

"More strippers?"

"If it sucks we'll leave," he says.

"Fair enough."

Chapter Six

The bullet hole is dark and lit with black lights, neon, and red and yellow

stage lights. The smell of glittered bodies, booze, cigarette smoke, human

sweat and perfume twists itself into my nostrils. The scent will take time to

leave the body and inevitably days later I will find and wonder where the

specks of glitter stuck to my forehead came from. It lacks the subtle allure

of Jacque's. The talent is low, whorey, and drugged out. The décor: a small

single-stage venue with a glass paneled peep show room with private

booths in the back. At the front stage a young, naked, black girl is

swinging herself around a pole. Rio and Corrine leave us to meet Loni at a

gay club on Bourbon Street. As a policy, women are not allowed inside the

bar unless they strip because the management presumes any woman coming into the bar is a hooker and cannot work the patrons without giving the owners their cut.

A lone waitress works the dance floor and takes drink orders after warning us the bar has a two drink minimum and we can't stay if we're "just looking." I ask her for an Absolut on the rocks double figuring this will satisfy the house rules on minimums.

"What's that?" she asks.

"Vodka."

"We don't have that."

"I'll take a Miller Lite with the bottle cap on."

"We only have cans."

"Okay."

"What else?"

"What else what?"

"Your second drink."

"What do you mean?"

"You have to order your second drink now," she says.

"Okay. Make it two Lites."

"Six dollars."

I give her a ten and keep three.

Seth sits against a wall not far from view of the stage. He is quietly hiding from the women prowling the bar for drinks and a dance. Roberto and Lenny are closer to the stage and tip dollars to the stripper whenever she crawls up to curl and arch her thin body in front of them like a cat stretching itself against the floor. Aaron is at the back bar taking in the peep show.

"Don't make eye contact with them...That's how they get you," Seth says suspiciously. "I've already spent twenty bucks."

"But we just got here," I say.

"I know. Damn gypsies."

When the song ends there is a smattering of applause. The DJ praises the black girl's dancing and asks the crowd to show their appreciation for her efforts. She is on all fours, collecting money from the first row when she gets close enough to Seth. I turn away when the dancer smacks her hand on the stage floor. "THIS ONE WON'T LOOK AT ME!" she yells. She waits for a moment and smacks the stage again.

I look at Seth and laugh.

The DJ's voice booms over the speakers, "Come on fellas, show some love to Lady Bree!"

She smacks her hand again and refuses to move on down the stage.

"What's the matter?! You don't like black girls?!"

Seth is speechless at first and tries to say something before she cuts him off. "Or maybe you don't like girls?!"

He stands up from his chair. "Alright...alright." He breaks open his wallet and thumbs through the bills. He turns to Lenny and Roberto and asks, "Anybody have change for a five?"

"Nope." Lenny laughs.

I shake my head and laugh too hard to say anything.

The stripper smacks her hand on the stage again.

"Shit...alright, alright." He walks up to the stage and gives her a five.

The tip transforms Lady Bree's demeanor. She is instantly sweet and appreciative. "Thank you darling." She smiles and bats her glittered eyelashes.

Seth mumbles something to himself and feeling exploited, sinks back down into the chair and scoots it away from the stage. "See what I mean," he grumbles. "Gypsies."

A white girl with glasses sits next to me. Her name is Aspen and she is wearing a Catholic school girl's plaid skirt and dopey black rimmed glasses. From a distance Aspen could be a mid-twenties blonde. The makeup doesn't hide the weariness Her eyes betray hard experience and tell lies about her real age. She is plain. But under the red-gelled stage lights her rough, fair skinned face is smooth and alive in its feminine angles. In a place like this her slim body will be enough to keep her working. I introduce myself as Lance Mannion and listen to her sell.

"Would you like a lap dance?" she asks.

"No," I say. "I'm not much for the physicalities but thanks for offering."

"Enjoying Mardi Gras?"

"Yes."

"You don't have any beads."

"I'm not a person who should drink with a noose around my neck."

"It's not worth it," she says sadly.

"What?"

"Killing yourself."

"Suicide?" I ask. "No, no, I would never kill myself. Deliberately. I'm just clumsy and the beads could be a problem sooner or later."

"Oh."

A faint track of newer skin runs the length of her wrist, a ghost of a desperate and younger decision.

I ask, "How's business?"

"Slow," she says with a forced smile.

"But it's Mardi Gras."

"It's slow tonight...either that or bad tippers. We pay for our time here."

"What does that mean?" I ask.

"To dance," she says. "We pay for our time on stage and all that comes out of our tips."

"I'm not familiar with the industry."

She stands up and pushes her chair aside. "Well, I'm next. Maybe you'll change your mind." She leaves the bar and disappears through a door next to a set of stairs on the stage.

I sit and drink while Aspen works her routine through a forgettable song. Seth disappears into the back bar in the middle of the performance. The chairs in front of the stage gradually empty. When the song is over the DJ asks for a round of applause and moves quickly to introduce the next girl before too many men at the front stage lose interest. Roberto and

Lenny give Aspen a few dollars. She is picking her clothes off the floor when I offer her one of my two drink minimum beers and a tip.

She smiles. "I don't drink." She gathers the dollars left on the stage and counts out the total in her head. "See what I mean? Slow and cheap."

I give her a twenty. "At the end of the day it's just a job right?"

"Thanks." She takes the money, kisses my cheek and walks off stage. "Happy Mardi Gras!"

Roberto is sitting behind me, takes a deep swallow from his beer and says with a smirk, "I'd wash that cheek if I were you."

"Fuck off. You're one to talk. Where's your nose been?"

I take a seat next to Lenny and we watch the next dance. The song plays and for a moment the girl seems to have lost the beat to start her routine until it becomes impossible to deny the truth that for her, there is no music playing at all.

"This one isn't even moving," Lenny whispers. "What kind of dance is that? That's not sexy. That's just sad. This place is creeping me out."

The dancer is blonde, semi-conscious, flat-chested and very high. Her eyes are almost shut and she is roaming the stage listlessly and with barely enough self-awareness to keep from tumbling off. On some

223

threshold level she is familiar enough with her body and the breaks in the song to fake her way through it all. She turns her back to the audience for most of the performance staying upright by feeling the mirrored wall in front of her and pressing her face against it. When she steps away to turn towards the audience she leaves hand prints and fog from her slow breath against the glass.

I don't notice the loud banging noise coming from the back room because of the sad spectacle in front of me, but eventually it becomes more frequent and too loud to ignore. A familiar voice is yelling from somewhere in the bar, "WELL SPARKY...I'M NOT LEAVING THIS TOWN UNTIL SOMEBODY JERKS ME OFF!"

I look at Lenny. "Uh...What was that?"

We watch Seth escape past the stage. "Uh...Time to leave," he says and is out the door.

Lenny, Roberto and I walk towards the booths in the back and hear Aaron and a woman fighting with each other in the peepshow room.

Lenny draws back a black curtain. Aaron is smacking his bare hands against the cloudy Plexiglass separating himself and a very pissed off stripper. They bark at each other like angry dogs between fences.

"COME ON SPARKY!" he yells and smacks the glass. "SHOW ME THAT ASSHOLE!"

"YOU SICK FUCK!" she screams and hits the glass with a shoe until the plastic heel breaks off. "I'M GOING TO GET THE BARTENDER TO BREAK YOUR FUCKING NECK!"

Lenny looks at me. "Hey man, uh...Let's get the fuck out of here."

I am dizzy and drunk and mesmerized at the unfolding carnage of this potential situation to say anything but "Uh, sure" to Lenny.

We grab Aaron by the shoulders and pry him off the glass while he continues to throw tokens at her. The coins ricochet off the window and fly into the bar like stray bullets.

A naked and fat boobed woman bursts out from a side door and is running to throw her lone shoe at us. She yells at the bartender before being held back by the other girls, "CAN'T YOU KEEP THE FREAKS OUT OF HERE! WHAT THE FUCK DO THEY PAY YOU FOR?!"

The DJ cuts the music.

The bartender turns to Aaron. "Hey! Is there a problem? If there is, we can see that the police take care of it." He walks out from behind the bar.

Aaron laughs and says, "Relax jizz mopper."

The bartender's puffed out chest belies the fact his self esteem appears genuinely hurt. He stops behind the bar for a moment to look at the stripper with sad and tired eyes. His shoulders slump from the weight of the abrupt silence. There is a tragic familiarity between him and Sparky. It is the shared truth they are trapped in this bar and he has grown sick of fighting every jackass tourist who harasses her while she dances for tokens in a plastic box.

Sparky insists, "DO SOMETHING JOHN!"

Aaron declares, "Sorry for the trouble. We're leaving." He digs into his pocket and throws a few dollars on the floor. "Go buy a new mop."

He roars and laughs as Lenny and I hustle him through the bar.

"IT'S THE BEST JOB YOU'LL EVER HAVE!"

Sparky continues to scream at the bartender.

Lenny barks, "You crazy fucker! What the hell was that about?"

"HA!...Nothing." Aaron is wild eyed and trying to put me into a headlock. "Did you see her face? Why the fuck would I want to see her asshole? I was just teasing. I didn't really want that. That's just wrong."

Aaron and his need to see an animated orifice is destined to get us into bad trouble as it has before. It is a good idea to take a break and collect our thoughts. Aaron wants to go to Harrah's to win some money for the bill at Jacque's. The others think this to be a grand idea and walk towards Canal.

"You're not coming?" Aaron asks me.

"I'm really not up for it. It's late and I think I need something to eat before I head back to the hotel."

We walk a block and a half together and part company at a corner pizza stand. The others order food and leave. I stay and have one pepperoni and one sausage slice before ordering two more slices and a coconut-flavored Hurricane. Half a block later I'm sick and make my way to a bar across the street to find something to ease the pains.

"Slivovitz," I say to the lady behind the counter.

"What?"

"Slivovitz," I say again.

"I don't think we have that," she says. "What is it? Is it a vodka?"

"WHAT?!" I cry. "NO."

"We got three-for-one beers."

"No, no. I need something stronger than that."

"What is it?"

"What?"

"Slivovitz," she asks.

"Plum Brandy. It's good for digestion as long as you don't mind taking a few years off your life."

She is unmoved by my plight. "Uh...honey I'm busy and we don't have any, so does that mean you want a beer?"

"No. That would just make me angry and pee more. Absolut on the rocks."

She shakes her head with watchful eyes.

"That's vodka," I huff.

She goes to the bar's far end to get a new bottle of Absolut. A Zydeco band is on stage whipping the crowd into foot-stomping and girl twirling frenzies. The band looks too young to be interested or skilled in playing this type of music in a bar with sawdust on the floor, but their speed metal version of "Jambalaya" catches fire and seems a perfectly crazed noise for this strange hour in the Quarter.

The bartender hands the drink to me. "Four dollars."

"That band is great." I swallow the vodka and pay her a five. "Is the lead singer blind?"

"No," she says, "just...eccentric."

The frontman's eyes are opaque. He is young, black and swinging a long braid of hair from front to back like a thick whip at the crowd. His accordion is screaming high notes like it's on fire and he has no problem moving around the stage without eyes. I get closer to the stage. A black girl standing next to me asks for a cigarette.

"I don't smoke."

"Too bad," she says as she sways and gazes at the lead singer. "For a vampire that boy plays a hell of an accordion."

I nod my head and I sip my drink. "Uh-huh...Wha--?"

She laughs me off and dances closer to the stage before asking someone else for a cigarette.

I walk back to the bar and order a few more vodkas until my stomach feels better. The night bleeds into my eyesight until I can barely see beyond the cracks of my eyelids. My head feels heavy with sleep and booze. It is time to go back to the hotel.

I make my way back to The W with very little trouble. A left here, a right there, two more lefts, some familiar if not blurry lights and landmarks and soon the dimly lit red "W" hanging above Chartres is pointing at the lobby entrance.

I am ferociously drunk and leaning on the walls of the elevator as it carries me up. My head has become a ball of lead. It is a slow search for my room through carpeted hallways, hands grasping and feeling the wallpaper like brail. There is probably enough light to follow the signs but my eyelids are barely open. Right from the elevator, left at the hallway, a quick right, and three doors down from the corner.

The keycard is lost somewhere in my back pocket and once I am able to separate it from a few balled up dollar bills and ATM receipts, I swipe it through the lock. The key doesn't work and I am anxious knowing full well it is never an easy task to convince someone at a hotel to let you in to your own room when you look and smell derelict. The red light blinks on the door lock while I carefully reconsider the procedure.

"Swipe goddamn you."

The red eye blinks in the dark.

"Swipe."

It blinks again, this time with more indifference.

I pull the card out and look at it to make sure I am using the right end and gently run it through the lock.

"SWIPE GODDAMNIT!"

The red light blinks.

I pull the key out, shove it back quickly, and push against the door with my right shoulder. "SWIPE!"

The lock stops blinking and there is no light, red or green. I grab the door handle and pull at it. A sudden shiver runs over my skin for a few seconds and my stomach heaves half a big spit. The door is awash with tacos, vodka, and pizza.

"Good Lord." I am dazed. Stunned. Staring at the lock. "I don't remember eating carrots." I brush the key card clean and give the lock one more try. I notice the number on the key is different than the number on the door.

"Holy shit. I'm on the wrong floor."

Panic. A clumsy escape for the elevator is my immediate solution. It occurs to me the civil thing to do would be to place an anonymous call to the front desk and report the need for a bucket, mop, and pine scented Lysol on the fourth floor. I realize they will know what room I am calling from. In considering the bad things I should be apologetic and claim responsibility for in this town, why should *that* be it? I suppose The W's luxurious nature lends itself to politeness whenever something base and common happens. But I'm not about to reveal my identity to the staff as one of "those" people. Better to hide and lurk in the shadows as a common drunk than open myself to criticism for being a despicable reprobate who lacks the intelligence to know where he is or the decency to bus his own puke.

I have only minor trouble with my own hotel room door when the lock opens. In a rush to hide into the safety of a bed I hit my face on the metal doorframe. Somehow I end up in bed. In my dizzy brain I have a slight recollection of being sprawled out on the floor, halfway in the room and halfway out in the hallway, laid bare, helpless, bruised, and painted in puke before finding the will to crawl into the room. No matter. For the most part I am safe for the night and relieved to finally rest my throbbing face on a cool pillow.

SATURDAY

<u>Chapter One</u>

There is a crossroads in Clarksdale, Mississippi 400 miles north of New Orleans. In the 1930's a young bluesman longing for fame and fortune had heard:

"If you want to learn how to make songs yourself, you take your guitar and you go to where the road crosses that way...where a crossroads is. Be sure to get there just a little 'fore twelve that night so you know you'll be there. Have your guitar and be playing a piece there by yourself. A black man will walk up there and take your guitar and he'll tune it...and

then he'll play a piece and hand it back to you...then you'll learn to play anything you want."

The young man, whose wife and unborn child's deaths were a catalyst for a hate towards God, searched within and then beyond himself to gain control of his life. Grief-stricken, he made a decision to call on the devil, and on a quiet windswept junction where highways 61 and 49 meet, he walked with his guitar and spoke an old incantation. The local folklore has it the devil manifested himself as a black man and tuned the guitar in exchange for the young man's soul. From then on his songs were filled with soulful lamentations and he played the guitar with an unearthly style never heard before. His musical career was short. In 1936 he recorded seventeen songs and shortly thereafter, rumor has it, the devil collected his due. At 27 the young man died after drinking a whiskey bottle some say was laced with strychnine. His name was Robert Johnson and his "devil" was a trickster deity who lurks at crossroads and entrances named Legba.

When I wake, Seth and Lenny are pacing the room. Seth is drinking a Hurricane and Lenny is pulling the cover off the bed across from me. They are talking but I can't make out what they are saying. I stare at them for a moment and hear nothing. For a moment I believe it has finally happened: *I've drank myself deaf.*

I sit up.

Lenny laughs and points to his ear. I put a hand to my head and feel a pillow of dried shaving cream in my ear.

"That's not funny...what if it doesn't come out?" I go to the bathroom, wash the shaving cream out and crawl back into bed. "I had the weirdest dream," I mumble. "I dreamt an old black man taught me how to play blues guitar. He looked like John Lee Hooker."

Seth sips on the Hurricane and yawns, "Maybe it was Legba."

"That's not funny."

"What are you talking about?" Seth says.

"Legba..." I reply.

"What's a Legba?" he asks.

"Wait...you said Legba."

"I didn't say anything," he mumbles. "What were we talking about?"

"Get out of my head."

"What the hell are you talking about?" he growls. "Jesus...go back to sleep."

"Like hell I will." I roll off the bed and plant my feet firmly on the carpet. "You try sleeping after the devil pops into your head to teach you how to play musical instruments."

"You've lost your mind," Seth says.

"Screw off."

Lenny groans, "Go back to sleep, you're still drunk."

"What time is it?" I ask.

"Almost 10."

"You guys are just getting in now?"

"No," Lenny yawns. "Aaron is still at Harrah's."

"Where's Roberto?"

Lenny laughs. "Upstairs in the other room," he says.

"What's so funny?"

"Somebody threw up on their door," he says and covers his head with a pillow.

"Savages," I say. "There's just no hope for this world. Nothing but bad mannered tourists in this godforsaken town. That behavior shouldn't be tolerated in a four star environment." I put my jeans on.

Lenny peers out of the cave he has created with his pillows. "Where are you going?"

"I can't sleep. I'm going to get something to eat."

Bad drinking leaves you vulnerable to nightmarish things: hangovers, crippling dehydration, relentless headaches, horrible breath, and sore dispositions. Somewhere among the inventory are bad dreams and death. The empty Absolut bottle sits on the dresser as I tie my shoes. I'll have to stop drinking so much some day, I think to myself, but today, is not the day.

I wander to Canal Street searching for the cure for a crushing headache and avoid the remnants of the morning ballet playing out yet again on Bourbon with their hoses and brooms. McDonald's is still serving breakfast and I slip in for some relief.

The evangelicals are half a block away and standing on Canal underneath the electric streetcar lines. They have just finished breakfast and are discussing their plan of attack for the day. It's an opportune time for them to be struck down by a street car or an errant power line. I can do without their tub-thumping this early in the morning. Brother Bob Whittaker is among them in his loud Old Testament glory. He is preaching to the air: "REPENT! REPENT!" and brandishing a picket sign above his head with a large photograph of the World Trade Towers smoldering in flame. His message below reads:

WHERE WAS YOUR GOD ON THIS DAY?

I feel a sudden rage to pull bricks from the side of the building and bludgeon him to death. All this place needs is that kind of distasteful rhetoric for a religious war to break out during Mardi Gras. It would really bring God's wrath down onto this town. New Orleans floods because it's below sea level and if this jackass isn't careful in using the Good Lord's name in such a vile way, a grand old biblical flood is liable to wipe the place clean of their ilk as well as all the "sinners". Maybe I can muster up a religious coalition of the willing: the Krishnas, Scientologists, Promise Keepers, and every other religious faction in the city to dispose of Bob Whittaker in order to appease God and preserve the spirited chaos we boozers abide by in this place.

I don't know where God was on that day.

It was Tuesday morning. I was in downtown Chicago and I was late for work. The lobby was empty and when I snuck past the front desk to disappear into my office a clerk popped his head out of a room behind me and said matter of factly, "Did you see what happened to the World Trade Center?"

"No," I replied.

"A plane accidentally crashed into it," he said.

"No shit?" I said and followed him into an office where everyone was watching the television. The towers were still standing when a rumor came over the news of a plane crashing into the Pentagon. I watched the second plane hit the Trade Center. My blood went cold and drained out. I felt empty. Smoke and dust belched up high into the Manhattan sky and made no noise. It was an odd thing. So much smoke and dust spreading itself into the clear blue air and no noise. Something that big falling down should make a sound, I thought, but it didn't. Then I realized I was watching it on television. It reminded me of mushrooms on my parents' front yard in Florida when I was growing up. They were grayish green and would fill up with spores until their heads swelled like paper balloons. In the mornings you might catch one blow itself up and a plume of spores would rise silently in the air to spread mushrooms into the world. They would pollute the yard and choke the grass. When another plane crashed in Pennsylvania everyone in the office left in a controlled and somber panic.

Chicago's Loop emptied quickly out of fear that an unaccounted plane could easily slam into the Sears Tower and bring this mysterious violence to our city. I stayed at the office after realizing the only way to find my sister in Manhattan was to email her and stay by my computer until she told me she was alright. There were no open phone lines into New York so I called my mother in Kentucky for any word on my sister.

There was panic and grief in her voice. "I-I can't get through to her office," she said.

"I can't either," I said. "I'm sure it's just the network. There are probably too many calls going in and out."

"I-I don't know where her office is," she said.

"It's in Manhattan," I said, "but I don't know where."

"Is it close to the World Trade Center?" she asked.

"I don't know."

There was a horrible silence on the phone.

"Mom---"

"I don't know what to do..." she cried.

"We'll find her."

An hour later my sister emailed saying she was with friends and that's all she could say. Our cousin at NYU was safe and my friends in New York emailed the same.

I left the office and went to St. Peter's Church off the corner of Clark and Madison. It was an unsettling walk. The Loop with all its routine and anonymous noise, its random car horns, street corner conversations, and trains, was still, abandoned, empty and quiet. The Church was full of people but quiet. With everything that occurred within the few short hours that morning, when it seemed like the end of the world we knew was at hand, some of us found ourselves in Church, not praying for ourselves but for other people; for strangers living and dying hundreds of miles away. Those few moments in a quiet church full of people made that day tolerable.

Churches are places of serenity. The buildings are very still and sometimes cold. When I am in them, I rarely listen to the rituals going on. I usually tune out the sermons and ceremony and participate because of experience and repetition. If you pass through a church with a troubled heart you will eventually realize the sound of your footsteps echoing against high ceilings and marble floors is significant because you are walking towards something beyond yourself in search of solace. I think if I hear my footsteps walking across marble floors in vast hallways when I am dead, I will know I am in heaven even before I open my eyes. The sound will resonate with me and I will know I have passed on and am walking within a house of God towards truth and beyond the religious dogma.

But if I hear Bob Whittaker chanting "REPENT! REPENT!" before I open my eyes, I will know for certain I am in hell.

Chapter Two

"I would like a jazz funeral," I say to Rio as she sits across from me sipping her vodka tonic. We are sitting outside in The W courtyard in lounge chairs and underneath umbrellas sipping icy concoctions and trying to piece together what transpired amongst us during the previous night's good timing. It's a little after noon and Corrine and Aaron sit with us.

"You shouldn't talk about things like that," Rio lectures.

"Why not?" I ask.

"It's morose."

"Talking about wanting a jazz funeral is morose?"

"Yes," she says and shakes apart the ice cubes in her drink.

"Aren't you sick of thinking about death?"

I pour myself a few swallows from the Absolut. A light humidity in the air makes frost on the glasses. "I guess we won't be going on any cemetery tours."

Aaron is drinking endless amounts of water and hasn't slept in over 24 hours which has dulled his enthusiasm for New Orleans to a respectable level for now. "I thought you wanted a Viking funeral pyre."

"I've changed my mind. I'm not Nordic and I don't think I would find rest in Valhalla." I take a deep sip. "No...I think a jazz funeral would be a lot more appropriate. That would be fun. Lots of music and dancing--"

"And drinking," Corrine interjects.

"How much would all that cost?" Aaron asks.

"I have no clue but you have to make sure whoever is in charge of the arrangements plays 'Many Rivers to Cross' for me."

"How about 'Crossroad Blues' ?" he suggests.

"Yeah...very funny," I say. "Wait until Legba visits you."

"Enough with all the dying," Rio says. "It's too nice a day to think about those things."

"Easy for you to say," Aaron groans, "you're not hungover. Why is that?" He asks as he takes a small aspirin bottle from the table and shakes out two pills.

"Because I don't stop drinking," she says.

"Where is Seth?" Corrine asks.

"He's still asleep," I reply.

"Wake his ass up," Rio orders. "I didn't come down all this way just to watch *you* drink."

"What did *I* do?" I say.

"Nothing." She snorts and giggles. "Yup...I'm still drunk. Rio is feeling fun-key."

Roberto walks into the courtyard. He is a mess and suffering noticebly from last night.

Rio laughs. "You look like crap."

He sits down, grabs a beer from our ice-filled garbage can, puts it on his neck and sinks into a chair. "I woke up in the swimming pool."

Corrine laughs, "You what?"

"I woke up in the pool," he groans.

"How the hell does something like that happen?" Aaron asks.

"Long story..."

He stuck around with Aaron at Harrah's until he blew $150 in thirty minutes playing blackjack and left to wander the Quarter for cheaper thrills. Somewhere in between the casino and The W he ran into some women staying at The W who were lost and insisted in calling him "Charlie".

"Why?" Aaron asks.

"Because they thought I was some guy they met earlier named 'Charlie'," he says.

He escorted them back to The W and worked his drunken charms on them until one woman proposed they meet at the pool for a late night swim.

"Ever heard of a succubus?" I say to Aaron as I pour Rio another vodka tonic. "There are swarms around here. They visit you in your sleep. Maybe you were passed out in the pool already."

Roberto looks confused. "A suck-your-what?"

I pass the drink onto Rio.

"Never mind," she says. "Is this going to be another 'And she gave me the money back' stories?"

"You want me to finish the story?"

Aaron says, "Let him finish the story."

"Anyway...so I was so drunk. But I went to the pool---"

"Were you naked?!" Rio asks

"NO. Would you let me finish."

245

Rio is stares into the sky, bored, but too drunk to resist this topic.

"Go on."

"I had shorts on and I went to the pool and waited for ten minutes. Then I went back up to their room and knocked on the door. The chick opens the door and she's like buck naked," he says enthusiastically.

"Was she hot?" Aaron asks.

"Yeah, she had a big ole' set of ---" Roberto stops and whispers, "...titties."

"Big ole what?" Rio demands with a raised voice. A couple sitting by the pool glares at our table. Rio notices this and lifts her glass to them. "TITTIES! TITTIES! TITTIES! YEAH I SAID IT!" She laughs and mumbles to herself, "Like no one is saying that word fifty million times in this town."

"Anyway," Roberto continues, "So this chick tells me she'll be down in ten minutes after she puts on her bikini." He seems lost in thought for a moment and stares out at the wall beyond our table.

"And then?" Rio asks.

"Oh," he continues, "so I go down to the pool and sit on the steps in the water. Next thing I know...it's daylight, I'm staring at the sky...and

I'm freezing my balls off wondering why I'm so cold?" Roberto leans back
and pops open the beer he's been cooling his neck with.

We sit patiently for a moment while he drinks his beer.

"And?" Rio asks.

"Nothing. I went upstairs and went to sleep," he says.

"Good story," Aaron says and grabs a beer.

"You had to be there," Roberto declares.

Aaron laughs. "I like his version with the succubus better."

"Now what is a suck-your-bus?" Roberto asks.

"Never mind," I say.

Rio declares, "Let's go somewhere."

"Where?" I ask.

"Let's just walk," she insists.

"How about some lunch?"

"Alright."

We leave Seth and Lenny asleep at the hotel and on my suggestion
dine at The Court of Two Sisters. It is well suited for surrendering a
hangover and easing into the day. The courtyard is canopied by tangled
tree branches. The trees spread into one another and hide little birds in their
wooded lace who chirp and sneak down to the tables before an orange cat

named Oscar spooks a few away. The civility of white table cloth and the

black tie and vested staff keeps the rowdiness of Bourbon Street at bay

long enough for us to quiet the mind and appreciate a good Southern meal.

A three man jazz ensemble is playing old standards and taking a few

requests next to the fountain while waiters and busboys outmaneuver

wandering patrons and the black iron trellises laced with purple, green, and

yellow. There are several stations: egg; carving; and seafood, and in

keeping with the idea that in New Orleans every meal is a feast, we start

out with the breakfast foods: eggs benedict, cornbread, biscuits and gravy.

Then we dive into more lunch fare: Jambalaya, sweet potatoes, Andouille

sausage, roast beef, fried okra, and pork ribs, finishing off with a bowl of

vanilla ice cream and praline sauce. It all goes down with a round of

bloody marys and a sweet rum inspired concoction Rio buys for the table.

The French Quarter sidewalk is an aimless stroll, narrowed and

lined with poles descending from the balconies above. On Royal Street, the

elegant curios are a contrast to the gaudy stores on Bourbon Street stocked

with t-shirts, hats, beads, and cheap souvenir clutter. The walk takes us

past art galleries, jewelry shops, and a curator of ancient weaponry that

captures Rio's unfettered interest in medieval violence. There is an instant

and primal recognition between her and a broad sword locked safely behind the shop owner's display case. She asks to see it, and the feel and weight of it are natural in her hands, maybe because of a familiar history in a past life. If it wasn't for her compulsion to thrust and swing it in such a small space, the shop keeper might have indulged her enthusiastic reunion with it for much longer.

At a Voodoo shop on Decatur, Rio is disheartened to learn how Voodoo is a benevolent faith. The shop has a variety of religiously significant tools for dabblers who have questions about the everyday use of oils and candles. An altar in the corner is burning incense next to a plate of oranges, a glass of rum and a cigar. I speak with the middle-aged woman caretaker of the altar. I've been blinded by lies, I am told.

"The devil belongs to the Christians," the woman behind the counter says.

"And Legba?" I ask.

"Legba is a Loa, a spirit; Christians call them saints. He is mischievous but not evil. *That* is a Christian concept."

"I think he may have visited me in my dream last night."

"Hmph..." She laughs. "And how drunk were you last night?"

"Who says I was drunk?"

"I can smell you."

"Huh...well, I don't remember," I say.

"But enough to see the devil you think?"

"Sure...why not?" I reply.

"You might consider your dream a good thing," she says. "Maybe you're being warned."

I ask, "From what?"

"That's for you to figure out," she says.

"Thanks," I reply. "What do I owe you?"

"Nothing," she says. "I'm not a priestess. I'm just a sales clerk."

I can stay and ask for a ritual, maybe something simple to keep "the devil" away. But why bother when it seems I can easily avoid spiritual hazards by not drinking until I hallucinate.

"In the end it's probably your personal demons that do you in rather than a man with horns and a guitar," I preach to Corrine as I follow her around a souvenir store near Jackson Square. I am carrying an imbecile sized beer in one hand as she gift shops for her mom.

"I've seen some weird stuff after too much alcohol." She squints and walks towards a far corner. "What do you think?" she says as she points to a gray sweatshirt hanging on the wall.

"It looks like all the other ones from all the other stores," I say.

"I'll wait until we get to the French Market," she says.

We head to Jackson Square to meet the others. At night the Square is closed and for some odd reason becomes the impromptu domicile for stray cats who hunt the rats and cockroaches. During the daylight the black gates and fence guarding Andrew Jackson's statue are spontaneously transformed into museum walls by artists hanging paintings and other work on the old iron bars. At the moment, it's overpopulated with slow strolling tourists, musicians, artists, fortunetellers, Venetian mimes and homeless. Some guy dressed as a clown is wobbly drunk with a bunch of other clowns and peeing in a cup right in front of the Cathedral. A white blur of something odd is slowly forming within the landscape before us. It is barely noticeable as Corrine and I squeeze our way through the crowd.

Corrine asks, "What's that smell?"

"Probably that pack of filthy clowns," I reply looking ahead of us. "We're down wind from the circus."

"Let's walk on this side," she insists and takes my arm.

I ask, "Where do you think we should go tonight?"

"Let's all have dinner together some place before we hit Bourbon," she replies.

"Hmm...Acme?"

"What's that?" she asks.

"Seafood. It's not far from the hotel."

"Is it all fried? I don't know if I could eat anymore fried food," she

says.

I stop and squint into the distance. Corrine keeps walking.

"I---uh...I don't...where else would you like to go?"

"What about the Italian restaurant at the hotel?" she says as she

fades into the crowd.

I walk to catch up with her. "The uh...the what?"

"The restaurant at The W," she says. I lose her in the crowd. "It

looks expensive. Maybe we should try looking for someplace-----."

Her voice evaporates.

I look for her behind me and make headway backwards into the

crowd before stopping in horror.

I gasp. "Good Lord."

The white blur has taken shape and an angel is standing silently on

the street half a block away from me, brilliantly white and wispy. She is

floating above the crowd in a long gown, her wings arched high behind the

shoulders and hands placed against her chest as if she is praying. She is

staring directly at me.

This is it. This is the end. Today I merge with The Infinite. God has finally come to judge me, and I am standing before this herald of the Lord at Mardi Gras cowering in fear with an imbecile sized beer and a heart feverishly pumping something through my body that at this point in the day is still mostly blood. This angel will no doubt report back to my maker with nothing but bad news and I will spend an eternity trying to explain myself and why I squandered my last days in the company of drinkers, addicts, prostitutes, hate mongers and heretics:

"But they're my friends," I would reply. "...Not so much the hate mongers and prostitutes, but the rest have some good qualities in spite of themselves."

And the Good Lord will smite me in the midst of all this revelry for making light of my final judgment. No. Best to be apologetic and beg for mercy for indulging your human weaknesses with a clean glass and some ice. Best to confess and admit I was down a bad path and would eventually turn back towards sanity and responsible behavior once the truth hit me, or until my money ran out.

"One more chance to fall in favor of your good graces Lord and I promise I will leave Seth's well-deserved punishment to your providence.

One more chance and I will never set foot in a strip club again without good cause or in good faith."

"And the booze?" the Lord would ask.

"Come again?" I would say meekly.

"The drinking, man, the drinking."

"It's not bad, really," I would say. "I was always under the assumption alcohol was proof you loved me."

"Just for that I should send you back as an oyster!"

"MERCY!" I would beg, "YOU CAN'T SEND ME BACK JUST TO HAVE MY SHELL SHUCKED AND MY GUTS SPREAD OUT ON A RITZ CRACKER AND BE EATEN BY A HEATHEN LIKE SETH! FORGIVE ME!"

"No, you must be cleansed before entering the gates of Heaven."

And with that the re-incarnation would begin.

Corrine grabs my arm. "What are you doing?"

I tug on her shoulder. "Are you seeing this?" I whimper.

She turns around. "Seeing what?"

"That." I point at the angel.

"I see it."

"YOU DO?!"

Corrine walks towards the angel.

"Don't!" I plead.

The angel stands perfectly still. Corrine waves her hand in front of the white face. She kneels down to lift the gown from the street. The angel is standing on a bucket. "Look," Corrine says, "she's wearing Reeboks".

I sigh and toss the warm beer into a garbage can a few feet away. "I think I'm getting sick."

"They're all over the place," she says.

Yes, they are all over the place.

Off in the distance a man with a thick shock of white hair is dressed like a revivalist preacher. A large sign behind him reads: "JESUS CHRIST IS ANGRY WITH THE WICKED EVERYDAY." He is channeling Jonathan Edwards and selling the Old Testament wrath to a curious but transient congregation:

"It is no security to wicked men for one moment that there are no visible means of death at hand! It is no security to a natural man, that he is now in health, and that he does not see which way he should now immediately go out of the world by any accident, and that there is no visible danger in any respect in his circumstance! The manifold and continual experience of the world in all ages, shows this is no evidence, that a man is not on the brink of eternity, and that the next step will not be into another world!"

"What's he saying?" she asks.

"We're all going to hell but we just don't know it," I say.

"Almost every natural man that hears of hell, flatters himself that he shall escape it; he depends upon himself for his own security; he flatters himself in what he has done, in what he is doing now, or what he intends to do! Everyone lays out matters in his own mind how he shall avoid damnation, and flatters himself that he contrives well for himself, and that his schemes will not fail!"

"These wackos are everywhere," she says as she pulls my arm. The Square is art and death masquerading on painted faces and grotesque bodies. A man in a black hooded robe flies by me almost clipping the alcohol halo spinning above my head. "Watch it asshole!" he growls. Apparently The Reaper wields his sickle on roller blades and wears wrap-around Gargoyle sunglasses to keep the Southern sun from baking his cool stares. I am not entirely convinced we aren't both already dead and facing

certain judgment. "Damn performance artists," I groan. "They've overrun

the place." We've accidentally wandered into performance artist hell where

talent, taste, and theatrical harmony are irrelevant and waiting for your

spare change.

I put two dollars into the angel's can.

The angel bends forward, bows at me and returns to her original

stone-faced and pious stance.

"I think these mimes have had enough fun twisting my mind. Let's

move on before we run into something you can't explain to me."

Corrine asks, "Are you okay?"

"Eh. I think I need a second to get my bearings."

She asks, "How about a drink?"

"Sure. Why not?"

Corrine buys two beers for four bucks from a guy selling water

bottles out of a rolling cooler. We find a spot inside the gated square

underneath some trees and sit down on the lawn not too far from Andrew

Jackson and his horse. I crack open both cans and hand one to her and raise

my drink. "Many happy returns."

"Cheers," she replies. "I would return," she says. "I like this place. Might be a great place to live." She lights a cigarette.

"It's not always like this but it has its charms. I kind of like it better when it's not like this."

"Right. You come down here a lot."

I ask, "Can I bum one?"

"You don't smoke," she says and takes out her pack.

"I used to."

"Oh right..." Corrine smiles. "With what's her name?"

"Who?"

"The girl in the picture from the restaurant. You knew her. You're holding a cigarette in the picture."

"I was?"

"Yeah. She wasn't just some random chick."

"What makes you think that?'

"The expression on your face. You recognized her. Ex-girlfriend? A woman can tell."

"Ex-nothing. Can I have that cigarette now?"

Corrine shakes the box. "I'm out. You can share mine." She passes the cigarette to me then pulls away. "Sorry, it has lipstick." She wipes the filter with a finger. "So who is she?"

I grab the cigarette and take a drag. "Just a girl I got mixed up with. We had fun. It ended. That's why they call them 'flings'".

She asks, "From here?"

I pass the cigarette to her. "Not originally. No. But we met here."

"Is that why you've been here so many times?"

"No. I just like it here. To visit. She was just one more reason."

Corrine takes a drag. "You should move down here you like it so much."

"Uh-huh." I look around the square at the fortunetellers, street performers, artists, mimes and magicians. The mules are sleepy. The sun's heat and the cool feel of grass underneath my palms occurs to me along with the cigarette smoke and the girl. I'm experiencing what Walker Percy's Binx Bolling called a "repetition". Finding yourself in a reenactment of a passed moment and trying to isolate, savor and relive the experience with hindsight. It is there for a second but dissolves.

"What happened? Is she still here?"

"I don't know. We agreed to let it go."

"That's too bad. You both looked happy in that picture."

"This place will do it to you." I take the cigarette from her hand. "What would you do if you moved here?"

"I don't know. I love the vibe. Maybe I'd paint or something."

"You paint?"

"I was a fine arts major before I dropped out."

"Really."

She shoves my arm. "Yeah 'really'. Don't you remember we had this discussion when we first met?"

"Vaguely? Were we drinking?"

"Uh, yeah. We were bombed. I got locked out in the stairwell and you found me but got us both locked out. We sat around waiting for help to arrive."

"Oh right," I say.

"Right."

"No, I remember…vaguely," I reply. "Why'd you drop out?"

"Too much partying."

"That'll do it." I hand her the cigarette and she takes a drag and puts it out in the dirt. "Yeah. You should come down here and paint." I take a nice long sip of the cold beer and with the nicotine boost feel well on my way to an afternoon of boozing. "Not too much partying around here to distract you."

"Right." Corrine shields her eyes from the sun and laughs.

"What?"

"Come here," she puts a soft thumb to my face and rubs my bottom lip. "You've got my lipstick on your mouth."

Chapter Three

The French Market has been around since 1812. The bazaar is ripe with all types of things most people don't need: folk art, black market compact discs, jewelry, toys, souvenir clothing, hot sauce, locally grown fruit, sunglasses, knock-off luggage and hats. There are new and old immigrant groups engaged in commerce here. The air is buttery thick with kettle corn and the mossy scent of patchouli oil, and different types of music clash in the market's narrow aisles among competing vendors.

Rio eyes a table two booths down. "That's what you need," she says.

A middle-aged white woman behind the display speaks with a heavy Eastern European accent. She has furnishings for old school vices:

pipes, cigar cutters, lighters, cigarette holders, cigarette cases, flasks, and poison rings.

I pick up a dull silver flask with three monkeys on it sitting side by side.

Roberto says, "You should carry that around to warn everyone you're a world class drunk."

I ignore him.

"Which monkey are you?" Rio asks. "See no evil, speak no evil, or hear no evil?"

"Do No Evil," I reply.

Rio laughs. "Fat chance."

"Fourteen dollars," the women grunts without so much as a glance towards our direction.

"I don't like her attitude," Rio huffs.

"Don't start," I mutter.

The woman turns back towards us. "You buy."

I make an offer. "How about nine?"

She shakes her head. "Fourteen."

"Ten."

"Twelve," she says without flinching.

"Fine."

I hand her the money and she slides the flask into a cardboard box and into a small red grocery bag.

Corrine picks up a ring. "How much is this?"

"Twelve," the woman says.

"That's a poison ring," I say.

Roberto asks, "What's it for?"

Rio grunts, "For poison, stupid." Her lips and tongue are a bloody red, a consequence of a sixty-four ounce Hurricane in a Styrofoam cup she is sucking the life out of. I am certain she will speak Spanish soon. She sometimes does this prior to a complete linguistic and communication breakdown. She will slur and refer to herself in the third person, speak Spanish-English while slurring and finally ease into more Spanish and refer to herself in the third person, in Spanish. "Idioto," she mumbles and ambles towards an opening in the crowd and the tables outside the market.

"Someone should follow her to make sure she doesn't cause any trouble," I say. "The Spanish aren't welcome around here. Some of these descended French could still harbor deep resentment to a Latin tongue."

"I'll go," Aaron says. "The patchouli is really giving me a headache." He cuts through the crowd and follows Rio from a safe distance.

Corrine buys the ring and manages to talk the vendor down to seven dollars on account they are both Polish. I find a table with French Quarter scenes painted on old slate roof tiles and pass on a purchase because they are weighty and will probably break since I am clumsy with booze.

Aaron, Roberto and Rio are near a booth selling trashy women's clothes. It's the perfect attire for the debauched population of young girls visiting this place. She entrusts her Hurricane to me while she walks around the other booths.

I take a deep sip. It is slushy, cold, and too sweet for my nerves. I am in a wretched brain freeze and put the cup on a stand next to the entrance of one vendor's stall. The Hurricane falls off the stand and onto the ground and splits from its Styrofoam bottom. Bright red goop oozes onto the vendor's carpet.

"You know what the problem here is," I say, "the bottom fell out."

Rio walks back towards us. Her tongue is wagging red and she squints from the bright daylight. "Where's my drink?"

I point to the red mush next to my shoe. "I'll have to buy you another one. The bottom fell out."

"Pinche pendejo." She gives me an angry look and walks past more tables eventually leaving the market with Corrine and Roberto in tow.

We round the corner near Jimmy Buffet's Margaritaville and see Rio drag Corrine and Roberto into the bar with a fierce and thirsty look in her eyes.

"I've seen her fight men," Aaron says.

"I'm not worth her punch," I reply.

"You think that matters to her? She's just looking for a reason."

"Duly noted," I reply. "I guess the first round is on me."

Buffet's serves its signature drink with a small plastic compass floating in it which always amuses me until you realize it's a sign to watch where you're going with the tequila. It's usually south and not necessarily tropical. In any case they make a decent drink and the compass is always something to carry with you to find your way north from New Orleans. We have a few, and the drinking continues at a fine pace. I decide to take in an early afternoon cordial of the usual. The vodka has cut nicely through the Hurricane and beers and my head feels light and cheerful. Seth and Lenny have made it past the three o'clock hour with enough rest and meet us at a bar near Decatur and St. Louis. The bar has machines stirring different colored Hurricanes so I stop and order one as further apology for Rio's lost drink and a round of beer for the rest of us. The bartender is a dimwitted white kid who can't figure out how to break a twenty to make change for a sixteen-dollar tab. Corrine takes pity on him and tells him to keep the change although Rio feels it necessary to give the boy long, condescending stares as he presses buttons on the register to no avail. After a few minutes of awkward silence Rio feels he's "earned it". We take the beers and move to the bar's tables and umbrellas on a balcony overlooking Decatur Street. It is a good day. The sun is warm and the breeze is blowing parade sounds throughout the city.

I sink into the chair when Aaron walks onto the balcony with more drinks.

"Good Lord," I gasp. "I think its way too early for me to be getting into this much alcohol right now. I haven't drunk any water since I arrived except the melted ice in the vodka but I don't think that counts, do you?"

"And I haven't slept in over a day. Drink," he says. "I'm feeling good. I was up about thirteen hundred last night and ended up leaving with nine. At least I didn't end up sleeping in the pool."

Roberto's eyes are barely open and his Budweiser is no longer beading over itself. He has been nursing the same drink for over half an hour and the beer is warm.

"Where's Seth and Lenny?" I ask.

"They called from down the street at a hot dog stand," Aaron replies.

We walk to the edge of the balcony. The air is suddenly awash with iridescent soap bubbles the size of balloons sailing from somewhere below us. I squint past the soap and see Lenny waiting in line at a Lucky Dog.

"I had one of those dogs at the airport last time I was here and I thought it might kill me," I groan.

"Really?"

"No. Well it was either that or the skull rattling hangover I was suffering through but I'm sure the hot dog didn't help."

There is a pained expression on his face. "They went down fine last night," Aaron says.

"Was this before or after the strip club?"

"Which one?"

"Jacque's."

"Before, right outside the door. Why are there always food vendors outside of strip clubs? Remember the barbeque grill outside that strip club in East St. Louis. Worst ribs ever."

"I don't think East St. Louis is known for their ribs."

Aaron pauses. "Can you blame me? I was ferociously drunk and saw 'St. Louis' and 'ribs'. Damn East St. Louis. Took my money and part of my small intestine. Not to mention a part of my soul." He finishes the beer and takes another from the table. "Ah, hell." Aaron toasts my beer bottle. "To good times."

There is an unspoken immunity wafting around us like the soap bubbles randomly orbiting our balcony. Mardi Gras is a welcomed distraction from new realities. Whatever is going on outside the city is unimportant and we can worry about it all when the good times end because here life is a fevered dream. It's drinking, and laughing, and gambling, and being seduced, and being frightened by the world's bizarre beauty like when you were a boy. Let the viscid absurdity of Carnival wash over you if only for a day or two. Make time to watch acrobats, mimes and magicians and beautiful girls and death pass before your eyes. We want nothing more than a moment to have a good time. The bill officially comes on Ash Wednesday just like the Good Lord intended but on a balcony overlooking the Quarter with beer and a warm breeze sinking deeper into your head, it's hard to care about Wednesday or any other day.

"I'll have to go back to California to remember what normal people are like," Aaron says.

Rio and Corrine leave the balcony to have their fortunes read by the mystics whose card tables, chairs, and umbrellas populate the real estate in front of the Cathedral. Rio tries to drag me from the balcony for a reading but I refuse. I remember Lisa sitting at a fortune teller's table when we first met. She got me into the habit of reading her horoscope on a daily basis in some metaphysical hope our paths would continue to cross one another. It took a while to stop reading her days when everything ended.

We drink until about three. After a few quick drinks to catch up, Lenny is beyond redemption. There is a suspicious and dark twinkle in his eyes from being seriously steeped in alcohol in such a short amount of time. His buzz from the night before has been resuscitated with the Hurricanes he's guzzling. Eventually he slides into Mandarin and Sevens and I know crazy, unrestrained impulses creep out from his brain.

He growls, "I don't want anymore frozen fruity crap. It's giving me a fucking headache."

"Maybe it's a hangover," I say.

"No, it's the ice. It's making my head hurt. It feels like my head is splitting in two."

Good for you, I think, maybe your skull is just an egg and you're beginning to hatch. You should really let the monster out more.

"You don't know what you're saying," he says.

"Did I say that out loud?"

His eyes fix on the bubbles floating above my head. "I can see what you're thinking," he says and swats at a few. Thin red veins are spread across his blood shot eyes. His brow furrows and he rubs the ridges around his eye socket.

I wave the waitress over and order a drink.

He grins. "Okay. Maybe just one more before we go to the casino." Aaron has convinced Lenny and Roberto fortune and luck favor them.

He slams the drink down and declares, "Let's go win sssome money!" and is off down Decatur Street with his wraparound shades and an ATM card.

Corrine, Rio, Seth and I skip the casino and head down Canal towards Bourbon Street. It's overcast but still very bright. On Canal the floats excite the euphoric crowds. The floats are enormous sphinx-like beasts. Their gigantic human heads and long animal bodies are weighed down with light and garland and men in masks and costume. Beads and throws fly off the decks like sparks off comets and the late afternoon sky burns with wild color and brilliance.

On the way to Bourbon Street Rio is lured into a bar playing her song. Eventually the bartenders invite her and Corrine to dance on the bar with a few other girls for free shots and beads. Mardi Gras has infected their brains and liberated their souls. The transformation is a beautiful sight: pretty girls dancing to a background of shiny colored bottles and an audience of Venetian masked bar flies. Corrine picks up a mask near her feet. She hesitates at first and tries to figure out which side is the inside as Rio, now incognito, whips beads over their heads like a lasso. I catch Corrine's eyes before she brushes aside strands of long brown hair trapped between her lips. She lets slip a smile and puts the mask on to transcend the familiar and become something different. Something unexplored. Something feminine. Something sexual.

"Sirens," the bouncer says as he minds the door but can't help looking at the bar. "You can always tell a girl's first time in New Orleans. Sumthin new comes out of them, sumthin fine, lyrical...you know? Music. Can you hear it, mah bruther?"

"Yes," I mumble to myself. "I've heard her music before."

Rio bends down, whispers into Seth's ear and tries to yank him up to dance. He swats at her and moves back.

"Odysseus," I say to him, "Can't you just enjoy the show?"

"What?"

"Nevermind."

Rio whispers something to Corrine. They laugh and Corrine winks and blows a kiss towards our direction.

Streamers shoot through the light. Confetti explodes the air. Beads fly from all directions. A few girls flash the howling inebriates and the place erupts in flash bulbs and back into just another chaotic French Quarter bar during Mardi Gras.

The girls retrieve their spoils and free drinks and we end up around St. Phillip and Bourbon Street. We stop in for a drink at Laffitte's Blacksmith Bar. It's not much to look at from the outside and could pass for a condemned woodshed from a distance. But it's worth at least one drink since there are always people having a good laugh in its dank. Even in the daylight it's dark and barely lit and if it is lit, it's mostly with candles. The tourist board will tell you it's the oldest bar in the country and was a blacksmith shop for the pirate brothers Jean and Pierre Laffite. They used the shop as a front for trading slaves and its seedy past is a perfect fit amongst the contemporary lewdness and decadence. It smells old, and if the bar were suddenly awash with light you might see dead pirates infesting the dimly walled corners like mold in old books. There is a fireplace inside and a small courtyard which is a perfect place to sit and watch the world go by. At first Seth isn't too enthusiastic about being in what he thinks is a "gay" pirate bar. But there's an open table in the courtyard so we grab onto it to settle in for a few drinks.

I take the plastic compass from Buffet's and place it on the table. Rio and Corrine talk about gay men and who in the bar are most likely "toppers." Seth is smoking a cigarette.

Outside the walled patio the Bible bangers make an afternoon run through Bourbon Street to condemn the gay and wicked with details of the torment they face upon their final judgment if they don't stop having sex with each other and start shagging like God intended. We are no longer moving and the alcohol settles into my brain. My eyes are heavy when I catch sight of the compass.

The needle spins wildly and stops.

"Did you see that?" I say.

Seth blows out a drag of smoke.

"Did you see that?" I insist.

"No. What?"

"The compass."

"What about it?"

"The needle went haywire. That only happens in the Bermuda Triangle or places where the principles of space and time as you experience it don't apply."

"You're seeing things. It's not even real."

"Yes it is." I put the compass in my hand and spin it around. All the while the needle points north. "See."

He grabs the compass and throws it into the street.

"YOU BASTARD!" I scream. "What if I need that to find my way home?"

"You said it didn't work."

Rio comes back to the table and asks, "What's up your ass?"

"Nothing," he mumbles. "Are you guys going to be here a while?"

"Yes," she declares.

"Well then I'm going." He gets up, takes his beer and walks out of the courtyard.

Corrine asks, "Where are you going?"

"I'll just see you back at the hotel," he replies, and is gone.

"Alright grumpy!" Rio yells. She turns to me, "Do you want to leave?"

"No," I say.

"Screw him," Rio says. "Maybe gay pirates make him uncomfortable."

"Maybe," I say. "But he's got some ego to think they would want *him*."

I watch Seth squeeze past the religious and shake apart the ice cubes in my glass. "I just realized, they always know more about hell than heaven."

"Who?" Rio asks.

"These fanatics."

"Why is that?"

"I don't know. Look at that poor bastard." I point towards a fat man in a tight gray t-shirt waddling a few steps ahead of Brother Bob Whittaker. The man has a speaker box strapped to his head. His face is hot and red and the veins in his forehead surface. The gray shirt has the words "JESUS IS LORD" in red letters and is wet with sweat around his armpits. The shirt appears to be the only thing keeping his stomach from splitting open and releasing a torrent of holy water and guts. The burden of being

Bob's pack animal is wearing on him. He looks about ready to drop from the effort as Bob prods him with the tip of the bullhorn through the thick crowd on Bourbon Street. There is too much feedback to hear what Bob is saying and his voice is hoarse. The only thing I hear is, "pornographers" and "child molesters" and "God hates faggots!"

I empty the glass.

"Who is that guy?" Rio asks half-heartedly.

"The guy with the bullhorn?"

"Yeah," she replies.

"Never mind him. He's a noisy and evil fuck," I say. "I've dealt with him before and he's deranged. Apparently you can't preach the Bible without preaching God's hatred. He and his goddamned parrots are dedicated to making sure we all go to hell."

"Huh?" Rio pauses.

"DAMN YOUR OILY HIDES!" I yell. "YOU'RE ALL SLAVES!" The fat bastard in the gray shirt seems to finally understand this as I catch his right eye squeezing a sad glance at me the way the mules tied to carriages at Jackson Square look at you on hot long July days. He continues shuffling along Bourbon Street with Whittaker's burden balanced on his head. There are a few laughs from the people in the bar.

Rio laughs, "I like this! I think you need more to drink. It brings out your honesty."

"So it is written, so let it be done," I mumble.

Corrine gets up and heads inside to get the next round. Laffite's is now louder and more crowded. Bob Whittaker has moved on towards Canal. Bourbon Street is beginning to bustle. It will get very thick soon and we will need to fight our way through or take a side street back to The W.

"You didn't do anything to him did you?" I ask.

Rio asks, "Who?"

"Seth."

"No. Not me."

I ask, "Did you say something to him?"

"Absolutely not," she replies. She lets slip an evil grin. "I think he's mad you and Corrine didn't wait for him to get up before we left."

"What?"

"Not so much you but Corrine…or maybe you too. Who knows with him?"

I ask, "What the hell are you talking about?"

"I think he's got a thing for her."

"HA! You're nuts. He doesn't even like people."

"Corrine got him to dance the other night when you were off screaming about flesh eating parrots and fighting your invisible enemies. He never dances. They had a *pretty* good time." Rio seems pleased with herself in revealing this to me.

I groan, "He'd have a better shot with the gay pirates."

She laughs. "Jealous?"

"Don't start anything," I say.

"Cockblocker."

"Fuck you, tramp. Just like you, my relationship with Corrine is strictly alcoholic and co-dependent."

"Uh-huh."

"You gotta be kidding me. Is that what he's pissed about today?"

Rio shrugs her shoulders.

I abandon the inquiry and don't want to know what secret torment she has unleashed upon him to get his blood pressure up.

Corrine brings back some Miller Lites and light brown colored shots.

"What is that?" I ask.

"Rum," she says.

"Hmm...normally I'm opposed to such blatant attempts to make me sick but we're sitting in a pirate bar so rum is perfectly in order."

We shoot the rum and the back end burns my throat. My eyes are a watery mess.

"SWEET JESUS!" I scream. "WH--WHAT THE HELL WAS THAT?!" I wipe tears from my eyes when my nose drips.

Corrine is laughing.

Rio is unsympathetic. "Gah...You're such a pussy."

I close my eyes and suck on the beer until the plastic cup is empty. The vapors from the shot float recklessly in the air and my skin feels hot.

"151," Rio says.

I can't bring myself to say anything. Dizziness spills over my brain. This is the second time in 24 hours I have drank 151 and it is not behaving well in my body. I have done my best to stay away from drinking it for any reason since my 21st birthday because it pummeled me into my bathroom floor. It took two days to fully recover from the poisoning.

"Stop thinking about the taste and just enjoy the ride," Rio says.

"It's shit!" I gag. I can feel the smooth hard wood floor in my old bathroom once again and my twenty-one year old face pressed firmly against the toilet seat.

"Where's Corrine?" I ask.

"She went to get you water."

To my horror Corrine comes back with water and three more shots.

I plead. "It's not even 5:30."

"We're not leaving unless you do that shot." Rio grins. "I think I could stay here all night if I have to. Besides, you don't look drunk."

The high proof is infecting my brain and my stomach bends into unnatural shapes. I am woozy but reason if I don't look drunk then I must be okay.

"Fine." I raise the shot glass over the table. We toast and drink. The vapors begin to rise and the rum stings my tongue. Rio and Corrine eye me suspiciously.

"Open your mouth!" Rio orders.

I shake my head and spit out onto the ground. My eyes and face burn and the taste sits on me as thick as paste.

She huffs, "Just for that you have to drink two." She unfastens her wallet and pulls out a twenty-dollar bill.

"No," I cry. "I-I'll drink anything else just not that!"

"Fine." She sneers.

A few rounds later I have drank a Bushmill, a Jim Beam, some Marker's Mark and a Wild Turkey.

"Never drink anything with an animal's picture on the bottle." I am about to expand on my theory when I lean back in my chair and feel my feet leave the ground. The New Orleans sky is before me and my head is plastered against the Earth. There is a faint chorus of "AHHHHS" and relentless female laughter. The Turkey gurgles up the back of my throat and I close my eyes. My head spins in the momentary darkness.

"Are you okay?" a voice asks.

I open my eyes and see the graying sky. It is early still, and it looks darker than it should be for five o'clock.

"Are you okay?" the voice says again.

I laugh, feeling very comfortable on the ground and mumble, "I-- uh---I--don't really know."

Chapter Four

An event horizon is the space where the universe as we know it touches the beginning of the darkness in a black hole. Nobody really knows what is beyond the event horizon. There are only theories. It is a place where gravity's force is so strong nothing can escape. Not even the purity of light. If you travel beyond the event horizon you will be sucked into a black hole's singularity-----a point when the infinite density and curvature of space-time changes physical laws as you understand them. The usual rules do not apply. It is believed that in a rotating black hole these singularities can be used as portals into other areas of our universe or even other universes and as such, infinite possibilities. It is said the shortest distance between two points is a straight line, which is not absolutely true when gravity bends space. Within a black hole the shortest distance between two points in space-time can be zero or nowhere; so theoretically you can sit still within a black hole's darkness and let space and time come to you.

"Jeesuz are you okay?" Corrine laughs.

I remain still on the ground, afraid to move in case I stir the nausea. "I'm fine," I say as she stands over me.

"Do you need help getting up?"

"You're very kind, but no. I'm just appreciating the color of the sky from the ground's perspective."

She bends down and pulls me back up. Rio makes a half-hearted attempt to pull me up and crashes onto her chair. "SSSIDDOWN!" she slurs.

Aaron grabs my shoulder and sets my chair upright. "Sit up before you fall over...look, just lean against the table."

"Where the fuck did you come from?!"

He gives me a confused look.

"What?" I ask.

"Stop leaning back...you're gonna tip over again," he insists.

We are in The W courtyard. The fountain is quietly bubbling over itself. A freshly opened Absolut bottle is staring at me on the table. The umbrellas are down and the sky is dark blue but clear. Rio is sipping a vodka tonic and waving it in the air like a trophy. A vodka on the rocks is sweating nervously on the table for me.

"Wh-What time is it?" I ask.

"Almost seven-thirty," Corrine says.

There is a long pause as I take in my surroundings to make sure I am not dreaming.

"What?" Aaron asks.

"Where? How long have we been here?"

They look at one another as if I've asked this question before.

"Nevermind." I look at my watch. It is 7:22.

It's happened again. I've traveled in time and no one knows it.

Aaron speaks, "You were saying?"

I look at him, mystified. "I was saying what?"

"Jazz funeral."

"That I want to have one?"

Rio yells, "GAWDDAMIT ARE WE TALKING ABOUT THIS AGAIN!?"

"I don't know..." I mumble meekly, "are we?"

"Are you alright?" Corrine asks. "That's the second time you fell today."

"No. I mean yes I'm fine." I mumble, "Nothing like a rum inspired time warp to set you straight."

They look at one another with some concern.

"Never mind," I say. I take the glass and a deep sip. The vodka has blended well with the ice.

"He must be okay," Aaron says. "He's drinking."

"Lord where did all these beads come from?!" I grab and yank at them and struggle to take them off. "It's not a good idea for me to be wearing these things when I'm drinking." I continue to struggle. "Sooner or later they'll end up hanging me with these!"

"Maybe he isn't alright," Corrine says.

I pull most off but tire from the effort and sit still with my drink.

"The boys at Laffitte thought you should have them." Rio smiles.

"What?"

She winks.

I am horrified.

"Wha-What did I---"

She laughs the type of evil pirate's laugh the brothers Laffitte must have made every time some unfortunate soul discovered they had been sold into slavery.

"I don't want to know." I look down at my shoes. "WHAT'S THAT?!"

"Your puke," Rio says as she sips on her tonic and vodka.

Corrine asks, "You don't remember throwing up?"

I reply sadly, "No."

Rio fills in the grisly details. After taking the fall at Laffite's the girls and I backtracked through the thick of Bourbon Street and passed by the sword shop which was now closed. She was disheartened until I metioned to her that during the Superbowl there were tanks stationed in the city to fight the terrorists and rumor had it that one or two were still roaming around. It seemed to liven her spirit and we went looking for them so she could "ride the cannon". Somewhere near the Hotel Monteleone I remembered the hotel's carousel bar and insisted on sitting down for a spin while the piano played "Rocket Man." We made a game of the experience as the three of us slowly orbited around the center of our micro-verse, a Filipino bartender named Nick. Each time we completed a full rotation we did a shot. To be clear, the carousel bar does not spin wildly like a children's amusement, but very slow, deliberate, and slight. As you sit, the scenery remakes itself without you. Motion without movement. Time passing without meaning. Your life is suspended in a queasy Jell-O mold of cigarette smoke, fragmented piano notes, girl laughter, non-sequential conversations with the disappearing and reappearing Nick, and rum, more rum. For the most part I like rum's effect on me when it's diluted. It fondles my brain and reminds me of floating in a purple and yellow sunset on a coral beach near the South China Sea. On that trip I was fondled by the alcohol and suspended in black water and Tanduay rum and sat peacefully in an inner tube processing the dark horizon. I was curious but not fearful of bull sharks feeding at the dusk and the unexploded sea ordinance from World War II that might drift by while I soaked. That rum binge was serenity in the midst of certain doom. But on the carousel at the Hotel Monteleone it was slow motion panic and certain doom. The shots of rum were going down at a pace bound to end in gastrointestinal violence. I survived three complete orbits and three quarters into my fourth revolution my brain righted itself and spun in the opposite direction than the rest of the bar. The oddly angled mirrors above the bar repeated our reflections to infinity. Whole at one moment, then split, and gone in an instant, and back as we made our landing approach towards Nick. *Where am I?* I thought.

Why am I dissolving? Am I invisible? Didn't I finish this drink? Have I just been spinning and drinking here forever? Panic induced nausea. I had to free myself from this unnerving activity and get to a toilet somewhere through the hotel lobby and past the display window of Tennessee William's desk. All the while I kept encircling the room in my own drunken loop and begging for a restroom as the annoyed hotel staff did their best to redirect my syrupy eyes to the men's room more than once. A vague memory of the cold floor, the stall door halfway open with my legs sticking out from underneath, the automatic toilet's refusal to flush on cue, sickness and darkness.

Conventional wisdom refers to an unconscious state as blacking out but I'm willing to go further than a black out and call it what it really is, a black hole. Excessive drinking has an event horizon; that moment in your head when you know you should quit because your body cannot take the poison anymore and there is no certainty the gravity within your next sip won't suck you in and send you hurtling towards an unknown part of the universe. When you come through the other end you may find yourself right where you were when the darkness took you. But most times you will find yourself lost within your head. This happened once before in Louisville during a romp at the Derby. My associates and I snuck two gallons of vodka disguised as water along with juices and ice to mix. I had my drink without the dressings and took in a good day at the races without incident until I drank an orange juice bottle mixed with Everclear from the cooler. I was standing in line under the hot Blue Grass sun to bet a two-dollar, trifecta box for the ninth race when I found myself scaling a chain-link fence next to a cabstand in front of Churchill Downs screaming like a rabid monkey. It was early evening and I was practically naked, incomprehensible, and belligerent. The Louisville police, who are familiar with all types of asinine behavior, were not amused someone had brought a wild animal to the track. If my friends had not convinced them I was human, I would have probably been darted with tranquilizers, carted off by animal control, and subsequently shipped back to Southeast Asia to live out my days in the jungle with a family of gibbons.

"I need to wash my shoes," I say as I leave the courtyard and make my way to the elevators. I am stale. Throwing up rid most of the alcohol from my body but I ache in my stomach for food, and a shower might do me some good.

The room is dim but the remaining daylight is creeping through the open patio doors and the wood blind windows. The beds remain unmade and pillows and blankets are strewn across the floor next to open bags, dirty clothes, and half a case of beer still chilling in the garbage can. It smells like Bourbon Street in here, and it's apparent housekeeping has neglected their duties. There is a bag of Krystal cheeseburgers sitting on the desk and two 32 ounce Coke cups beading water and leaving a mark on the desk table. I take my shoes off, dig into the bag for a burger and eat one and some fries. The food is still warm and grilled onions fill the air in the room. I go to the patio doors to open the blinds.

There is labored breathing coming from underneath a dark corner behind the bed next to the windows. Then a whisper, "What are you doing?!"

The comforter slides from the bed and is swallowed by the shapeless dark.

"Seth?"

There is a pause and a grunt. "No."

I reach for the switch on the wall closest to me and flood the room with light.

Lenny screams. He is curled up in a ball and buried within the comforter. "Turn that off," he moans. "It hurts my fuckin eyes."

He is in his shorts and sandals and not much else. He crawls over the bed to grab his wraparound shades and yanks at my beads. I fall forward and land in a pile of bags.

"I TOLD YOU TO KEEP THE LIGHTS OFF! ARE YOU DEAF?!"

"No you crazy bastard so stop yelling!" I shout back.
He grunts and stands me up by the shirt before petting my head and using my beads as a leash. He smacks my face and takes a deep breath.

"They're looking for me..."

"Who?" I ask and try to unwind his grip from my beads.

"THEM." He lets me go and sniffs the air until it leads him to the Krystal box in my hand.

"Where's my food?" he asks.

I point to the desk.

He grabs the bag and a drink and climbs back over to the corner of the bed. "Very good," he mumbles to himself and devours the burgers and fries. "So fucking good," he says with a full mouth, "very good." It is an awful display watching this half naked beast eat tiny cheeseburgers. I might vomit again.

I ask, "What *happened* to you?"

292

"I won," he laughs between the open-mouthed chewing and heavy breathing.

"Won what?"

He belches loudly into the air. "Money."

He reaches into his pocket and whips out a hand roll thick with twenty-dollar bills. He holds it up and waves it in the air.

"How much is that?" I ask.

"900."

"Are you drunk?"

He shrugs his shoulders.

I ask, "What happened?"

He takes a deep sip from the Coke and burps. "Oh, man that's good! I took a leak on the streets and the cops came after me. Do you know those mothers have horses and whips?" He grunts and laughs. "Jesus, that must be a Southern thing. I freaked out and threw some twenties in the air and kept running. Then I ducked into Krystal."

He pauses to clear his throat and breathe. "Is that bribery?" he asks.

"I don't know," I reply. "The laws are different here. It's all Napoleonic Code. I wouldn't put it past the authorities to use horse whips.

That'll definitely get your attention." I pick the other Coke off the table, take a sip and quickly spit it out. It is thick and spicy. "Aww--What--"

"Oh look," he brays like a mule, "you're full."

I grab a napkin and wipe my tongue. "What the hell is that?!"

"Rum and Coke. Some chick loaded my cups before I found the hotel."

I can't seem to escape it, the rum. The smell queers my head. "I need a shower," I reply.

He leaps up and pushes me aside. "I gotta shit." He peels off a twenty from his bankroll and flicks it at me. "This will take awhile."

I keep the money, turn the T.V. on and set my head down on a pillow. There is a news documentary about the uprising in Afghanistan's Qala-i-Jangi prison. A CIA officer was the first American to die in combat during the invasion. He was killed while interrogating prisoners. It took seven days and a lot of bombs to put down the revolt. Among the surviving prisoners was an American fighting for the enemy. There was footage of the CIA agent interviewing the American hours before the uprising, an irony not lost on the documentary filmmakers. After the first thirty minutes I turn the T.V. off and nap.

At around 8:30 the room is empty. I am dimwitted and take a cold shower to shake off the dullness. I find a clean pair of jeans buried in my backpack and a black, long sleeve sweater that smells like laundry detergent. It reminds me of home. I take some vitamins and two asprin to neutralize the free radicals in my head. I can feel them, conspiring, conniving, and stealing electrons from one another----bad molecules taking from good molecules----morality playing itself out on atomic levels.

In the courtyard the coven of drunks have gathered en masse and are eager for the evening after steeping themselves in booze for most of the late afternoon. It is dark and the fountain continues to bubble and gush. Hushed roars rise and fall in the distance over the rooftops and along Bourbon Street. Carnival is the riptide swelling violently underneath the streets this time of year. You will only know its danger all too well once you place a foot into the water. Drunks scramble everywhere, drinking feverishly and consuming the life around them. There is a glass and a half left in the Absolut bottle and I make sure to pour myself a tall one before Rio realizes we are running out. For the moment, as with most French Quarter buildings, the only refuge is the courtyard. We are protected by the history in its walls and the sentiment for older, more deliberate times.

"Maybe you should slow it down. It's only 9," Seth suggests to Rio. She is pestering him and trying to pinch his nipples. He isn't upset yet. And you can tell by the slow and drowsed glances in his eyes he has done shots. Lenny is running around the courtyard talking to strangers, smoking their cigarettes, and giving them money for the drinks at their tables. Roberto and Corrine trade chilled Jagermiester shots. Soon the dark green bottle empties itself out.

Lenny creeps up to the table and is wobbly. He grips the oversized umbrella stand and swings around it like a drunken ape. "Whaddya got?"

I ask,"Huh?"

"Whaddya got?"

I am sinking down into that familiar funny feeling. The glass is sweating in my hand. The courtyard lights and spinning ice make small kaleidoscopes on the table.

I reply, "Vodka?"

He fans out a few twenty-dollar bills from his bankroll and smacks me across the face with it.

"You goddamn beast!" I yell. "Those fuckers at Harrah's should never give immigrants money!"

He runs off laughing to himself and discovers a dimly lit corner with unopened beer from an abandoned table. "You got nuthin! NUTHIN!"

I am mesmerized by the kaleidoscopes.

"What do you all wanna do?" Roberto asks.

"Let's eat. I'm starving," Seth says.

"Where?"

"I dunno...but not Bourbon Street," he replies.

Lenny brings back two Rolling Rocks and a Dixie beer. "I have some Krystal upstairs."

"I hate Krystal," Seth says.

Rio has a curious look on her face as if she has discovered something amazing she had not known before. She laughs. "Yeah right...when have you ever had crystal?"

"Many times."

Rio snorts. "Like when?" she asks.

"Just a couple of days ago on the way down here."

"Bullshit."

"No, it is shit," Seth says.

"You had crystal on the way down here?"

"Uh-huh."

Rio is stunned. "I had no idea."

"Sometimes I get it with cheese but it doesn't help."

Rio is perplexed. "Uh...What?"

"What?"

"Cheese? What the fuck do you do with the cheese? Smoke it?"

Seth replies, "Smoke the cheese?"

She asks, "Does it make it better?"

"Better?" Seth rolls his eyes and shakes his head. "I just told you it doesn't help. What the hell are you talking about?"

"Crystal," she says.

"Yeah, Krystal," he replies. "Lenny's got some upstairs if you're really hungry. I don't know if there's cheese but there's definitely grilled onions."

"What the fuck are you talking about?"

He groans, "Krystal."

"You smoke meth?" she asks.

Seth blurts out,"What? I'm talking about the hamburger place you cocaine-crazed bitch."

Rio laughs. She is nearly in tears. "Oh my God...," she continues to cry, "...for a second there I thought we might have something to build our love on."

"Ha!" I laugh. "Can you imagine him on drugs?"

Rio says, "It might improve his personality."

Seth snaps, "So what's your excuse?"

"Aww don't be mad. That was funny." She plants a big kiss on him.

Seth cringes, "Get away from me."

"Come on," I reply. "Pretend you like girls."

Rio's blue eyes are sloppy and look focused in opposite directions. She has one leg on Seth's lap and both arms wrapped around him. She is trying to stare deeply into his eyes. "For the record sir," she slurs, "I don't like cocaine...I just like the way it SMELLZZZZ----"

Lenny brings a mix of different beers to the table.

I groan, "That is going to give me a headache."

"Which one?" Lenny asks and lights the cigarette that's been dangling on his lips forever.

"Any of them," I reply.

"You couldn't take anything else?" Rio asks.

He says with a shrug, "That's all there was you needy bitches."

I finish the Absolut and open the beer. "This is horrible. I need vodka." I put the beer on the table and stand up. The ground gives way like a trampoline and it takes me a moment to adjust to the soft earth. "That's not good," I say as I look at the solid cobblestones around me. "The floor is melting."

Rio taps her fingernails against her empty glass. "What part of a human body do you think would taste the best?"

I laugh. Seth peels Rios' arms off of his shoulders and steps away from the table.

I take the empty glass from her and set it on the table. "Let's find something to eat."

Chapter Five

Bourbon Street smells like the inside of a pig's stomach and it cannot be helped at this time of night. You can taste the pork in the air and the smell is turning the sky into strange colors. There is simply not enough water and sanitation to match the rate at which ingredients are being stirred into the human stew cooking within the street. The action is too chaotic and grubby to avoid the mess. Garbage bags overrun the sidewalks. The alcohol bleeds freely from them and the plastic cups of fruit punch, rum and beer are forming slick puddles. Broken beads roll and spread over the concrete like marbles. The footing is dangerous. I don't see the vomit but I know it's there because it hangs in the air like a ghost, dampening my clothes, turning my head, and queering the stomach. There is noise; joyous profanities, random clapping, laughing and relentless shouting. Loud music blows out from the bars and mixes with other sounds on the street. The "OOOOO's" and "Ahhh's" and redneck "Yee-haws!" can be felt blocks away and pass over you like waves at the beach. Somewhere on the street or above my head there are ladies getting naked, beads offered and thrown, and pushing and shoving. There will be many fights and unsolicited groping going on tonight. The police know it but will allow the weirdness and quasi-criminal conduct to persist as long as nobody gets beyond control. They have a rough job and cannot arrest everybody, just the serious brawlers and defecators. I barely process the chaos around me. Bourbon Street is a flash of neon bright in some places and too dark and formless in others. This is a watery masquerade and everyone is pretending to be something other than their selves as they swim the Quarter in full accoutrement and garb. It seems like everyone has a costume, feather boa, giant beads, and mask. Some can barely tread the water and others are already drowned. There's one poor bastard passed out on the foul earth in a doorway with a beer stand in it. We all take pictures next to the body until the lifeguards haul him away for his own safety. Everyone rejoices and continues to stir the gumbo with more yelling and drinking and pushing and laughing.

I am worried I will not be able to get a drink. Nothing fancy, but just something to keep the feeling going. We make a quick stop for some 32 ounce Miller Lites. Most of the beer spills out of the cups while we bump, push, and stumble through the crowds. I am soaked with alcohol from the knees down.

Eventually we make port at a restaurant with live Cajun music. Lenny is dancing with Rio on a makeshift dance floor between dinner tables while I pass the time for the thirty-minute wait at the bar trying to drink some shots Aaron has bought to make me sick.

Out of nowhere a crazy Asian woman charges at me screaming, "OH MY GOD IT'S CHARLIE!"

We butt heads.

I might have simply deflected her assault, but am clumsy with booze and unable to stand my ground.

We fall back. Me on my head and she on her face, beads swing and flail, the restaurant goes from vertical to diagonal to horizontal. My skull makes a hollow sound against the bar.

The woman is helped up by a man I take to be her husband because he has the weary eyes of a man who's wife is always a drunken wreck. She seems alright and is laughing, but holding her forehead above her right eyebrow. I am massaging my brain when he takes a good look at his wife and yells: "Jeezus Christ, Julie! You're bleeding!" The laughing stops. The weeping begins. Blood flows unchecked.

Steady your mind, jerk. You're a horrible drunk. This is all you need. To have a complete stranger accuse you of mortally wounding his wife with a headbutt. Whiskey and dizziness clouds my brain. The man is upset. In my present state my only defense to an onslaught of drunken and angry blows will be to curl myself up the way an armadillo would until he wears himself out.

The woman stops crying. "BUT...YOU'RE NOT CHARLIE!"

"I am not!" I plead, hoping my startled overreaction will garner some sympathy from the bar and establish a convincing foundation of innocence.

"Are you all right?" the bartender asks.

"Yes, I'm fine," I reply.

Her husband shakes his head. "He's not talking to you, jackass." He takes a wet towel from the bartender to clean her cut.

"Huh...well then...." I say. "Mistaken identities are commonplace when you've been drinking for over twelve hours. I'm certain she meant no deliberate harm but you should really learn to control your booze before you do some serious damage."

The girl is dazed but calm now and pressing the wound with a wet towel.

"You're only hurting yourself," I mumble and grab my Absolut and ice.

The man continues to clean and apply pressure to her forehead while the bartender digs up some band-aids from behind the bar.

"...I guess I'll be leaving," I say as I slip through the crowd and head straight to the dance floor.

Dinner starts out as a civil affair despite the apparent chaos in the restaurant. The house band has switched to Blue Grass and the music is frenzied and louder. More people are on the dance floor and dinner tables get knocked and bumped with the grind. I think we are all very hungry and a little drained from drinking. The noise makes it easier to focus on the food, and less on each other. I order a fried shrimp Po' Boy, dressed, along with a small jambalaya. The sandwich is bland and needs heat so I dowse it with the hottest bottle on the table and wash it all down with a cold beer. I can tell the day has worn on us from the blank and slow-eyed stares at the table and in order to salvage the night someone must take the initiative to do something irrational in order to shake loose the beasts within. I order

the very worst tequila the restaurant has for the table. It goes down horribly

and quickly rouses everyone into contorted faces of momentary illness.

Then, within the booze clouds and dizziness, the beasts emerge, violently

happy.

Roberto blinks spastically. "It's too bright in here." His eyes are

closing up which means soon he will be blind and guided by only voices

and feelings.

Lenny eyeballs the chandeliers hanging above our heads.

"Is it last call?" Roberto continues. "Why are all the lights on?"

Lenny replies, "You don't know what you're talking about. Your

eyes are shut."

I am emboldened by Roberto's momentary vulnerability and made

stupid by the tequila. My brain sizzles and spins. I reach across the table at

Roberto's plate with my fork and stab it into his burger. "Are you gonna

eat that?"

He doesn't react.

Lenny snorts. "Aw, man."

Roberto is now awake. He mumbles something to himself before

grabbing Lenny's water glass and throwing it at me.

Seth glares at us. "Cut it out you fucking morons," he barks. "You're getting me wet!"

I pick up a napkin to dry my shirt.

Roberto keeps eating, silent but vigilant. He's seething. Ready to boil over and gut me on the dinner table.

Lenny looks at me and shakes his head.

The waitress, a kind and very patient woman, comes by to check on us. "Hmm...do you need some more napkins?" she asks.

I wring the water out of my shirt sleeve. "Yes," I reply.

"Alright, but you boys behave yourselves," she says.

"Maybe you should sit on this side," Corrine says.

"Fuck that...I'm not changing places with him." Seth growls.

"No," I reply, "I'm sure it was an accident." I pick up a dry napkin and throw it at Roberto's face. "See...I'm a nice person."

"Here we go." Lenny grins. He has witnessed these aberrant and asinine displays between me and Roberto before. At times we cannot help but fight; familiarity breeds contempt. The reckless consumption of alcohol makes that hatred quick to surface in moments like this. We have known each other too long and seen one another in our best and worst moments as people. That is probably why we are still friends in spite of it all, because who else besides these drunks at the table can appreciate the twisted bond. Drinking is how we've shared our joy and numbed our heartbreak. As with any long term relationship bad blood festers every now and then especially when the blood is mostly booze. Once in a while there has to be a blood letting.

Aaron pushes his plate aside and leans over to me. "C'mon...fight against your natural instincts and stop being a jerk."

Roberto picks up the water carafe and dumps it on my plate. "He can't help it."

Water and ice land in my lap.

There is an uneasy silence. The mood is ripe for hostility.

The waitress comes by. "Did you spill again?"

"Yes, ma'am," I reply. "I have a nervous disorder..."

"More like a drinking problem," Roberto says.

I eye him and consider my next move.

"It's still a disorder!" I yell and lunge at him over the table knocking plates of food, glasses, and water all over the floor. Lenny pulls me back onto the ground. Seth and Aaron grab Roberto and move him away from the table. The girls are silent and the waitress has run away to the bar to get the manager.

"I think we should wrap things up and leave," Aaron says. "Everyone's getting cranky."

"Fuck him!" Roberto shouts.

Lenny grabs me by the shirt and whispers, "You're a fucking asshole dude."

Roberto yells, "He's not an asshole, he's a goddamned fucking train wreck!" He wrestles his way out of Seth and Aaron's hold. "Let me go!"

Rio steps in. "Alright." She points at me. "You. Leave."

"Why do I have to leave?" I ask.

"Let's go," Lenny says. "We'll meet up with you later when everything has calmed down."

"But why do I have to leave?" I ask.

There is silence and mean stares.

"Fine," I reply and reach into my pocket to throw a balled up twenty dollar bill at Roberto.

He shakes his drunken head. "You're fucking hopeless dude."

Rio orders, "Stop it."

I slur, "It's for the food jackass."

"Stop." She says again looking at me.

"You don't have to worry about me," Roberto says. "I'm not starting anything...I'm not getting arrested for this jerk."

"Come on stupid," Lenny says as he and Seth hustle me out of the restaurant.

After dinner I feel ill. Lenny and Seth don't say much. I've no doubt what is on their minds; I am completely out of line and am a jerk off because I believe drinking excessively entitles me to behave poorly. What little food I was able to eat has not settled right and is sloshing around my stomach refusing to digest and process. We make our way back to Bourbon Street and are at Pat O'Brien's. It is standing room only and the crowds continue to thicken. I prefer the courtyard at O'Brien's much more during the off peak times when you can get a table and enjoy their signature drink without the people. There is an endless line for the restroom. While I wait, a guy a few feet in front of me collapses after downing one too many drinks. The light in his eyes burned out before the Hurricane glass hit the pavement and shattered, spilling ice and fruit juice everywhere. He is helped up by his friends and moved out of the line but it doesn't make a dent in the wait, so we cross the street to seek out a more accessible venue and some breathing room.

A fight breaks out across the street from the side entrance outside Pat O'Brien's on St. Peters Street. Two white boys get into it with two black bouncers. Judging by their alcohol-impaired balance, the white boys are hopelessly outmatched. A shorter guy grabs at a bouncer from behind and the bouncer doesn't hesitate to spin around and put a solid fist to his jaw. There is surprise in the man's face until his eyes glaze over. His head bounces against the curb before his body deflates onto the pavement.

The survivor is shown no mercy. His best punches have little effect, but this epiphany is a split second too late. He is beat senseless and thrown out into the street.

When they finish laying waste to these patrons a bouncer runs up to the first man he knocked out and kicks him in the head.

"Jesus Christ." Seth says.

Lenny turns away. "Eeewwww! That's just not right," he mumbles.

We stand by for the aftermath and watch the police arrive to shove the onlookers aside and make arrests.

"Let's get out of here," I say. "Seeing something like that is just bad for the buzz."

We cross over to Royal Street to look for a cowboy bar Seth is certain has a mechanical bull. He says it will take our minds off the violence and we can sit and drink cold beer and watch good looking drunk girls dry hump the bull while "Urban Cowboy" plays on a giant movie screen in the background. He is pretty sure it's on Royal, but after one or two passes down the street I am convinced the bar is somewhere else. We settle for a bar that doesn't look too crowded and where the patrons are greeted by a black gentleman wearing a very fine velvet green blazer and white gloves. The bar is old, dark wooded, and English. The backroom has better lighting and sinks into a lounge with chairs and small tables surrounded by fox hunting paintings and horse pictures on the walls. It is too old world and too stuffy for my mood until a krewe dressed in safari clothes settles into the far corner with butterfly nets, walking sticks and toy rifles. They are middle aged and mostly from Mississippi except Wayne, who later introduces himself to me as "an Arnout" of the Louisiana Arnouts who bravely fought the British beside Andrew Jackson in the War of 1812. We come to his attention before all that when a woman named Marie from Wayne's krewe tries to convince a young blonde girl sitting next to us to show everyone her boobs. "Honey, you better show 'em while you got 'em," Marie says before making the blonde stand up, "because one day gravity will just kill 'em like it done me." Then Marie lifts her shirt up to reveal her worn out chest. This gets the whole room worked up and pretty soon they chant for the blonde to undress.

The blonde is red faced, tipsy, and might just be convinced to give us all a show if she gets drunk enough. She laughs. "But my Dad would kill me."

Marie rolls up her fingers in one hand and raises the hand to the crowd. She points to the tiny space between her thumb and index finger. "You see that?" She declares. "You've got to loosen up girl."

"I don't get it," the blonde says. She is now wearing a fake pair of naked boobs someone from the krewe has given her "just to get comfortable with the idea."

"You've got to loosen up, 'cause your hole's too tight."

The room chants and claps again until everyone realizes the blonde won't budge.

"It's Mardi Gras!" Wayne yells at us from across the room. "Your girl should loosen up."

"She's not with us," Lenny replies.

"Where ya'll from?" the room asks.

"Chicago," I reply.

"Hey Chicargo!" Wayne yells. "Where ya'll from?"

Seth looks at me and shakes his head.

"We're from Chicago!" Lenny yells.

Wayne walks across the room and plants himself at a table next to Marie. With their toy rifles, butterfly nets, and safari outfits the krewe's theme has something to do with hunting for Osama. "What're y'all supposed to be?" he asks.

Marie interjects, "Is this your first Mardi Gras? Ya'll should really wear costumes."

"We are wearing costumes," I reply.

Marie asks, "What're ya'll supposed to be?"

I point at Seth. "I'm him."

"And who is he?" she asks.

"He's me," I say.

Marie laughs. "Ya'll are real silly." She turns her attention back to undressing the blonde.

Wayne and Marie are Mardi Gras dinosaurs and really into the debauchery and sex and sinfulness of it all. They are fully aware and experienced in the knowledge and ways of the secret orgies and hard drugs hidden above our heads and behind the balcony doors in the Quarter. These are things most of us visitors will never know and only catch glimpses of when the excessiveness spills out onto the balcony in stark nakedness to throw beads. We trade shots before Wayne offers to share a joint with us. I decline. I've been away from the Gulf Coast for too long and living up North has made me suspicious of doing drugs with Southerners. He offers to buy me another drink which I also decline.

Wayne insists, "Look Chicargo, I'm gonna buy you a drink whether you like it or not. I'm from here and you're gonna accept it and embrace the idea. I don't know how they do things up North, but it's just our way."

"No thanks, really," I say. "I've been drinking too much. If you don't back off I might have to eat your liver to replace mine."

"Christ! Can't you just get over it and have another drink with me so we can move on with the goddamn party? It's not like I'm asking you to do a line of coke off Marie's ass!"

"Thank God," I say, "because I shouldn't try something I might really like."

I look at Seth whose bored expression makes it clear he is ready to leave.

"Alright Wayne, one more drink. But after that I've got to go."

I have a shot of Bushmill with Wayne at the bar. He recites some stories about his own first real Mardi Gras and how dropping in for a few days won't really give you a taste of the season. He spits out a phone number and asks me to repeat it back to him so I don't forget and invites me to visit next year to "do this thing right." Before we leave he insists on giving me some homemade booze he is carrying in his costume's canteen. He hands the canteen to me after the bartender forgets to give him a large plastic cup for me to carry on our way back to Bourbon Street.

"I can't take your canteen," I say. "What if you die of thirst?"

"It's cheap shit." He flashes the inside of his jacket at me. "I got another one in my vest," he says. "That one's almost empty anyway and it's been a bitch drinking and carrying this shit around all day. Take it. That's an order."

I sling it around my body and salute him. "Very well, sir."

I thank him for the drinks and the canteen and he wishes me luck.

We make it back to O'Brien's and meet up with Rio and the others. There is no room to move and because of this, me and Roberto are within arms length of each other. We get more drunk and uncertain of each other's motives, so I offer him a truce for the evening which he begrudgingly accepts since I am not willing to offer an apology. In honor of our accord, we take a few drinks from Wayne's brew. It is pungent and awful, but with a vodka chaser it goes away quietly. I abandon the beer regiment for the evening. It is making me full and pushing my bladder's limits every time I put one down. Getting a drink from the bar is impossible and I enjoy the vodka very quickly which makes me drunk and ornery. We leave when the courtyard becomes uncomfortably packed.

Outside O'Brien's it is not much better. There is nowhere to drink except on the street. A young kid, around sixteen years old, is throwing up half a block off of Bourbon. His fingers are dug into the steel wired mesh screens of a restaurant long gone out of business. The clutch is an instinctive act; an involuntary response infants make when they grab their mother's clothing for safety. This naïve faith does not go unpunished or unnoticed in this place. Some older and experienced visitors file past him and laugh out loud, "WHOA-HO! Welcome to Mardi Gras, kid!" They, like everyone else, have little sympathy for this spectacle aside from stepping away from the puddle. Vomiting is as much a rite of passage in New Orleans as drinking a Hurricane and eating a Po' Boy. It's a sacrilege to not have at least one anecdote to share about just how viciously the French Quarter kicked in your stomach during a nightmarish run of drinking. The tale you spin hides an undeniable and horrible truth, and one

317

that probably won't hit you until your third day or a good epic purge. The dark truth is that Mardi Gras' allure has little to do with pleasure itself and more to do with a shot of pleasure chased with sadomasochism and pain. You can really forget what your life is about after a few hard days of it. Mardi Gras is an endurance test, and as with any great American marathon the reward for most enthusiasts is being able to say you made it across the finish line. For the moment the finish line seems further away and a faint whisper is telling me I've run this race once too often. I'm pushing my luck in returning here to spoil myself with vodka. In my obedience to the thirst, I always forget that after a few days in New Orleans the city begins to drink you. Mardi Gras makes fools of us all. There is no escaping the shame and public displays of buffoonery. There is too much bad intentioned drinking in Southern culture to avoid being swept away by a mixed drink and beer flood rising like a tsunami at the beginning of St. Charles Avenue. It carries the floats and crazies towards Bourbon Street.

One drunken Floridian is more than eager to reassure me of the normalcy in all this. "Oh, you know us Southerners, we just like to get drunk and act all silly." She tells me this before she crashes the stage at a piano bar we slip into to escape the crowded mess on Bourbon. She and a middle-aged swingers' krewe slowly torture the decent folk in the establishment by stripping waist up to dance to Tom Jones' "You Can Leave Your Hat On." The drooping, freckled folds and orange flesh swing together and against one another without shame or end; and the milk has long since gone bad. At grand Southern events like this, any Viagra and alcohol crazed group of semi-retirees feel emboldened and even entitled to show us law abiding, internet savvy perverts a live display of the debilitating effects of a life long devotion to sunbathing and poor eating habits. It is more than apparent that these rowdy nudists have been here before. After too much time in New Orleans your skin no longer fits your body. It is either too tight from the bloat of gluttony or too loose because of your evaporating spirit. Either way, it doesn't fit. It greys, gets stained, torn, and worn out. After one too many Fat Tuesdays the body is just another costume like the masks, capes, boas and hats. There are many strange and beautiful things to marvel at in this bar in New Orleans tonight, but elder nudity is not one of them. There are the young sirens, New Orleans' virgins, dancing on the bar with boas and beads and discovering something new in their voice and their potential to spin charms on a willing crowd. There is the Sammy Davis look alike wearing a Superman costume who appears from nowhere to not only sing, "Sitting on the Dock of the Bay," but to bang out a drum solo in the middle of his song. And there is a dwarf from the audience named Hermie who jumps on stage to kick out a rousing version of George Michael's "Faith." By the song's end he has thrown his entire soul into the music and succeeds in whipping the bar into a mad frenzy when he declares to this bohemian Mardi Gras court something already apparent to us all:

"Hey, I'm a fucking midget...I GOTTA HAVE FAITH!"

The bar gives him a standing ovation and he exits stage left with his body pouring sweat and his arms raised in triumph.

Amen, brother Hermie. Amen.

Outside the bar, a meaty bunch of Brother Bob's parrots have dug in their position at the corner on Iberville. One stands and holds a large wooden cross with "JESUS IS LORD" painted on it. The others wave large signs bearing happy thoughts such as:

"THE FEARFUL AND UNBELIEVING AND ALL LIARS SHALL HAVE THEIR PART IN THE LAKE OF FIRE!"

And

"FEAR GOD AND GIVE GLORY TO HIM FOR THE TIME OF HIS JUDGMENT IS COMING!"

Bob is nowhere to be found, but another Bob with a bullhorn is praying aloud to the air. This is young Bob, New Bob, Bob 2.0, the future of the movement no doubt; making his bones by throwing himself straight into the mouth of Hell at this godless hour in the Quarter. He begins his sermon by yelling to everyone within earshot, "God...we pray our actions here give some glory back to you! We live in grace, even here, and we are not afraid of death, because death is the blink of an eye and from our work in your name we know we will wake up in paradise!"

I laugh and think it brave for them to be here at this time considering they are stuck in the middle of hundreds whom they are condemning as sinners. We can easily turn on them like drunken cannibals, devour them, and crucify the ringleader on one of those big crosses they're carrying.

Rio growls, "They're taking up valuable space."

"Stay away from them," I say. I can tell she is hoping someone will start a fight with her.

She laughs. "They don't scare me."

There is the beginning of a shouting match between a few onlookers and New Bob as he continues blasting the crowd:

"This War on Terrorism, this world alliance, do you know what it is?! It's the beginning of the loss of individual Christian freedoms! And I don't need conspiracies to tell me what to expect because scripture has told me these things would happen. Signs are upon us and to say they are anything else but the end is blasphemous! You're all fools...Satan is manipulating your leaders' minds with terrorism to bring his final plans into effect, and you're all fools! Your leaders are already in league with the devil, and have conspired to trick and betray you! You can't see it because your souls have been bought out by booze, drugs, sex and the lies these things tell you about yourself. While you sit idly by, getting drunk and sodomizing one another, the real world has become a unity of heretics throwing its full weight against our nation's true Christians to stop evangelism and ban real Christian witness! But I for one am not going to compromise my faith at this time for "peace." I'm gonna fight you all wherever I can. This is my Crusade! God has called, and I am answering!"

"They're insane," I grunt. "No person in their right mind would stand on Bourbon Street at Mardi Gras at two in the morning and declare a jihad on these drunks." I've been taking shots from the canteen and the taste is sticking to my cheeks. My brain stings, my jaw clenches and my eyes begin to water. "No telling what sort of crazy ideas are running through their brains right now. They may be outnumbered, but you've got to be wary of people like that. They're dedicated enough to stab you in the heart with their wooden picket signs just to prove to themselves you're a vampire."

Most of the on-lookers give only passing attention to these agitators when a vocal group of costumed drinkers dressed as gay superheroes grab and pull at the signs, trying to knock them down or take them away. They are particularly interested in the ones saying: "God loves faggots so much he gave them AIDS!"

New Bob and his faction drive back the crowd by swinging their signs.

A thickly bearded man points at Wonderwoman and yells, "That's private property! You touch it again and I'll exercise my right to defend myself!"

New Bob sees this and points his bullhorn at their direction. "Wait, brother, wait. I don't want these people to get the wrong idea about us. We are not about violence. Violence and the evil it seeds is the last resort of a desperate minority. So I want you all to know that I wouldn't kill a faggot," new Bob yells at the crowd, "but I don't have to save one either!"

I know this shouting match will accomplish nothing because these fuckers only comprehend the kind of motivational violence baboons use to establish social order: teeth gnashing; extremist posturing; loud noises; and the occasional abortion clinic bombing. There is more pushing, mostly unintended because of the surge of people who are ignoring the unfolding melee and just trying to pass through the narrow corner to get a drink. Something is thrown, followed by a random shove, and then a fist. A corner pocket of violence erupts within the larger mayhem in the Quarter.

Rio gets excited and grabs me by my shirt sleeve. "Holy Shit! I wish I had my sword!" she yells. "LET'S GO GET SOME!"

I brush her aside and take a drink from the canteen.

The fighting goes on without Rio's contribution. Mounted police rush in and square off the corner. A large part of the street opens up. The NOPD separates everyone and makes arrests. Nobody messes with the horses until Supergirl punches a horse in the ass and runs into the Mango Mango pizza shop to evade arrest.

The horse and officer give chase and duck into the restaurant's open doors. Patrons inside scramble out with paper plates of pizza flying from their hands and total disbelief in their eyes. Supergirl looks terrified as the cop deftly manuevers the beast's girth in such a small space to pound him against the counter top several times until he screams with pain and apology.

Rio is stunned. "*THAT* WAS AWESOME."

"*That,*" I say, "is aggravated battery. Horses are people too goddamnit! Especially around here. Even I know better than to fuck with a horse. They should handle this breed of trouble makers old school and charge at them all with long spears and bayonets."

Rio is still awed by the scrum. Her big blue Valkyrie eyes are wet with tears of joy. She seems to be talking aloud in slow motion. "You think they'll let me ride that beautiful horse?" she asks.

The brick façade of the building behind her stretches up and bends down, ready to swallow her up. My feet are frozen and I sink into the street. Dizzy, hot and afraid.

"Why are we so far down from O'Briens? What are we doing here?" I ask.

She points behind me. My associates are gathered a few blocks down from us off Bourbon Street at a storefront entrance. They are yelling at something hanging on the wall above their heads.

I can't make it out. "What kind of animal is that?"

Rio laughs. "Are you that drunk?"

"I don't know..."

It is Roberto, and he is climbing the Two Dragons Oriental Spa's steel window mesh storefront. The lunatic is grabbing and pulling at it and rattling the cage. My associates are trying to talk him down. He rang the doorbell but was turned away once the establishment's proprietress saw he was uncontrollably rabid, horny, and drunk.

"That's not good," I say as I hear him bark and yelp like a crazed dog. "Someone should call the police before he gets into that place and harms those poor Asian girls."

Seth tries to grab his foot but pulls his shoe off instead. He yells, "Get down from there before you get arrested!"

Roberto spits out slurred gibberish and laughs.

Lenny picks the shoe off the ground and fires it at him. It misses and seems to drive Roberto into even more frenzied pulling and yelling. Lenny picks up the shoe and fires off another shot. *What in God's name has gotten into him,* I think, *and why are my feet sinking into the street?* The asphalt is definitely changing into tar, breaking down into its base, soft, gooey elements and swallowing me into black, smelly quicksand.

"You guys really shouldn't have drank that shit." Rio is shrinking from view. The bricks behind her grow into a massive shadow and I can barely make out her face inside the darkness.

"What stuff?" I ask.

"Your canteen cocktail," she replies.

"Wh- what the hell are you talking about?"

She pulls at the canteen around my neck to make her point and takes it in her hand. "Ugh...it smells horrible," she says and lets it go. I look at an empty cup in my hand I've been using to siphon off shots from the canteen. The liquid is milky.

The brain pops and sizzles. Gray matter braises within the alcohol juiced confines of my skull. Smoke is rising. My head fills with warmth and questions. I can taste the drink in my throat.

In the Philippines there is a drink made from coconut sap, local botanicals and herbs, but it is very temperamental and must be consumed only in the morning when it's still young because by the afternoon it will turn from clear to white and will make you violent, drunk, hungry, and blind. On one of Roberto's annual visits to his Motherland, he drank it while it was still in its infancy and the end result was a sad moment where the village drunkards fed him someone's dog. *Lycanthropy no doubt. The organic properties of this mystery drink have triggered something in his brain and the dog has come back to haunt him.* Poor bastard. Unless he's leashed and muzzled, he'll be wrangled by animal control and shipped off to the ASPCA to be euthanized. Otherwise the cops might snare him and he'll end up in a dirt pit in the bayou, forced to fight other dogs to the death. Either way it will be a sad and barbaric end.

I stare at the cup and watch the liquid slosh around in my hand. "Where did--"

Rio yells, "Don't hurt him Lenny!"

Lenny takes off his beads and fashions the bunch together as a crude horsewhip. He swings them at Roberto. "Get down here, you crazy fucker!"

"Get down before they call the cops!" Seth yells.

The heat from the drink is searing my brain and a cold sweat breaks over my body. I lunge for the light post to hold me up. "FORGET THE POLICE!" I scream. "WE NEED A PRIEST! THAT GODDAMN DOG IS NOT GOING TO EXORCISE ITSELF!"

Everyone stops and stares at me. I am wobbly and sporting a glorious wreath of nausea atop my head. They seem unconcerned by the toxic cloud of alcohol forming above me and turn their attention back on

Roberto. I unwind the canteen from my neck and drop it to the ground. The Quarter is breathing and I try to wrap my mind around the controlled riot taking place one block over between the horse police, the Gay Superhero League, and New Bob's apostles. I can hear it all, the late night free for all, sirens and yelling and bullhorns and mayhem. I am standing and riding the waves of cement as the street inhales and exhales. The French Quarter is tired of us all.

"HOLY SHIT!" I shout. "FORGET THAT DERANGED SAVAGE, YOU IDIOTS! CAN'T YOU SEE? THIS FUCKER'S ALIVE!"

Rio looks perfectly happy surfing the earthquake with her Styrofoam Hurricane and watches the drunks save the drunk. I struggle to stay upright and push against the canteen to right my balance. The street shakes and shudders. Legs wobble and give out. Marionette strings snap and I collapse into the pavement.

I am on hands and knees feeling for something familiar on the street. I grab onto the curb and drool. "Somebody call a priest." The city's heart pumps wildly. "WE NEED A FUCKING PRIEST I TELL YOU!" The pavement buckles and pops. I dig my nails into the ground and wait for the eruption, "Oh Lord...We need a priest..." Cold sweat. My head reels backwards. The body twists itself into odd involuntary shapes. Paralysis spreads. Legs freeze. Abdominal muscles go tight. The face contorts itself into an open mouth retch. My jaw is stiff until...release: the Po Boy, the jambalaya, the beer, the cheeseburgers, fries, vodka, bourbons, whiskey, tequilas and if the Lord has any mercy...the canteen cocktail. My arms and legs go numb.

"AWW GROSS!" Rio shrieks. "That's a lot of puke! Are you okay?"

I shake my head. My stomach is deflated and I am dizzy.

"Wow...that stuff jumped on top of you!" She examines the canteen from a distance and kicks it aside like an unexploded land mine. Canteen cocktail pours into the street. The cracked pavement laps up the spilled drink and mess. "Do you need something?"

I nod weakly. It's hard to breathe and I feel chunks of potato in my nose.

"Well let's go to that bar across the street. Here." She throws cocktail napkins at me. "You left some on your chin."

I nod again and wipe myself down before she helps me up. "You're an angel," I groan.

"Don't breathe on me."

The bar is forgettable. After some bad drinking they all seem the same in the Quarter. I remember talking to Seth before coming here. He was drunk and getting antsy just standing outside the Oriental Spa waiting for Roberto to stop howling at the moon. We looked on as Lenny continued to throw shoes at him.

"Just one more weirdo in the Quarter," Seth said. He reached into his pocket to get a cigarette. The box was empty. He turned to Rio. "You have a cigarette?"

"No," she said.

"I'm gonna go around the corner with Corrine to get cigarettes," he said. "We gotta leave before the cops show up."

"I like your thinking," I mumbled. My legs were still burning from the heave and had given out on me. Rio was holding me up by the belt loops on my jeans. "But is it wise to leave this man behind?"

"He'll be fine once the cops dart him."

"Damn fascists," I said. "Can't they see he's in the throes of something beyond their provincial understanding?"

"They might show him mercy," Seth replied, "but you shouldn't mess with the hookers around here. They'll gas him for sure."

I sighed. "Maybe it's all for the best. This place already has too many werewolves."

"I'll meet you at that bar."

I made a sign of the cross and gave him my blessing. "Go with God."

"You're an idiot," Seth said before he and Corrine wandered off into Bourbon Street with their arms around each other's waists.

The bar has a one drink minimum. And although I really don't feel the need to put myself in further jeopardy since all I wanted to do was wash my face in the bathroom, a drink had to be bought, so I order the usual to restore my head to the familiar. It does not go down easily.

Roberto was finally persuaded to come down off the fence when Aaron promised to take him to the closest strip club they could find. I stare at my glass, my head getting heavier and being drawn down onto the sticky table. Lenny is eating chicken fingers and hot sauce, and the sour, vinegar smell from the bottle makes me dizzy. The glass of vodka looks daunting and too big to finish so I put my head down and stare at it, hoping it will somehow drink itself.

"He can't sleep here," the waitress says to the table.

Rio looks at the waitress and raises a finger at her face. "He's not sleeping," she says, "he's just resting."

"His eyes are closed. That tells me he's asleep," she says.

"His eyes aren't closed goddamnit he's just Asian! Are you a fucking racist? Is this what our goddamned country is coming too? You people better get your shit together because we're all in this together!"

The waitress says nothing.

Rio sneers at her. "Who are you gonna believe, lady?!"

She is stunned and backs away from the table.

Rio growls, "Yeah, just back off!"

The waitress lingers for a moment, unsure of what to do.

Rio glares at her and shakes a chicken finger in her fist. "I'm not looking for a reason."

The waitress takes the check and places it on the table across from us and walks away.

"What's her problem?" Rio says. "We bought the drink minimum. We should be able to sit in peace."

I manage to lift my head. "Forget her. This place is a dump anyway. I'm leaving."

Lenny asks, "Where are you going?"

"Back to the hotel. I've had enough of this place. I spend good money here and support the local economy so I can have a license to throw up in the street and pass out at these fine establishments and this is the thanks I get?" I smack my hand against the table.

"STOP... jackass," Lenny says. "I'll walk you back to the hotel. Just let me finish my--"

"I don't need your help. I could find my way around this town blindfolded."

"Fine by me," Lenny says.

I stumble off the bar stool and almost face plant into the floor. I reconsider his offer. "Duly noted."

We leave Rio at the bar to wait for Seth and Corrine. The waitress is already intimidated and has left us alone. No telling what nightmarish behavior Rio will display towards the woman if she continues to antagonize her. I'm surprised how tolerant Rio was with her, but that sort of impolite banter could be deceptive. Rio might have already decided in her own mind that the opportunity for rational talk was over and is just waiting for the right moment to grab a pool stick from the corner wall and swing the blunt end like a battle ax into the waitress' face to emphasize the point.

I carry my drink from the bar. It is still a full glass and would be a waste to let it turn warm.

Lenny walks me through the Quarter while I protect my drink from the jostling crowd. It is almost three o'clock but the streets are still thick with people. The hotel is quiet and cool. Red candles burn in the lobby windows. While we wait for the elevator I hear laughter and voices creeping out from the courtyard and through the hallway's French doors. I feel like joining them, whoever they are, but reconsider and set my drink on a table next to the elevators.

"Don't do that," Lenny says, "it'll leave a watermark."

I pick up the glass and set it on the floor. When the elevator arrives, I bend down to pick up the glass. The Earth moves. I drop face down against the ground.

Lenny laughs and tries to help me up. "Forget the drink," he says.

"No," I reply and prop myself up to reach for the glass.

He lets me go and reaches for the elevator to hold the doors open. "Would you forget the fucking drink?" he says.

"I almost got it."

"I'll kick it over."

"Don't do it," I plead.

It's within my reach.

Lenny grins and nudges the glass further and further away from me with his foot.

I try to grab his leg. "No, don't you dare do it---"

Lenny shrugs his shoulders and kicks the glass over.

"AHHHHHHH! YOU GAWDDAMN SAVAGE!" I scream. "I'LL EAT YOUR FUCKING LIVER FOR THAT!" I scramble to grab the glass as it rolls across the floor. Absolut is pouring out and the ice cubes drop one by one. The carpet drinks up the vodka. I touch it and put wet fingers to my lips. "What kind of horrible monster are you?!" I moan. "You'll pay for this..."

Lennys says, "Man, you really need some help," and pushes me into the elevator from behind with his foot. I am not moving fast enough so he kicks me in the ass hard. "Get in there, you sorry bastard."

The laughter from the courtyard stops and the elevator doors close.

SUNDAY

<u>Chapter One</u>

Sometimes when you open your eyes to meet a Sunday it is best to keep them closed until your Saturday stops moving. There is some faint light in the room coming from the building across the street. I am moribund and my skin feels gray. I blink slowly for a moment, fix my eyes on eternity and am prepared to die in this bed. The ceiling is leaning to the left and snapping back in swirls of light and shadow.

I close my eyes. *"That is not good,"* a voice says. *"Still drunk...you are still drunk..."* In the darkness I feel the mattress make slow but graceful twirls across the hotel floor. My deathbed is a coffin slipping carelessly on ice. A funeral on ice. A jazz funeral on ice. Finally, *me on the rocks... the vodka drinking me.* I picture it clearly in my mind. Open casket. My cohorts dressed in all their finery. They tug me across an ice rink with a Zamboni and purple, yellow and green beaded ropes at the Superdome while Louis Armstrong sings "What a Wonderful World." Giant Styrofoam crayfish, oysters, grenades, and multi-colored parrots twirl in rings like a dance at the Ice-Capades. Strippers follow, pulling off their clothing bit by frilly bit and leaving wafty trails of glittered jasmine and baby oil in their wake. Bob Whittaker and his rotten ilk are chanting, proselytizing and condemning me from the penalty box. A spotlight. Seth stands at center ice. The crowd goes hush. He gives an abrupt but touching eulogy, his voice echoing throughout the dome:

"The stupid bastard lived well and died horribly. Now he's the Lord's problem. Who needs a drink?"

They Zamboni my coffin down Canal Street with a jazz band playing, "When the Saints Go Marching In." The New Orleans Department of Streets and Sanitation Ballet Company hoses down the ice--- a symbolic gesture to cleanse my sins. I have a place at St. Louis Cemetery No. 1 where The Voodoo Queen, Marie Laveau lies, and am ready to haunt the French Quarter; another restless spirit but without the mortal coil. Or maybe I could be put on display at The Presbytere in Jackson Square, preserved in alcohol and paraded as a float at Mardi Gras. My hangover-death would become an annual celebration, reenacted at passion plays by unapologetic Bacchanalians drinking Imbecile-sized vodkas. They would throw beads and doubloons at my corpse to pay the Boatman before I am ferried across the Mississippi River to the boisterous tunes of the Natchez' sweet wail. That's all a funeral procession is when you really think about it. Your final parade. A chance for people to toss throws at *you.*

"Hmm...all things considered, would it be so bad if you just gave up the ghost?" the voice suggests. *"Just give up..."*

The thought barely finishes festering within my brain's dizzied cracks when the room shakes, and the bed turns upside down violently. I am on the hard floor in my underwear and slowly crawling on hands and knees in the dark towards the oasis of the bathroom's cool tile; crawling over clothes, shoes, crushed plastic cups, paper bags, empty beer cans, liquor bottles, and beads.

Beads?

"OH LORD!" I scream. "WHERE THE HELL AM I?"

I am terrified. Am I really in my hotel room? Or am I really on Bourbon Street, lying in filth and crawling over mounds of garbage: naked, lost...confused; booze-addled and trapped in this semi-hallucinated state of denial and totally convinced I made it home last night. A pillow case is stuck to the back of my head. It is soft and bulky and can only belong to The W. I have bled from the take down with the crazy Asian woman from the restaurant and the pillow case is stuck to my hair. *Ignore it*, the voice says, *you have more urgent matters to attend to than a mortal head wound.* I struggle to push aside the sliding glass door to the bathroom but eventually press on with the crawl. Tectonic plates continue a horizontal slide across the Earth's crust. The room shakes. The toilet looks sideways. New Orleans has been thrust into zero gravity overnight and I will have to vomit upside down if I am to keep things civil, clean and orderly. Warm thick saliva fills the insides of my mouth. My stomach is a fist, ready to unleash itself on the floor along with a few feet of small intestine. My face goes cold. The toilet is within arms length, resentful and hissing. "DON'T START WITH ME, YOU FU-HU-CKING BEAST!" I gasp and take a deep swallow of hot saliva pooling in my mouth. My chest seizes up. Vomit flies onto the mossy colored floor. It is a dark and bloody sight. *Oh sweet Jesus, your insides are finally coming out.* Pain is in command. Muscles go stiff. A shudder. A spasm. Empty heaves. My heart stops racing, my eyes stop watering, and my lungs stop burning. Those are not my organs but a digested Hurricane lay spilled upon the floor.

The tile is cold and wet against my face. The Earth has stopped quaking and it is quiet. I smile in all my dizziness. There is always a strange calm following the gastric violence of a good purge. I give up the fight to get off the ground, sleep on a towel on the floor, and dream about a carnival on a boardwalk near the ocean.

I am standing on a garbage mountain at the foot of a giant Ferris wheel near the ocean. People from the Carnival begin to gather at the mountain's foot. I walk down and follow, watching them shuffle away and towards the water. There are five Buddhist monks dressed in red and yellow robes. They are grabbing people from the crowd, placing hands on strangers' heads and shaking them vigorously. It gives me the fear, so I hide behind the people looking on and try my best to blend into the crowd. A monk stops. He looks towards my direction and drives himself forward, pushing and shoving his way at me. He grabs my head, makes me kneel and says something I don't understand. He shakes my head violently, helps me to my feet, and walks back into the crowd.

"That'sss it?" Lenny slurs as he clings to the bathroom doorway.

"Well yes. I don't know. But I better wake up from this goddamn nightmare pretty fucking soon."

He is adorned with beads and drunk and wearing a Jester's hat. He has just come in and is clutching a 24 ounce Miller Lite Tall Boy in a brown paper bag close to his chest in one hand and something else in the other. His lips and face are covered with white powder.

"You've finally done it haven't you?" I say.

His eyes roll around his head. "What?"

"Rio has dragged you down and you couldn't help but do a face plant into the yayo."

"What the fuck are you talking about?" Lenny catches a glimpse of himself in the mirror and shakes an oily white bag at my face. "They're beignets you moron."

"Oh..."

He tries swatting at the cap 'n bells orbiting his head. "Jeezus Christ." He laughs. "Where did I get this hat?"

There is a moment of quiet followed by Lenny tearing at the beignets through the white bag. Fried dough and powdered sugar is wafting through the air and my aching belly has a strong urge to head to Café

DuMonde for coffee and doughnuts. I stare at the bathroom lights from the floor.

"Want a beer?" he asks.

"You're a horrible person. No."

He flashes an unopened pint of Absolut at me.

"AH! My hero!"

He shakes the bottle. "I'm sorry for kicking your drink over."

"No you're not."

"Ha! No I'm not."

"Well I'm sorry for threatening to eat your liver."

"No you're not."

"No I'm not."

"Well I'm going to drink these beers on the patio and go to sleep," he says and vanishes into the room with the bells jingling.

"What time is it?" I ask.

His voice trails into the room. I think I hear him say four-thirty.

I pick myself off the floor and grab one of the green bathrobes hanging on the door. The televsion is on CNN and the volume is turned way up. I look for the remote control but can't find it with all the crap on the floor.

"Goddamnit! Why is this fucking thing always on?" I search the screen with my hands looking for a button to turn it off. The director of Homeland Security is on the television explaining to the American public how duct tape can be used to protect your home in the event of a poisonous gas attack. "This fucking thing is always on!" I scream and slam the set against the back wall over and over again until the screen burps a flash of light and goes black.

Outside on the patio Lenny is smoking a cigarette and drinking his beers. I grab the bottle of Absolut off the desk table. It looks good for a few drinks or one really tall one and I make it to the patio without hurting myself on the junk spread all over the floor. After dropping me off, Lenny lost the others and went out for a nightcap and couldn't remember where the hotel was. Along the way he gave into his charity and passed out his blackjack winnings to strangers in the streets and a poor white girl from Canada who lost her way and stood crying at Bourbon and Canal looking for her friends.

"What the hell was all that noise?" Lenny asks.

I reply, "I think I killed the T.V."

"Eh…good riddance," he says.

I wave the Absolut bottle at him.

"No thanks," he replies.

"Thanks for this. Good Karma for you," I say and pour myself a glass.

"I need it." Lenny shakes his head and the bells jingle. "I feel like crap. I've got thisss film all over my skin. It jusss gets thicker and dirtier each day I'm here."

"Huh?"

"You know...that sssmell?" He sniffs his arm. "That French Quarter funk. Jeezus Christ you're a messsss...Look...look at you. You're sssspilling your drink."

"What?"

Lenny shakes his head. The bells jingle. He looks around. "Whatsss that fucking noizze?" he asks.

"Nothing. You're hearing things."

"Are you shurrre?"

"Positive."

There is silence. Lenny rolls his eyes up and back. "Quit fucking around...There it isss again."

"So you're a little dirty. It's Mardi Gras and we're in New Orleans." I lick the vodka off of my hand. "You'll probably have to burn all of your clothes when you get back home...you know...just to be safe."

He lights a cigarette. "I think I need to ssstop drinking for awhile."

"That's unfortunate. But this isn't an after school special."

Lenny thinks about it and opens up the second can. "I guessss I can worry about all that later."

"Absolutely. There's always later."

He leans back in his chair and feels the Jester on his head. "Hey...where'd I get this hat?"

I admire his willingness to soldier on through this debauched endeavor we find ourselves in. But I know what he's thinking. It's an underlying fear of the tipping point where such blind obedience to the booze robs you of common sense and you can no longer help yourself. Perhaps we've already passed the point and just don't appreciate it.

After my drink I crawl into the shower and turn the hot water temperature up very high. It is the only cure I can fathom to clear my head and wash the smoke, sweat, and alcohol from my skin. The cut on my head is scabbed over but some other physical ailment has surfaced. The inside corner of my left eye is darker than the other. It is a bloody red. The

346

delicate capillaries have burst and the darkness is spreading beyond the whites in my eye. *What does that mean? Too much pressure from the vomiting or the pounding headaches in my brain? Is the vodka forcing the blood from my head? Or maybe this is the beginning of a more sinister deficiency.* Vitamin C is needed in my diet. Perhaps I will eat the limes bartenders keep pushing on me with my drinks.

I put on my jeans, grab a clean shirt and a pull over. Lenny's powdery mess of beignet spread all over the carpet has inspired me to head to Café Du Monde for a coffee and breakfast.

There's no one out on Chartres. Two blocks before Jackson Square, a mime dressed in a thin black suit and flaming red bowtie stands on a soapbox. He has horns on his forehead and a black bowler hat held upside down in one hand. I stare at him for a moment.

"Why doesn't this surprise me?"

I walk up to him.

His big, black, glossy eyes are focused on the horizon towards the waterfront.

"Don't you ever sleep?" I reach into my back pocket and drop a few bucks into his hat. "A little sympathy for you...get some rest. You'll be busy for the next forty days."

He grins a twisted bridge of yellow teeth at me and tips the hat onto his head.

I shudder.

His rotten jaw opens wide and awful to pantomime exaggerated laughter and applause.

"Cut that out," I say. "This is your fault. Can't your devils stop pestering me?" I turn around and wobble down the street to the cafe and cross the square next to the Cathedral.

The sky is becoming light. In the distance a soft yellow glow sneaks out from underneath Café Du Monde's green and white awning. The Vietnamese servers straighten their paper hats and uniforms and wipe down tables in anticipation of the morning surge. It's almost five-thirty and the café is busy with early birds and noisy drunks. I get three beignets and a medium coffee to go. The peace and quiet of the riverfront is a good place to get my bearings. I can find an uninhabited bench and watch giant ships go by. A long freight train snakes its way along the river and blocks the water. It is going east and seems endless so I walk west along the tracks and towards the Aquarium. There is a statue by the river far from the café commissioned by Drago and Klara Cvhanovich in 1964. It is one statue with two faces. On its river face is a woman dressed in a long robe with a raised arm calling out to the Mississippi's open waters. She is a gatekeeper. On the opposite side of the monument and facing the French Quarter is an immigrant family. They stand huddled and reluctant at the land before them. The inscription at their feet reads:

Dedicated to the courageous Men and Women who left their home seeking freedom and opportunity and a better life in a new country.

I sit on a park bench and wait out the train crossing. The bench is cluttered with a motley assortment of beads, doubloons, plastic cups, bottles and beer cans. I clear a spot and sip the hot coffee.

After another five minutes the railroad clears and to my unhappy pain the horizon is blooming with the eager sway of giant crosses and signs. Bob Whittaker is across the tracks. His flock of parrots are holding a prayer breakfast on the riverfront and he is standing on a bench and lording over them.

Bob cries out through his bullhorn. "It *does* matter who you are and what you do to prove your commitment to Jesus. You must prove your worth in order to gain the salvation and paradise promised through Jesus Christ the Lord because God is coming. Oh, yes he's coming...and he does *not* love everyone! Who told you that lie? The media? The Pope?" Bob

takes a sign from the crowd and brandishes it at them. "To those who say

God loves everyone I say to you, 'Where was your God on that day?!'

Where was he?"

The parrots flap with applause.

Bob continues. "If God really loved everyone why would he

abandon this country at a desperate hour? Why? I'll tell you why...because

September 11th was the beginning. It's your wake up call to take this

country back from those who would keep this a godless nation. God

doesn't hesitate to send death and tragedy to right a wicked people. The

Bible tells us he sent godless people to kill his 'chosen people'. What

makes you so special? What makes you think he wouldn't send godless

people to kill us and make his point? If he must use this false god and these

rag heads to do it, he will. The gathering of false religions against America

is God's judgment upon a wayward people. This is the price we pay for

allowing this country to ignore and repudiate God. We let the ACLU and

the federal government throw God out of our schools. And God is angry!

We let abortionists kill babies. And God is angry! We let faggots and

lesbians and pagans secularize America. And God is angry! Mark my

words...God will continue to tear down the wall of his protection and allow

Satan and America's enemies to give us what we deserve unless you distinguish yourself from his enemies. Unless we fight to return our country to its rightful place as a Christian nation. The armies are amassing at Armageddon...which side are you on? The Tribulations are upon us, and I ask you again: what will you do to identify yourself as worthy of his protection and his salvation? Which side are you on?"

Someone shouts, "We're with you, Bob!"

"Thank you, sister...I know you are." He reaches down into the crowd to touch a woman's raised hands. "But if you're with me, you need to show God what you believe and march through these sinners and fornicators and idolaters and show them by any means necessary that we will *not* let them destroy our country."

A voice shouts, "I DIDN'T SEE MOHAMMED ON THE MAYFLOWER!"

"That's right." Bob sneers. "I'm not above exacting some vengeance against those who would harm my soul. And I'm not above using my hate against those who sin against my God. So...I say...I say to you...if you're with me..."

"WE'RE WITH YOU, BROTHER BOB!"

Bob gets down on one knee and aims the bullhorn at his legion. His voice goes low. He delivers a hushed plea, "...if you're with me...then join me now..." the voice grows stronger, louder, "...and we will take back this land and this world in His name..." Bob rises to his feet, "...one parish at a time...one city at a time...one state at a time...and ONE NATION AT A TIME!"

The parrots are inflamed. They are spoiling for the fight. Ready to crush the world with their charge. They pump their crosses and signs at each other.

Bob stabs his red fists and bullhorn into the air and delivers a battle cry to stir their hearts: "CHRISTIAN RULE!" he shouts to the field of crosses. "CHRISTIAN RULE WITH VICTORY!"

They sing it back to Bob:

"CHRISTIAN RULE WITH VICTORY!"

"CHRISTIAN RULE WITH VICTORY!"

I need to leave New Orleans.

I need to be in a different climate, one of familiarity and deliverance. I am sick of drinking, and sick of Bob, and sick of his hell-bent prescription to cure the sick with tribal theology. Years before he prayed for some horrible event to bring us out from our secular existence and into the light of his rancorous judgment. Prayed the type of prayers he knew God answered when queers and dopers got AIDS. Bob's long hoped for day of reckoning has arrived. His cacophonous fire brand is finally relevant and makes sense because the Anti-Christ is hiding in a cave somewhere on the border between Afghanistan and Pakistan. War, Famine, Death and Pestilence will ravage the planet. Insecurity and religious war will breathe life into his murderous Deity. And the parrots will believe him because they are lost and frightened about what the world has become and Bob looks prophetic, infallible and comforting with a vengeful God and terrorists driving them towards a personal salvation. They will continue to pray for nothing less than bad times for us all, for New Orleans to be made an example of, to be plunged into darkness, ravaged with locusts and frogs, and for the Angel of Death to kill its first born sons.

I get up from the bench. Plastic cups and beer bottles surround my feet. I kick a few beer bottles over until I nudge one that doesn't move. The sound of its full and tight virginity is familiar to me. It is a sick and uncontrollable impulse, this thing of mine. I am outside my body, watching me pick up this unopened 12 ounce bottle of Miller Lite sitting on the ground next to me. It is not my beer, but here I am reaching for it, reaching for it and not sure what I am going to do with it once I feel the cold weight of it slushy and heavy in my hand. I raise it up and twist the top to watch the beer spread itself over the rim with giggly white and gold pearls. It smells sweet and tart in the cool morning air. I close my eyes and breathe it in.

There is an odd silence.

Bob has stopped yelling.

Gasps and a fearful hush fall upon the parrots. Bob can barely raise his head to look around. He is red faced.

Foamy.

Rabid.

Bleeding.

The bottle is no longer in my hand.

The bottle is no longer in my hand because I have thrown it at Bob from across the tracks. On any other occasion I would have drunk that delicious goddamned beer.

The parrots shuffle towards Bob to see if he's alright.

"FUCKING IDIOTS!" I yell. "HE'S THE ASSHOLE WHO'S KILLING JESUS!"

Blood seeps through Bob's fingers. He shoves a woman trying to towel the dark red split on his mouth. His black squint grows hot with tears and red when he sees me.

I creep backwards.

The communal bewilderment is gone and the parrots are bloodthirsty.

Someone shouts, "GET THAT SON OF A BITCH!"

There is a low roar.

I stumble over a garbage bag lying open on the grass, get up, and run. Brother Bob's army scatters to cross the tracks.

Across Jackson Square is the Cathedral. Cutting through is dangerous. The Square has bad karma. It was a military courtyard a long time ago and a place for public executions for a time before that. I disregard the bad history, run straight through to the Cathedral and in remembering my Victor Hugo yell frantically, "SANCTUARY! SANCTUARY!! SANCTUARY!!!"

The doors are locked.

I pull at them and look over my shoulder, *Figures…that hasn't worked since the 15th Century.*

I dart to the right. Fear and adrenaline fuel my alcohol impaired body to an apex of physical endurance rarely experienced after such a nightmarish bout of drinking. The Quarter will be my defense. I'll lead these humorless bastards on an absurd hunt through a labyrinth of strip clubs, gay bars and sex shops. Northeast is a good direction, it's quiet, and everything looks the same, easy to lose them, there, I think. Or get lost yourself. I can run and hide in a cemetery but might be trapped within those high walls. If they catch me they can easily dispose of the body and double bury it in some ancient mausoleum no one ever visits. Head back to the hotel? No. I passed Chartres blocks ago and the streets are thick with parrots. *They are everywhere.* Stick to the big streets and you'll make sense of your dilemma and get your bearings.

The high arched entrance to Louis Armstrong Park is in the distance.

A man is pointing furiously and running at me from Rampart. "HE'S HERE!"

"Monster!" I turn around and run. "You'll stay away from me if you know what's good for you!"

Go down. Go down Bourbon Street.

I get close to Lafitte's Blacksmith Shop and stop.

The man from Rampart has caught up with me. "HE'S HERE!"

I grab two plastic, neon red half yard glasses from the garbage covered ground. Their long necks and fat bulbous ends make for excellent flanged maces in a bind. "GET BACK FREAK!"

He steps aside at first but tries to corner me.

I hit him with the fat sloshy end.

He is stunned.

I hit him again.

The cheap plastic explodes on his head. Gastric napalm spreads into the air. It lands and sticks everywhere.

The man stops to consider what has just happened to the both of us. He whimpers, "What the hell is this?" and breathes in the fumes.

A shared gag.

"OH GOD....IS--IS THIS---?"

Someone's bad Mardi Gras vomit just rained regurgitated pink and yellow chunks all over us. Ghastly odors fill the street.

"OH GOD!" I scream. "GAH! THAT'S AWFUL!"

He cringes from the smell and covers himself up.

My favorite pullover is a mess.

I club him with the other half yard glass. "FUCK! SEE WHAT YOU MADE ME DO ASSHOLE! NOTHING GETS OUT BILE!" I drop the glasses and scream mad obscenities and run back towards the river. It's expansive and vast. I can keep running until my body gives up.

Close to the Cathedral is a taxi. It drifts like a ghost through the streets. It looks like a converted hearse from the fifties; somber, black, heavy and long. It sloshes around, a big manta ray of death and deliverance, slow and graceful with long, sharp tail fins. The white painted stenciling on the car's door reads:

"J. WALKER CAROLAN'S LIVERY SERVICES, LTD. SERVING THE GREATER NEW ORLEANS AREA AND OUTLYING PARISH. EST. 1999"

I wave until the car pulls up. The window slides down and a middle aged black man smoking a cheroot cigar gives me the once over.

I can barely breathe and lean against the doorframe with my hands.

"J. Walker Carolan?"

"No," he replies. He looks over his shoulder and past me. He says dryly, "You got troubles."

"Apparently. How much to the airport?" I ask.

"Twenty-four bucks."

"Fine." I pull on the door handle. The door is locked.

"You ain't got no bags or anything?"

"No." I pull on the door handle again.

"You got puke on you."

"Yes I know. It's not mine." I take the sweater off and roll it into a ball.

Bob is getting closer.

"You got a ticket?"

"FOR GODSSAKES MAN! OPEN THE DOOR AND JUST DRIVE THE FUCKING CAR!"

"Hmm..." He mumbles, "I don't like your attitude. Goddamned tourist." The window slides shut and the car lurches into gear.

I hold onto the driver's side mirror and plead, "I'LL GIVE YOU FORTY BUCKS! JUST PLEASE TAKE ME TO THE AIRPORT!"

He stops the car and speaks.

"What?!" I ask.

He rolls the window down and says calmly, "Fifty."

"OKAY, fifty."

"Deal." He says and unlocks the door. "Don't get no puke on my upholstery."

"I know. I know."

I jump into the backseat.

He opens his hand out. "Ahem."

I drop the money in his hand and he points to the seat belt.

"OH FOR GODSSAKE MAN JUST DRIVE!"

"Your funeral."

The hearse tears through the narrow streets. We pull further away and the roar and sight of the French Quarter fades from the rear window. Once past Canal I breathe deep and sink into the cool vinyl seat. I slide the window down to get some air. *"Seth and the others will do fine without me,"* I think as I throw my pullover out of the window and onto Poydras, *"My abandonment is a minor betrayal. All for the best really. It's only Sunday and they'll have plenty of good times without me. Besides, this place could use one less drunken tourist."*

Chapter Two

A man wearing a sandwich board is standing on the cement island

separating commercial traffic from the regular traffic at Louis Armstrong

New Orleans International Airport departure terminal. The sign reads:

"'Walk while ye have the light, lest darkness come upon you'---1 John, 1."

No time like the present, I think to myself. The air is thickening

with menace. A tragic uncertainty hangs over the soul of this city. A place

like this suffers willingly for other people's sins and the world needs New

Orleans to eat our sins at a time like this. The misanthropes and Bad

Timers have crept into the Bohemian realm and it is no longer a sanctuary

361

for me. It's time to split, until the world's weighty doldrums begin to sink in once again and renew my contempt for seriousness, temperance, and the new, grotesque bureaucracies of American life: the metal detectors, xenophobia, terrorist alerts, and daily headlines filled with grim rumor and conjecture.

The local news over the car radio is reporting that the F.B.I. in conjunction with the Transportation Security Administration and highly informed experts are preparing a national threat assessment for the next five years.

I don't need government officialisms to assess the threat. I have seen the threat. Long dark days lie ahead. The forecast calls for high pressure anxiety and cold sweat panic over a yet unknown doom. *What next?* I think to myself, *and for how long must we endure these bastards dear Lord?* Things always get worse before they get better. People like Bob don't go away quietly. They linger to spread their disease. They hold witch trials, blow up abortion clinics, get television shows, write shitty books, publish newspapers and run for public office to influence and infect the fearful with lies. They drag everyone down into their medieval warrior cult and soon humanity is back in the dark ages and the Earth is flat. I suppose I can tolerate all of it if I can stay drunk until the New

Renaissance, but New Orleans has shown me, the veil wears thin. The anesthesia is finally beginning to burn off and a bad hangover is beginning to take hold, one to last for years. My mouth is dry and stale from the relentless drinking, and I am sick, rotten and spooked. Blood is circulating poorly in my veins and the aphids are burrowing themselves into my skin to do battle once again. No telling what havoc a pressurized cabin at 32,000 feet will unleash on my already dehydrated and alcohol impaired brain. I will have to self-medicate to lessen the suffering in my head before I set foot on the plane.

Flights leaving Louisiana are expensive on such short notice but I will pay just about any price to get the hell out. There is a 10:15 leaving New Orleans with a one hour layover in Birmingham, then onto Chicago and arriving at 2:30 in the afternoon at Midway. I have just enough left on my debit card for a one way to get me home and order Chinese once I get back to the Northlands. Payday is Tuesday and I have some loose cash and comps I can muster if I need some good cheer from the winter boredom.

The lines at the security checkpoint are long and I am more than obliged to walk naked through the metal detectors as long as it will speed along the process and allow me to sit and rest. After passing through with my driver's license and ticket, I am asked to take my shoes off and have them inspected by hand, but after seeing the muck lodged inside their crevices security sends me on my way without a hassle.

I feel better once I'm past the checkpoint and sitting on a stool at The Live Oaks Bar in Terminal B. No way those religious fundamentalists will be allowed to get in here even if they know where to find me. The NTSA and Louisiana National Guard will make damn sure of that. They'll be shot dead as soon as they set foot in the place. The Feds aren't going to tolerate any nonsense around airports.

I order a morning cordial and read a complimentary Sunday paper to pass the time. The front page has a national story about a need to increase defense spending at home and abroad and the possible activation of more National Guard units to be deployed for the war effort. Locally there was a bomb threat made against an unfinished mosque nobody paid much attention to until some irate neighbors complained about it going up in their backyard. Behind my back at the metal detectors is a red sign with white lettering hovering above a heavily armed soldier's head. It reads:

"SECURITY IS NOT A LAUGHING MATTER. ALL JOKES ARE TAKEN VERY SERIOUSLY."

The joke is on us. Me, Brother Bob, and the parrots. We've been driven mad with the fear and it's feeding the suspicion and hate we keep buried with our history in order to begrudgingly live with one another's freedom and not destroy the seemingly incompatible patch worked fabric of what we think this country is about.

There is a small article about the Louisiana Derby. After reading it, a visit to Louisville and Churchill Downs on the first weekend in May seems more than certain in my mind. It will give me something to look forward to, and get me through the winter and the two annual events preceding a hot Chicago summer: St. Patrick's Day in March and Opening Day at Comiskey in April. Those rituals tease and excite the soul but will no doubt have to be celebrated and endured in the cold as they are every year. No. Kentucky in May will have to be it for now. It is something to dream about and plan for. I'll take another few days off from work and reunite with the coven of drinkers in the warmth and in grand Southern fashion.

The flight to Chicago is surprisingly full and boards at 9:50. It is open seating and although I sit in the back to avoid any large groups of people traveling together, I still end up stuck in a section overrun by a few drunks who have continued to drink and collect beads throughout the night and into the morning. There is a row close to the bathroom. It seems inconspicuous enough. A heavy black woman is sitting next to the window and the other two seats are empty. I take the seat on the aisle and sink into my place with a full vodka glass I've carried from the bar. At around 10:25 we are still on the ground and I am lightly sauced. We wait for a few passengers who are held up by the long lines and security checks. When they finally board the plane, a good old boy with a bag too big to fit in the overhead bin or underneath the seat meanders all the way to the back and gives me his best smile.

He asks, "Anyone sittin there?"

I groan, "No."

"Mind if I sit in the aisle? I've got this bag..." He has a lazy eye and reeks of beer and cigarettes and I have the feeling he is one of those people you meet who are incessant talkers on planes.

"Sorry, no. I've got a medical condition that requires me to be no more than ten feet away from the bathroom with no obstructions."

"Huh?"

"I've got a doctor's note."

"Oh, never mind then, my bad," he says. "Wouldn't want you to die on my account. I'll just squeeze on in the middle there if I can."

366

We sit on the ground for another forty minutes and are able to order drinks because of the wait. I try my best to tune out the people still celebrating their wild time in the Quarter and bite the plastic cup in my hand when the man nudges my shoulder. He is flicking a Bic lighter on and off against his boot and giving me a shit-eater's grin.

I sip the vodka and chew the ice. "You realize that sort of behavior doesn't fly anymore."

He puts the lighter away and says, "Yeah, lots of shit don't fly no more. 'Specially A-rabs." He laughs. He pushes aside the plastic cup a flight attendant has given him and drinks from his beer can. "Hayward Michaels."

I raise my glass at him. "Seth."

"Leavin so soon? It's not even Tuesday."

"Why would I care about that?"

"Mardi Gras, man."

I give him a puzzled look.

He is incredulous. "Fat Tuesday? Hurricanes? Drinking? Beads? Tits?"

"Oh...Carnival. I really don't have time for that kind of nonsense. I'm just passing through from Atlanta en route to Chicago."

"You from there?" he asks.

"Me? No, like I said, just passing through. I'm leaving the country. Atlanta, New Orleans, Chicago, Bhutan."

"Buhwhat?"

"Bhutan. The last Buddhist kingdom on the planet."

"Hmm..." He eyes me suspiciously. "You Buddhist, huh?"

"No. But I'm a firm believer in ahimsa"

He nods in confusion.

"Besides, it doesn't pay to be anything nowadays. No, I'll just sit on the fence and wait for the winner. Might as well wait it out in Bhutan right? Beautiful country out there. Bucolic. Expansive. Just me and the monks."

Now he seems even more confused about the direction of our conversation.

I swirl the ice and drink the Absolut.

"What's your excuse?" I say.

He asks, "Fer what?"

"Mardi Gras?"

"Can't. Gotta work. Construction. They got me workin a big park project in downtown Chicago. Figures I'd end up havin to go in the dead of winter."

I look out the window across the aisle from me at the mid-morning sun. The airfield is thick and green, and even though I am trapped in this flying, aluminum sausage breathing poisonous, recycled oxygen, I know beyond the window the air is soft and jasmine. "I hear the city is sinking," I say.

He asks, "Chicago?"

"No, New Orleans."

He nods and takes a long swig of beer. "It'll all just vanish one day."

I think about New Orleans and Mardi Gras and Lisa.

After she disappeared I took a shuttle bus to the airport and tried to sleep as it darted in and out of I-10's rush hour traffic. I held onto my roller bag. It rocked everytime the driver applied the breaks and the stop and go kept me awake until I thought about our last day in the Quarter and the beautiful lie that would no longer be there if I came back.

Lisa wanted to walk down Royal in a red dress she bought from a boutique on Magazine Street. And I wanted what she wanted. We held hands like real people and she pretended she was in love.

There was a gallery window with a large canvas of a sunflower field painted thick with oil colors that caught her eyes. A sleepy, white scottish terrier sat dutifully in the doorway warming himself in the sun.

Lisa squealed "Max!" and let my hand go to kneel down and play with the dog.

"Who?" I asked.

"Max," she said again. "He looks just like my puppy at home. Just scruffier."

The terrier rolled onto his back and Lisa scratched his belly.

"Aww...you're just like Max. So cute!"

The sunflowers in the window watched us like a hundred eyes. It broke my heart to see Lisa in her red dress petting that dog in the gallery's doorway. In New Orleans we lived audaciously. We had never lost anything. For the moment, her beauty was unblemished by the burden of consequences, but that was about to change. I felt like a thief for taking her away from the truth of what she meant to someone else and a liar for pretending it didn't matter.

On the shuttle I had the kind of rest people pray for when they tell you they would like to die in their sleep given the choice; to die in comfort and a place of dreams. When I woke there was a lush field of grass rushing past my eyes and for some unexplainable reason I thought I was dead and in my afterlife.

Just moments before I was dreaming of New Orleans.

In love.

In beauty.

Now I was dead and in heaven.

It was only after the shuttle bus hit a bump and I knocked my head against the window that I realized I was staring at the same field of grass I see now outside the airplane running along the winding road to the airport.

The green looks different on the other side of the airport's barbed wire fence and the vodka is going down fast.

Hayward cocks his head and shrugs. "You were saying?"

"The sinking," I reply, "...after that, the world won't be the same."

"No it won't," he says and sips on his beer. "Welcome to the new normal."

"I hear it gets pretty crazy here."

Hayward grins. "This town? You have no idea. You may fall in love with her but you'll never know her. Not really."

The flight attendant, an older woman, is handing out plastic pilot wings to some kids two rows up when, as a matter of routine and habit, I shake the empty cup of ice. She was mildly pleasant when I boarded the plane but the wait on the tarmac has worn on her. She is blonde and I imagine from her looks she has seen better days a lifetime ago when her future showed some promise after placing second in a local parishes' beauty pageant. Now she is stuck in a dangerous job and tired of being ordered around like a cocktail waitress by the troublemakers up front.

She huffs, "Would you like another drink?"

It is coincidental, but she's mistaken my cup shaking as a boorish demand to refill my glass.

"Would you like another drink?"

I consider her question and the harsh look about her face. She has judgmental eyes and maybe nothing is coincidental after you spend too much time in New Orleans. Maybe this irritable woman with her plastic wings is the Lord's herald, or maybe something more sinister. On the religious calendar we are on the verge of Lent; forty days and forty nights of fasting, sheer will power, abstinence and self-denial. The same forty-day sabbatical the Good Shepard took to fine tune his soul, strengthen his

mind, and protect his body against the temptations of the flesh the Devil

flaunted at him before he began a historic ministry. The moment seems

right. Make a choice. Be the good Catholic boy I was raised to be and

follow the rules for once. Deny the flesh and its extracurricular needs. No

meat on Friday. No booze for forty days. Go clean and give up the vice to

cleanse the body. Go to church every Sunday and on Good Friday. Go to

confession to cleanse the soul. Resist the temptation. Slow it down.

Meditate. Reconsider your life's direction on all its levels, and for forty

days let sobriety and the Good Lord take you to wherever it is you are

supposed to be.

"Sir?" The flight attendant picks up the napkin and empty cup.

I am lost in thought about the prospect of the renewal I will

experience after behaving myself for the next forty days.

The endless possibilities.

The predictable outcomes.

It is exciting and horrifying.

"SIR!"

"Yes?"

"Would you like another drink before take off?!"

I catch a glimpse of Hayward for a second. He is staring forward and trying his best not to laugh for some reason. I think he thinks it funny I am being pushed around by this mad woman with plastic wings. A tiny smirk creeps out from beyond the edge of his mouth. He looks at me with his good eye and shrugs.

"Sir?" she demands.

My glass is empty and according to the tenets of my own religious handicap I still have until Wednesday to live it up.

"Sure," I reply. "Why not?"

The End

ABOUT THE AUTHOR

Michael Crame lives and writes in Chicago. He is currently working on his second novel, *The Library at Orchard Hall*.